P9-AQS-613

DEMOLITION

DEMOLITION

Nick Oldham

**SEVERN
HOUSE**

For Belinda

First world edition published in Great Britain and the USA in 2022
by Severn House, an imprint of Canongate Books Ltd,
14 High Street, Edinburgh EH1 1TE.

Trade paperback edition first published in Great Britain and the USA in 2023
by Severn House, an imprint of Canongate Books Ltd.

severnhouse.com

British Library Cataloguing-in-Publication Data
A CIP catalogue record for this title is available from the British Library.

ISBN-13: 978-1-4483-0694-7 (cased)
ISBN-13: 978-1-4483-0697-8 (trade paper)
ISBN-13: 978-1-4483-0696-1 (e-book)

All Severn House titles are printed on acid-free paper.

MIX
Paper from
responsible sources
FSC
www.fsc.org   FSC® C013056

Typeset by Palimpsest Book Production Ltd.,
Falkirk, Stirlingshire, Scotland.
Printed and bound in Great Britain by
TJ Books, Padstow, Cornwall.

ONE

A few years ago, Marcus Durham kidnapped a business rival. It was just one of those incidents – *minor incidents*, Durham argued to the Crown Court judge – designed to teach someone a lesson. It wasn't meant to be anything more than that, he insisted further in his defence, throwing himself on the mercy of the court. There was no ransom demand or whatever, so it wasn't like a real kidnap – except, of course, it was. Durham had picked two of his best men, who he knew could be trusted, who liked to kick and punch people and keep their gobs shut, and with them by his side, he went to Josh Price's house, crashed through the front door with sledgehammers and dragged Price out, screaming and writhing, just as he was eating his tea with his wife Maggie, daughter Hannah and spaniel Poppy; the former two screamed a hell of a lot and the dog, squealing, went to hide under a chair.

They trussed him up, blindfolded him, hurled him into the back of a van and drove to Durham's building yard out in the sticks in the Ribble Valley, where they manhandled the petrified man into a shipping container and sat him on a chair on a plastic sheet – *for effect, sir*, Durham had pleaded to the unimpressed judge – and gave him a vicious beating to within a whisker of his life before locking him in the container to bleed, suffer and repent at leisure on his misdemeanour.

Price had been naive enough to outbid Durham at an auction for a derelict barn located between Garstang and Longridge on the slopes of Beacon Fell. Durham had intended to buy and renovate the property for himself, and prior to the auction he'd put the hard word around the building community that the place was his and he fully expected to get it at the reserve price and not a penny more.

Clearly, that was a memo Price didn't get.

Not that he would necessarily have taken any notice of it because he and Durham didn't get along anyway, so he gleefully outbid Durham by £20,000 and the smug 'Fuck you' look he'd given

Marcus when he held up his bidding paddle pretty much secured his fate.

No one – *no one* – got away with looking at Marcus Durham like that.

'I'm sure you get where I'm coming from, Your Worship, don't you?' he'd said to the judge. 'It's a matter of respect, isn't it, boss?'

Even that did not impress the judge, who, being of the Crown Court, should have been addressed as 'Your Honour' and certainly not 'boss'.

However, Price's kidnap following the property auction wasn't a very well-thought-out plan, not least because it was obvious to all concerned, despite the use of balaclava hoods, who had kidnapped him. Plus Durham didn't really have an endgame worked out as regards Price's fate. All he really wanted to do was scare him shitless, make him sign the property deeds over to him (for which he would willingly have paid him that reserve price, less ten per cent for all this inconvenience) and let that be a warning to him: tread on my toes again, scumbag, and next time my steel toe-capped work boots will kick you into a vegetative state and you'll spend the remainder of your life sucking soup up through a straw.

Durham never got as far as having the property signed over to him and releasing Price because about an hour after delivering the beating and incarcerating Price in the container, the cops turned up en masse at the builder's yard as Durham was stepping out of his office in the Portakabin. Two Heckler & Koch MP5s were rammed into his face and firearms officers were screaming at him and his two guys to hit the deck.

Which they did – face down. Fast.

Durham twisted his head to see a smart-arse detective superintendent called Christie lean over him and take great pleasure in arresting him with very much that same smug look on his face as had been worn by Price in the auction house, the look that said he'd got one over on Durham.

In spite of his heartfelt pleas to the Crown Court and a pretty wily barrister, Durham's tale of woe fell on deaf ears, and the judge sentenced him to eight years, meaning that because of the vagaries of the British justice system, he was out in four and wore an ankle tag for two years after that.

As far as the parole board and his probation officers were concerned, he emerged from prison a reformed character.

Actually, he didn't.

He went straight back into his property renovation and restoration business with a canny new partner, but not before revisiting Josh Price (after the ankle tag had been removed, obviously) and making him disappear – a neat trick he'd learned from a London-based gangster with whom Durham had shared a cell for a few interesting months in Manchester Prison, a guy who had a great sideline in making people vanish into thin air for good.

The trick, of course, was that Josh Price's disappearance could never be linked to Marcus Durham in spite of any speculation.

But the best thing of all for Durham was that his new partner was able, through a series of shell businesses, to acquire the property that had been so humiliatingly snatched from his grasp by Price, obviously at a cost well below market value because Price's widow (although she didn't yet know she was legally a widow as the seven years required by law had not passed; all she knew was that her husband had disappeared off the face of the earth) desperately needed any cash as Price's own business dealings were far from straight-forward. He was just as much a rogue as Durham in many ways, though much less violent, and he certainly hadn't deserved to be kidnapped initially and then, some six and a half years later, be fed into a stone crusher where his bones were ground to ash to become part of the hardcore underneath the HS2 railway that was under construction from London northwards.

Rumour had it that at least four other bodies were under the tracks already.

Durham then spent a considerable amount of cash renovating the coveted property because he had always intended it to be his home.

And now it was, and no one could prove he'd acquired it other than legally and above board.

At six thirty that Monday morning, as he dipped his toe in the water of the swimming pool he'd built outside the house, he had thought fleetingly about the chain of events that had led to the property eventually – and rightly, he thought indignantly – becoming his. He was not troubled by any of these recollections because Marcus Durham didn't do conscience.

He looked across the expanse of the heated blue water, one of the very few infinity pools in any property in Lancashire; in fact, Durham didn't know of any other personally and, being in the business, he thought he would have heard.

One thing he was certain of was that there was definitely no other property with such a pool that had such stunning views as this: sweeping way down from Beacon Fell, across the wide-open plain of Lancashire, west to the coast some twenty miles distant. From here, on a clear day – and today was such a day – Blackpool Tower was visible directly ahead; to the north were the clearly defined mountains of the Lake District and to the south the mountains of North Wales.

A seriously perfect location.

Durham sighed contentedly.

The weather was good and today would be the hottest day of the year – he was going to fucking well enjoy it to the max.

He dragged off his sweat-stained T-shirt, damp from a decent workout in the home gym, then slid off his shorts to stand there completely naked on the edge of the pool, hands on hips, proudly displaying his manhood and well-muscled body, salon-tanned as there had been no holidays abroad this year. He hoped there was some nosy parker out there in a house, equipped with binoculars, watching him.

Good luck to them, he thought, giving his groin a jaunty jerk before diving smoothly into the perfect water, loving the way it seemed to caress his heavily tattooed skin.

For a guy in his mid-forties, he was proud of his fitness, and the twenty-metre-long pool provided him with a good follow-up workout after the gym.

Twenty minutes later, he came to a stop and swam across to the long edge of the pool, where he contentedly rested his chin on his hands and surveyed the wonderful view down to the coast.

Yep, he thought, people could call him a heathen, a fly-by-night chancer, a rogue always on the lookout for a good deal; yes, he was a bit reckless with the dosh and unforgiving to those who got in his way, and yes, he was pretty lucky to have fallen in with his current business partner who did an excellent job of controlling him . . . Marcus Durham knew all these things, but he also knew that he must have some kind of arty-farty streak within him to be able to appreciate this awesome view. So he wasn't a heathen, after all.

He was so preoccupied in picking out the landmarks on the coast – the tower, the windmill at Lytham – that he failed to hear the soft, padded approach of the person who was dressed from head to toe in a forensic suit with a hockey goalkeeper mask covering the face.

'Mr Durham?'

With a splash of surprise, Durham spun in the water.

'Fuck're you?' he demanded, instantly registering the forensic suit and mask and just as immediately understanding its meaning – particularly so when the person's right hand came up and in it was an ugly-looking black pistol held by a hand in a latex glove, a hand also encased, as was the gun, in a clear plastic bag.

Durham reacted instinctively and dived under the water, knowing that, in spite of what appeared in films or TV crime dramas, the truth was that bullets fired into water of any real depth were quickly sucked of their energy and propulsion, and anyone on the bottom of a swimming pool would be unlikely to be killed by a slug from a handgun. Already, as he went under, he prayed that whoever this intruder was would waste at least some bullets trying to kill him underwater and that maybe – somehow – he would find the strength to launch himself out like a killer whale and tackle this person.

As he dived with his eyes open, he heard the gun fire twice. He twisted his head to see the trail of the bullets in the water close to his face, but obviously losing their killing force and momentum as they crashed into the density of the water.

Durham powered his way to the bottom of the pool, the deep end being just short of two metres, and he held himself, paddling madly to keep himself down while looking up and seeing the shape of the intruder, gun in hand, clear yet shimmering at the edge of the pool.

Durham knew he didn't have much time.

Before diving, he had not managed to inhale a complete lungful of air and already he was struggling as the combination of stress, fear and adrenaline increased his heart rate and took their toll on the small amount of oxygen in his system.

Keeping down, he pushed himself away from the deep end, propelling himself with a desperate surge towards the shallow end, in the vain hope that if he moved quickly enough, he might out-manoeuvre his hunter.

In truth, he wasn't really thinking straight now. He was just reacting to the situation, floundering, his brain a swirl of confused thoughts and strategies and possibilities, all with one simple aim: survival.

As his fingertips touched the wall at the shallow end, he knew he didn't have anything left in his lungs and that either his next breath would be an intake of warm water or he would have to shoot upwards and draw air – and he was already realizing that his brief hope of rising with the deadliness of a killer whale was a forlorn one.

He twisted.

His lungs burned.

He saw the menacing shape of the forensic-clad figure had simply walked along the edge and was still there, biding time.

As his lungs tightened, he knew he would have to go up now or take the first breath of a drowning man.

Durham braced himself like a sprinter at the starting blocks.

Then he went for it, had to. His plan was to go for the attacker's legs, whip them from under whoever it was, topple them, disarm and overpower them.

One thing was certain: Durham wasn't going to go down without a fight.

He counted.

On 'three' – the very last moment before his lungs filled with water – he surged up out of the pool and dived for the legs of the intruder, floundering like a wet seal as he came out and completely missing as the person simply stepped back out of reach.

Durham lunged again – missed again – and somehow found himself to be utterly exhausted by the stressful experience which, so far, had probably lasted only a maximum of ninety seconds, as the fresh air rushed down his gullet to his greedy lungs.

Wearily, he drew himself up on to all fours, his closely shaved head hanging between his arms. He coughed, spluttered and finally raised his face to look up.

'Fuck're you?' He wiped his mouth with the back of his hand. 'Fuck d'ya want? I haven't done owt. Who the fuck're you, ya—'

His words stopped abruptly as the intruder loosened the cord that had pulled the forensic hood tight around their face, then pushed it back.

The hockey mask was slowly removed, then dropped on the concrete.

Durham squinted. It took more than a few moments for recognition to take place as the intruder glared into his eyes and waited for it to dawn on him.

He swore again, gulped and took another breath before saying – in very much the same pathetic, weedy tone of voice he had used when speaking to the Crown Court judge some years earlier – 'Look, c'mon, we can sort this out, OK?'

'In what way, exactly?'

The intruder raised the automatic still encased in the plastic bag. Durham could see the two ejected shells side by side in the bottom of the bag.

This time he swore inwardly.

That little touch, the bag around the gun, plus the forensic suit, meant only one thing: a professional approach, someone who wasn't going to leave a trail for anyone, someone intent on not getting caught . . . yet he knew that if he couldn't get out of this alive, there would be bullets in the pool as well as in him. It was just the empty shell casings that would not be found.

And then he thought it wouldn't matter either way.

Because the cops thought he was a shit-bag to start with and they'd put no effort into finding this person who was about to execute him.

'Stand up!' The gun jerked. 'Stand on the edge of the pool, facing me.' The voice was resolute, unwavering.

Slowly, Durham got to his feet. Naked, he stood upright, but this time he felt totally vulnerable in his birthday suit, not like he had only a few minutes before when he'd waggled his penis to the world. His hands covered his cock and balls. 'Come on,' he whined, 'surely we can put this right. I'll do anything. Please.'

'Move back so your heels are right on the edge of the pool,' he was instructed.

He shuffled back a couple of inches.

The gun was aimed at his body mass.

He started to cower.

'You know what this is for,' he was told.

There was no fancy shooting. No headshots. Destruction of the heart and lungs was just as effective, and in less than a second four bullets slammed into his chest.

He toppled backwards into the water. His killer walked to the edge, looking dispassionately down as Durham flailed for a few moments, then stopped moving and floated across the pool, bleeding profusely, clouding the water with red.

The killer stepped back, picked up the mask, refitted it, pulled the hood back into place, then left.

TWO

To James Twain, the Supermarine Spitfire was a thing of true beauty.

At first, it had been nothing of the sort, just a jumble of broken, twisted metal, fragments of wings and an engine, but as Twain had walked around the old barn in North Yorkshire some four years earlier – a building he intended to demolish and rebuild into a classy country home – kicking straw and seeing old tractor parts strewn around, he'd yanked back a tarpaulin sheet and his mouth had dried up immediately. It was the find of a lifetime – the remains of a World War Two Spitfire, that glorious, gorgeous fighter plane that had played such a vital role in the Battle of Britain and beyond. Some parts of it were easily recognizable, such as the fuselage and propeller, other bits less so.

But James Twain knew exactly what he was looking at.

He had struck lucky on a couple of other occasions when assessing properties to buy.

Once he'd discovered an old Aston Martin – again under a tarpaulin – in complete disrepair, just a piece of junk to most people's eyes, but Twain had seen through this, its potential, and made an offer on the property he was surveying that explicitly included anything that might be found in it. It was an offer the family of the dementia-riddled old man who owned it was more than happy to take to cover spiralling care costs.

He'd rebuilt and renovated the Aston and it now sat proudly on a plinth in a display garage alongside his current home – Far End Barn on the outskirts of the village of Thornwell – and he had already refused a cash offer of a third of a million for it.

Once, in another barn, he had also found the husk of a Benz from the turn of the twentieth century, but he had donated that, once renovated, to a motor museum down south because he didn't much like it.

The Spitfire, though, was his best find ever, even though it was in more pieces than an Airfix model kit.

On discovering it, he had again made an all-encompassing offer to the estate of the deceased owner, and the plane and the barn became his.

Doing a bit of research just to satisfy his curiosity, he discovered that the owner had been a second unit director on a couple of war films made just after WWII; he had snaffled the plane after filming but, over seventy-odd years, had done nothing with it other than allow it to deteriorate and rot away.

It became Twain's obsession, and after four years and a huge chunk of money, he was on the cusp of revealing it to the world at large and maybe putting it up for auction.

At eight thirty that morning, Twain unlocked the door to the immense workshop behind his house and stepped inside, flipping on the light switches because there were no windows in the building. As the lights pinged on, the Spitfire was illuminated in all its wartime glory.

As ever, it took his breath away. Not just because of its undoubted beauty, timeless looks and fine lines – a masterpiece of engineering and design – but because it was his.

He liked owning things.

Rolling his neck muscles – he was amazed just how much that neck-hold from the previous evening's encounter had made everything ache – and also massaging his throat around his windpipe, where he could still feel the point at which the sharp tip of that steak knife had been pressed, he walked slowly towards the plane, looking at it longingly yet critically: had he missed any minute detail? Was there something else that needed doing before it was unleashed upon the world?

He circled it slowly, his eyes roving every panel, every rivet for a fault.

No. It looked tremendous.

Satisfied, he moved over to the workbench next to which, settled regally on a rig, was the rebuilt and reconditioned powerhouse of the Spitfire, the Rolls-Royce Merlin engine which was the final piece of the jigsaw. The engine now worked sweetly, and Twain estimated that another three months would probably see the first trials of the plane in the air.

His mouth went dry at the prospect; his lips twitched and pursed.

He needed to hear it again, the engine sound so synonymous with the Second World War, either striking fear into the heart of the enemy or as a symbol of hope against tyranny, depending on which side your loyalties lay. Whatever, it was a sound forever linked to the Supermarine Spitfire.

As he had done with the plane, he circled the engine slowly, marvelling at the engineering, shaking his head with admiration.

Then he couldn't resist it and decided to fire it up.

It took a couple of turns before the engine caught, literally spitting fire, but when it did, that noise reverberated around the workshop, filled his ears, numbed his senses and sent a shiver through his whole being.

Just a great start to the day, which he knew would be fraught with moaning minnies and whingeing old folk with nothing better to do with their time than have a go at him.

So at least James Twain died with the feeling and sound of the Spitfire engine pulsating through his bones and veins.

Because the problem was that it was so overpowering the sound muffled everything else, and there was no way he could have heard anyone sneaking up behind him or sense a presence.

In fact, the last thing that Twain sensed at all was the massive pain as the huge spanner crashed down on to the crown of his head in his bald patch and felled him instantly.

His knees buckled and he swooned to the sealed concrete floor of the workshop.

The repeated blows to the head were completely unnecessary and he didn't feel any of them because he was already dead when his face hit the ground.

THREE

'You should be able to solve all this nonsense – that's if you're anything of a detective, like folk round here say you are.'

Henry Christie bit his lip and felt his back creak painfully as he thrust the sponge into the bucket of warm soapy water, then stood upright with more creaking of the joints and began to wash down the brass plates that bore the names of the local people who had lost their lives in two world wars and other conflicts. The plates were attached to a fine stone memorial in one corner of Kendleton's village green, which on the previous evening had been pelted by more than a dozen rotten eggs. The stench was very unpleasant.

As he began this task mid-morning, he tried not to look at the old lady in the wheelchair who had made the somewhat cynical remark about his deductive prowess.

Mrs Veronica Gough was a sprightly, bright, very with-it eighty-nine-year-old, and she had learned only recently about Henry's past as a retired detective superintendent. Mrs Gough, as spokeswoman (she was always firm about that title) for the very unofficial but quietly powerful group that called itself the Village Council, had homed in on Henry to try to get him to use his super-investigatory powers to look into several instances of criminal damage and anti-social behaviour that had plagued the village of Kendleton lately.

Henry had already allowed himself to be coerced into being part of the village clean-up campaign, an initiative pushed by a subgroup of the Village Council which had taken on a 'Brighten up Kendleton' project which included planting flowers as well as cleaning anything that needed cleaning which wasn't too high for members to reach, as most of them were in their seventies and eighties and had balance issues. Henry – one of the younger members, and taking his role seriously as an upstanding member of the community, a responsibility he believed came with being the co-owner of The Tawny Owl, the only pub in a ten-mile radius – had volunteered sponge, mop, bucket and bubbles where necessary.

This subgroup was – obviously – overseen by Mrs Gough, although she wasn't in direct operational control of it. That task had been delegated to Mr Darbley, the local butcher, and Henry, who had once managed complex murder investigations, was happy to let that happen. His days of people management in any capacity were long gone; he didn't hanker for them to return and was quite content to be told what to do.

Earlier that morning, the case of the rotten eggs smashed on the war memorial had been brought to his attention by Mr Darbley, and Henry promised he would sort it out. He was just about to begin when Mrs Gough spotted him. She was out on patrol in her 'all bells and whistles' wheelchair which, local folklore would have it, was turbocharged.

'Completely disgusting,' Mrs Gough said passionately. 'Fancy desecrating a war memorial of all things. Most people might consider these minor crimes,' she continued, commenting on this latest instance of criminal damage, 'and the police – excuse me for saying – are completely inept, but these incidents are a blight on the village. Have you ever heard of the "broken windows" theory?'

Henry nodded: he had. It was the idea that visible signs of crime in urban areas lead to further crime unless tackled. He knew it well from his police problem-solving days.

'So you'll know that if we don't do something now, crack down on it, the village will become a ghetto before you can say boo to a Christmas goose.'

The spate of incidents to which she was referring – including the one Henry was trying to clean up at that moment – involved a lot of egg-smashing on residents' houses and car windows, some tyre slashing or just deflating, and, ironically, broken windows; plus, Henry knew, there had been numerous nitrous oxide or laughing gas canisters found discarded around the village, that being the in-vogue, accessible go-to high for youngsters seeking a quick hit by inhaling what was a potentially mind-wrecking and occasionally fatal substance. A small gang of teens, all dressed in black sports-wear – hoodies and jogging bottoms – were the culprits; they had started to gather and roam in a feral pack around Kendleton and neighbouring Thornwell, often ending up out of sight in a clearing in the woods by the stream, sharing spliffs and inhaling gas.

And depending on how the wind was blowing, the pungent aroma of weed often wafted across to Henry at The Tawny Owl as his senses picked up that once whiffed, never forgotten stink – which he disliked intensely. But he hadn't bothered too much. At first, instinctively as an ex-cop, he had felt the urge to wade in, sort them out, but he had realized how counterproductive that could be and that he and his pub could easily become a target for the kids. Instead, he took a metaphorical chill pill and let someone else worry about it – like the village bobby, PC Jake Niven, whose job it was.

To Mrs Gough's remark about broken windows, Henry replied, 'I'm not sure we've reached that stage yet.'

'You mark my words – if this isn't nipped in the bud, we're doomed – this community, this society we live in,' she said like an ominous soothsayer.

Henry screwed up his face but still didn't turn to look at her, just continued to wash down the nameplates on the memorial.

Then he took a step back to admire his handiwork. He was pleased with it, doing his civic duty, but then he frowned as he realized to his shame that this was the first time he had ever read the names on the memorial and was slightly irritated with himself.

There were two plates.

One related to those who had died during the First World War, fourteen of them, all soldiers killed in action. It listed their names, ages, ranks and the believed dates and locations of their deaths. He thought fourteen sounded a lot for such a small village, and their loss must have been devastating; then he remembered how many other towns and cities sent groups of young men en masse to war, most of whom never returned.

Even as he stood there, well over a hundred years later, he felt emotional at the thought.

From the names listed, it looked as though three main families had formed the recruits: two from the Broughtons, two from the Denmarks, three from the Felice family, a total of seven brothers, plus seven more from seven different families. Their ages ranged from seventeen to twenty-one, and half had died at the Somme in 1916.

Something strange, unsettling and sad seemed to shroud Henry as he read the names, and he swore softly to himself.

As he continued to scan the plaque, he saw that the name of the village was written as *Kendleton-with-Thornwell*. He had always thought the two were completely separate entities.

'Kendleton-with-Thornwell?' he said out loud, now allowing himself a glance at Mrs Gough. 'I didn't know that.' He obviously knew Thornwell was the next village along from Kendleton but had always believed them to be unrelated as such.

'Originally,' she said. 'Boundary changes in 1974 divided them. That said, they've always been divided, really. Thornwell's always been the poor relation, a bit like St Annes is to Lytham,' she said, referencing the side-by-side Lancashire coastal resorts.

Henry made no comment on that particular debate; he quite liked both places.

He crouched down slightly and continued to read the names of the WWII fallen on the next plaque: six in total – two soldiers, two airmen and two sailors. Then one more from the 1982 Falklands conflict, a soldier killed on Goose Green.

But there were five other names on the list, separated from the military personnel by a gap with a star etched into it.

Henry peered closer.

They were called Higham – Peter and Elsie – and their deaths were recorded as *Civilian bomb attack* on a date in December 1941. The next three, underneath the Highams, were German names with corresponding dates for their deaths.

His interest suddenly piqued even more, Henry started to turn to Mrs Gough and asked the question on his lips. 'What's the story concerning these people?' He pointed at the plaque.

'Ah, well, there *is* a story there,' she responded, about to tell him something eagerly, but at that moment both looked sharply around at the sound of a quickly approaching car coming from the direction of Thornwell.

It was an oldish but pristine Mercedes two-seater convertible, low and wide, with a woman at the wheel. Henry recognized it because the evening before he had watched the woman being driven away from The Tawny Owl by her husband after what Henry described as an 'altercation'.

It would be some time before Henry got an answer to his question about the names on the war memorial.

The evening before had been nice and steady.

Once the surge of excitement had abated in the community at the relaxation of lockdown rules and most businesses began operating more or less normally, The Tawny Owl's trade had reached pre-pandemic levels, meaning that 'steady' meant 'busy'.

Fortunately, Henry and Ginny had managed to hang on to most of their staff, whereas many other pubs and restaurants had struggled to keep their people or get them to return.

Henry Christie had originally moved in to live at Th'Owl, which is how the place was known locally, while still a serving detective with Lancashire Constabulary, even though it was against police regulations for officers to reside on licensed premises. Much to his surprise, he had got away with this misdemeanour and had lived there with his fiancée, Alison – who owned the business – and her stepdaughter, Ginny. Following Alison's untimely, tragic death, Henry had been left the business in her will, but he had quickly signed fifty per cent over to Ginny and they had run the place together ever since.

But now Henry was seriously considering signing the whole thing over to Ginny, whom he adored, and disappearing off into the sunset. He had itchy feet and an urge to do some travelling. That said, he had quite nicely settled into his role as landlord, really loved most of Kendleton's whacky inhabitants and didn't really see himself moving on.

So he was conflicted. Which was not unusual for him.

'*In due course*,' he promised himself internally as he poured another pint of Guinness for the local GP, Dr Lott, who waited eagerly on the other side of the bar. Once more, Henry had successfully managed to etch a proper shamrock in the froth as opposed to what usually looked like a dick jizzing. As he completed this task, he realized that his itchy feet were probably more due to what had recently happened in his professional and private life than a true urge to travel.

Professionally, he had just come to the end of a long but temporary contract as a civilian investigator with the police, during which he'd uncovered a long-standing criminal conspiracy and, vaguely connected to that in a roundabout way, he'd ended up coming face-to-face with a contract killer who fortunately hadn't been paid to kill Henry but had ruthlessly murdered two people either side of him. If nothing else, it had been a wake-up call that he could so easily have ended up on a mortuary slab, too. That thought had chilled his bones.

On the personal side, he had been semi-publicly dumped by his lady friend, one Detective Sergeant Diane Daniels, which had humiliated him.

Those two factors, plus the end of his contract, had combined to make him consider doing a runner from normal life for a while.

That he was also having a 'bit of a fling' (as he'd heard it called) with local millionairess and widow Maude Crichton, who was much keener on things than he was, made him also want to go into hiding.

However, as he passed the dark pint across the bar to Dr Lott and saw the look of abject pleasure on the older man's face as he lifted the glass and remarked, 'Well, at least it doesn't look like an ejaculating penis any more,' before taking a long, satisfying slurp, Henry couldn't feel anything other than contentment.

Maybe his days of romantic tomfoolery were over (and maybe he needed to draw a line under his non-serious relationship with Maude as he felt he was leading her on a bit) and his days of 'nicking folk' were also over but, he thought, so what? He had much to be thankful for.

'Thanks for that, Doc,' he smirked, taking the compliment.

'You're welcome.'

Henry gestured with a nod across to the table in the bar at which

Dr Lott and four of his friends were sitting. He had noticed them clustered around what looked like an old edition of a local newspaper, discussing something intently and casting occasional glances in his direction. 'What're you guys up to?'

Turning away from the bar, Dr Lott said, 'Join us for a moment, Henry.'

Henry nodded at Jack, the barman, and came from behind the bar, having to stop in his tracks to allow a customer to pass on his way from the dining room to the toilets, then he went over to the table at which Dr Lott had resumed his seat. The doctor pulled up another stool from an adjoining table, which he patted, and said to Henry, 'Sit.'

Henry sidled in and looked around at the five guys who he knew pretty well by now.

Dr Lott, obviously, although he was not Henry's GP.

Then there was Dave Darbley, the village butcher; Johnny 'Wren' Aston who ran an agricultural machinery business (Henry assumed the 'Wren' nickname was because Johnny sounded very much like Jenny); Roger 'The Rabbit' Tyson (Henry got that moniker) who was an ex-military man; and finally Leonard Barr, the only black man among them, who'd had a long and illustrious career as a musician – a saxophonist who had toured and recorded with some very well-known artists. Not one of them was under seventy, and as he sat down among them, he felt like the sprog. But the common denominator that linked them was that they were all widowers and their meet-up in Th'Owl was the highlight of their week.

'So, what's appertaining, guys?'

He glanced at the newspaper spread on the table, then up across Leonard's shoulder towards the bar where the customer who was on his way to the toilets seemed to have been waylaid by one of a group of men standing close to the bar, drinking. The man had his hand on the diner's chest and his face into his face. He looked angry, and Henry sensed something untoward was close to erupting.

However, the diner sidestepped and carried on towards the loos.

Henry frowned, then turned his attention back to the men around the table.

'This is what's appertaining!' Leonard tapped the newspaper with his fingertip and pushed it over to Henry. 'What do you make of it?'

'Yes,' Dr Lott said. 'You're a detective, and it's about time this was solved, don't you think?'

Henry peered down at the newspaper and saw the headline THORNWELL MURDER MYSTERY, under which was the subheading *80 years on and village still refuses to reveal murder suspect.*

Henry knew immediately what the story was about – the murder of a young man shot in the back of the head on his way home from the only pub in the village, The Swan's Neck; a murder never solved and a story wheeled out from time to time by the local press whether it needed to be told or not. Cynically, Henry thought it seemed to appear only on slow news days.

'You do cold cases, don't you?' Roger Tyson challenged him.

'This isn't cold, it's ice-age.' Henry grinned. He only knew what details had ever been reported in the press over the years, but he was sure the crime had been thoroughly investigated at the time and reopened officially at least twice since – and all before his time in the police. Without reading the paper, he recalled the basic problem was that there was a dead body, no witnesses and no apparent motive, and a village full of people who wouldn't or couldn't talk to the police. Yes, it was true that Henry had spent the last few months working on the Cold Case Unit, but this murder certainly wasn't on the list of that unit's priorities, not least because anyone who might know anything about it was probably dead now.

'So you're saying you're not interested?' Roger asked accusingly.

'I'm always interested in solving murders, but this is a no-go.'

'Even with today's scientific advances?' Dr Lott asked.

'Even then,' Henry assured him.

The five men glanced at each other.

Henry frowned again, wondering what was coming here.

'Well,' Dr Lott said – clearly the spokesperson or ringleader – 'we've decided, us five' – he gestured around the table – 'that we want to investigate it. We want to reopen the case.'

'I think you might find that to be a problem,' Henry began, trying not to giggle.

'Freedom of Information request,' Johnny Aston declared. 'That's where we'll start.'

Henry shook his head. 'Best of luck with that.' He felt immediately bad on seeing the deflated looks on the men's faces. 'Look, tell you what, I'll see if it's possible to root out the actual murder file, even though I don't work for the cops now, and see if there's anything I can give you from it. How does that sound?'

They all suddenly perked up at that news, and Henry was about to say something more when once again his attention was diverted by a sudden scuffle breaking out by the entrance to the toilet corridor between the diner who'd gone for a pee and the other man who'd initially blocked his way.

Now the latter guy – Henry knew him as Dale Renshaw – had the other one, James Twain, in a headlock in the crook of his left arm while punching him repeatedly, though not especially effectively, with uppercuts from his right fist and they were both pirouetting in a circle as they grappled each other and Twain, the one in the headlock, tried to free himself.

'Shit!' Henry sprang to his feet, strode towards the ruckus. 'Oi! Oi! Come on, fellas.'

Around the scrapping pair, everyone else had quickly stepped back, almost to form an arena, to gawp.

Henry threaded his way through and stepped between the fighting men, both of whom were quite a bit younger and much fitter than him. Nevertheless, he managed to prise Renshaw's grip off Twain's neck and shove the two roughly apart.

Renshaw teetered backwards into a couple of his mates, while Twain stepped away.

Henry could see fury blazing in Renshaw's eyes.

Twain, however, seemed calm, smug, rolling his neck like a fighter.

'This stops now,' Henry shouted – ineffectually, it seemed, as far as Renshaw was concerned because he immediately writhed free of his mates' grips and lunged at Twain, but instead managed to swing his fist into Henry's back.

Henry spun on him and Renshaw did retreat, realizing his error. 'Out, now – you're barred, Dale.' Henry pointed to the exit.

Renshaw's lips curled back from his teeth, snarling as he nodded, then glowered at Twain. 'I'll get you,' he growled. 'This isn't over.'

He then stomped towards the door. Henry watched him leave, then turned angrily to Twain who held up his hands, palms out, in a pacifying gesture.

'I didn't start this, Henry. I didn't say anything and I never hit him back,' he pleaded. 'My wife's in the dining room, and we're just out for a nice, quiet meal, that's all. No trouble. You know us. *He* started it.'

Henry, even after the short tussle, was breathing heavily – and seething.

He nodded, accepting Twain's word, jerked his head, and Twain returned a nod of thanks and headed back to the dining room.

Taking a deep breath to steady himself, Henry's head rotated towards Renshaw's companions at the bar, who all backed off, nothing to say. Henry gave them a nod of warning, which they seemed to accept, then spun on his heels to follow Renshaw out of the pub only to see him walking towards the village. He watched him go out of sight, aware from his experience in the police that, very often, troublemakers ejected from premises frequently hung around to take part in an ambush later.

As satisfied as he could be that Renshaw had gone, and massaging his back where the guy's fist had connected with his rib cage, he returned to his duties behind the bar where all now appeared to be peaceful.

Until just after ten p.m.

Henry had just handed Dr Lott another perfect pint when a shout and a crashing noise came from the main dining room, followed by another shout and a scream. Henry started to move as Meg, a young waitress, shot out of the room, beckoning Henry urgently to get in there.

He sidestepped from behind the bar and hurried over as Ginny rushed out of the kitchen, also alerted by the sound of the commotion.

He was curious about what to expect but already knew instinctively this had something to do with James Twain.

The restaurant had begun to thin out by this time as the last food orders had been at nine o'clock, and Henry estimated there would only be a handful of diners left and all of those would be couples.

He hadn't been expecting trouble at all that night. There were rarely any problems in The Tawny Owl, and most times if there was a fracas of any description, he was usually the target of it anyway.

He entered the dining room, avoiding customers scurrying out and looking daggers at him, clearly upset by what was happening. Even in those fleeting moments, it went through Henry's head that any problems could easily affect trade; any bad-mouthing spread like wildfire around these parts, and it only took one spiteful person to over-exaggerate or give a shitty review on TripAdvisor to knee the business in the bollocks. So to speak.

Henry saw the problem and stopped in his tracks as one does when a man is pinned to the wall by a woman holding a steak knife to his throat and looking as though she was eminently capable of slitting said throat with the serrated edge – a possibility made even more likely when she snarled, 'I'm gonna make you bleed, you bastard.'

Henry knew the couple slightly. They were occasional customers at The Tawny Owl who usually drew no untoward attention to themselves, were always well mannered and behaved, even though Henry had always sensed a certain aloofness between themselves and others reflected in their apparent unwillingness to get into much banter with 'mine host' (him) and a lack of conversation between themselves at the table as they dined. Henry never minded too much – he'd spent a whole career dealing with people who didn't want to speak to him – and on the plus side they always went for the most expensive items on the menu. They seemed to like lobster and the best steak, so clearly were not short of a bob or two.

The man – currently pinned to the wall – was James Twain, the one who'd been involved in the balletic brawl a short time earlier; the woman was his wife, Celia. They lived in a big, converted barn somewhere beyond Thornwell.

The Twains were in their mid-forties. James was squat, muscular, with one arm full of tattoos from shoulder to wrist. Celia was slim, pale and attractive, but with a stern air about her. Henry didn't know much about them beyond that. He'd once eyed James with his 'detective head' on and put him down as a Jack-the-lad, a reckless chancer but with a charming front, maybe a likeable rogue, but that was just Henry's suspicious estimation of him based on nothing more than feeling and instinct – in other words, his people radar that had served him well when he'd been a cop.

Twain's business was property renovation, and he was responsible for making silk purses out of sow's ears by buying up and modernizing many derelict farm buildings around north-east Lancashire over the years and converting them into desirable properties.

However, that didn't necessarily make him well liked around these parts, not least because the prices of these conversions were way above what most locals could afford. Twain had also renovated a number of pubs that had closed or fallen on hard times; he had demolished them, much to the chagrin of locals (who complained vociferously, though when the buildings had been pubs, the same people had never actually used them), and after much to-ing and fro-ing with parish and city councils and some preservation groups, Twain had rebuilt them as luxury apartments.

Henry had thought good luck to him, but it was obvious that Twain's steamroller approach had rubbed people up the wrong way, and Henry had heard him be referred to as 'Mr Unpopular'.

Henry was aware that the latest conflict getting people's backs up was Twain's purchase of and plans for The Swan's Neck, the pub in Thornwell, which after years of neglect, bad management and lack of investment had closed its doors, then mysteriously been razed to the ground.

Twain's plan was to flatten the whole area – the pub had a very large car park and beer garden out back – and build a small, exclusive housing estate. The proposal sent the local community hurtling into the stratosphere, and a pressure group calling itself 'Save Our Neck Action Group' – SONAG for short – under the redoubtable leadership of the wheelchair-bound Veronica Gough, had meetings at The Tawny Owl to plan their response. Henry could see they were a very vocal group but also that they didn't really have any teeth, just like many of their ageing members.

The Twains had arrived at The Tawny Owl on the evening of the steak-knife incident well in time for their pre-booked table and had been met and shown in by Meg. Henry had noticed their arrival but had been busy behind the bar and pretty much forgotten they were there until an order came through for a bottle of the very best Champagne. He had been the one to take the £185 bottle of Pol Roger 'Sir Winston Churchill' through to their table and make a flashy opening and pouring of the silver-bubbled liquid with the flourish of a French waiter.

'Nice choice, nice choice,' Henry congratulated them.

Neither responded other than with disinterested shrugs. Henry forced a smile, detecting more than a little tension between the couple, screwed the bottle back into the ice bucket and said, 'I'll leave it with you.' For that price they didn't have to acknowledge him . . . and they didn't.

Henry next saw James Twain going to the toilet, then a few minutes later in a headlock.

Half an hour after that, Celia had a knife to her husband's throat that was capable of slicing through rare steak as easily as through butter.

* * *

'Whoa, whoa, whoa!' Henry said, approaching the couple with his hands patting down fresh air in a gesture meant to convey peace, love and understanding.

The point of the knife was sticking in Twain's throat just by his Adam's apple, not quite deep enough to draw blood, although with only a little more pressure Henry knew it would slide in and sever the carotid artery with ease.

Twain was backed up against the wall, his chin angled upwards, a glint of fear in his eyes as he looked at his wife who was right up against him, keeping the knife steady as she snarled into his face.

She completely ignored Henry who was approaching very cautiously, hands still spread.

'You bastard,' Celia said, frothy, animalistic spittle coming from her lips. 'You cheating bastard.'

Twain's face twitched, not daring to respond.

Henry stepped around the chair Celia had been sitting on, now overturned, presumably as she shot to her feet, knife in hand, to attack her husband. James Twain's chair was also upended and, doing the maths, Henry guessed he must have shot to his feet maybe a second or two after Celia and backed off only to find himself trapped against the wall with an enraged, knife-wielding wife right in his face.

'I'm not the only one,' Twain managed to retort through gritted teeth. His nostrils flared wide, and rivulets of perspiration dribbled down his forehead and from the hairline at his temples.

'You're the bastard, though,' she said.

'Hey, hey,' Henry said, firmly enough to burst into their bubble.

Now, other than Ginny and Meg at his shoulder, the dining room had emptied as the remaining customers fled.

'Mrs Twain . . . Celia . . . please put the knife down,' Henry cooed.

For a few seconds, the tableau was motionless, like a painting, with just Celia's jaw rotating, and it could have gone either way, but then her shoulders sagged and slowly she swivelled to Henry. It took more moments for her eyes to properly focus on him. Henry knew 'red mist' syndrome when he saw it – that curtain of intense, uncontrollable rage that can come down and transform anyone from a placid human being into someone capable of sticking a knife into another's throat.

He knew it because he'd been affected by it several times.

'Mrs Twain,' Henry said again, 'please.'

Her eyelids flickered as she came out of that terrible mindset and seemed to realize what she was doing.

But James also realized her attention and determination had been diverted, and he took full advantage of it.

He grabbed her right wrist and twisted it away from his neck, taking the point of the knife in an arc away from the danger zone, but then he continued to twist, forcing her down on to her knees as her fingers opened and released their grip on the knife. Twain plucked it away and tossed it on to the oak floorboards. He was moving quickly now as he regained the upper hand, and he swept the knife away with a foot while he continued to force her arm back, bending it to snapping point at her elbow as he now glowered down at her with his own rage.

She screamed at the pain.

For a moment, Henry was certain her arm would break. He stepped in fast. 'Enough!'

James Twain raised his face, the ferocious expression still there but with an additional nasty grin that conveyed he was now enjoying himself.

'Back off,' he warned Henry.

'No way, not a chance. You let her go now,' Henry told him, then over his shoulder he called to Ginny. 'Police, now!'

'Gotcha,' Ginny responded.

James still held Celia in position, pain imprinted on her features. With just one extra jerk, he could have broken her arm in a place that would probably have been impossible to reset without extensive micro-surgery.

A position of absolute power.

He kept looking at Henry, sizing him up, but then a wider, boyish grin came to his face, and he relaxed, changed his grip, released the pressure and began to help Celia to her feet like a good husband. 'Nothing to see here – just a bit of a tiff,' Twain said, easing her upwards.

'Whatever,' Henry said, unimpressed. 'You need to pay and leave. You're both barred from here now.'

Twain shrugged. With a sneer on his face, he took out his wallet from his back pocket and, with finger and thumb, extracted a thick wad of notes.

'Should be enough,' he said and contemptuously scattered the money across the table.

He grabbed Celia forcefully by the arm and started to march her out on tiptoes.

Henry stepped in their way. 'Let her go.'

'Let her go?' Twain exploded, affronted. 'She had a knife to my throat – or didn't you see that?'

'I also saw you almost break her arm and earlier get involved in some sort of fight by the bar.'

'It's OK, Henry,' Celia said. Tears streamed down her face. 'I'm fine. I will be fine. Just a silly argument that got out of hand.'

Henry said, 'Be that as it may, I'm not having a woman dragged out of my premises by a man, husband or otherwise . . . so . . .' Henry leaned towards Twain. 'Let her go, OK? And then if she wants to go with you, it's her decision.'

'Not your business,' Twain said stubbornly.

'My place makes it my business,' Henry corrected him.

Twain's nostrils flared again at the challenge implicit in Henry's words. He swallowed and licked his lips, eyes on Henry. Seeing that the owner of the establishment meant what he said, he released Celia's arm, taking his fingers off one by one.

Henry gave him a nod. Twain ducked past him and headed for the exit, shouldering Meg out of his path.

Celia's face was tear-stained. Her make-up and mascara were smudged. She looked deadbeat and hugely embarrassed.

'Are you OK to go with him?' Henry asked.

She nodded. 'Yeah. Sorry.'

She seemed to be on the verge of saying something more but thought better of it and left. Henry followed her out on to the front terrace and watched her descend the steps and get in the passenger seat of the Mercedes sports car that Twain had already fired up. He was irritably dipping his foot on the accelerator pedal, revving the engine.

When she was in, before she had a chance to fasten her seatbelt, Twain tore away, throwing up gravel. Henry watched the car disappear and turned to go back into the pub when a movement by the rose wall caught his eye. He stopped, peered into the darkness and saw the figure of Dale Renshaw arise from the shadows. He was also watching James Twain drive away.

Henry stood upright, his back creaking again, dropped the sponge in the bucket and watched the sports car come in his and Mrs Gough's direction.

'That is a tart's car, that,' Mrs Gough said.

'What do you mean?'

'Seventies tarts and dolly birds used to drive around in them,' she explained. 'Just look at old films and adverts.'

'Oh, right.' Henry frowned, still not completely understanding what she meant.

The car slowed at the entrance to The Tawny Owl car park, but then Henry got the impression that Celia Twain had spotted him by the memorial, swerved slightly and drove towards him.

The convertible roof was down, and Celia was wearing a scarf fastened up around her head and a pair of large circular sunglasses. She pulled up on the road by the edge of the village green.

'Mr Christie! Henry!' she called unnecessarily.

He gave a wave of acknowledgement, wiped his hands dry down the sides of his jeans and walked towards her. He could hear the electronic whirr of Mrs Gough's wheelchair behind him.

'Mrs Twain, how are you?' Even as he approached, he had his suspicions about the big sunglasses, though, of course, they could just have been for driving as it was a sunny day.

Or was she wearing them to mask a black eye and swelling?

As he got closer, he could see that, despite the cover of the glasses, his suspicion had been correct, and he would have laid odds that if they came off, at least one black eye would be revealed along with swelling around the cheekbone.

His blood began to simmer.

'I'm all right,' she said airily.

Henry got even closer, and her injuries were more apparent. 'Really?'

He couldn't take his eyes off the very obvious swelling and bruising on her left cheek. Not only that, but as Celia was wearing a short-sleeved blouse, he was able to see lines of circular purple bruises and red welts down the fleshy parts of both her slim arms. Henry recognized this type of bruising from the many domestic assault cases he'd dealt with over the years, the result of being gripped ruthlessly, usually by a man. It looked as though James Twain had grabbed her, dragged her around and maybe slammed her against a wall and punched her.

Henry wondered if there were more injuries under her clothing, perhaps on her ribs, that he couldn't see.

'Did he beat you up?' he asked bluntly.

'No, no, no,' she said hurriedly. Henry knew the words were a lie, even though she added, 'Gave as good as I got. Drunken quarrel. These things happen.'

'Doesn't look like that to me,' Henry said, unimpressed. He had dealt with many women over the years who'd made light of things like this, trying to shrug off horrific assaults of the kind that sometimes ultimately proved fatal.

'Well, whatever,' she said, brushing his concerns under a metaphorical carpet. 'It's a private matter between me and my husband . . .'

'Which went public last night.'

'Be that as it may,' she said primly.

'I can get the local bobby to call round,' Henry suggested firmly. He'd asked Ginny to contact the police the night before, but she hadn't been able to get through. 'Just to have a word in James's lughole.'

'You'll do nothing of the sort. That would just exacerbate a delicate situation and wind him up,' she said, a tiny quiver of panic in her voice as the prospect of a cop at the door seemed to worry her. 'Apart from anything, he's in his workshop now, messing with his beloved plane . . . bloody engine's been on all morning, loud . . . he'll be annoyed to be disturbed . . . However, I didn't stop because of all that. I just came by to offer my – our – apologies for last night. It just got a touch out of hand . . . too much of that lovely champagne,' she said by way of an excuse, then added, 'No police, OK?'

'OK,' Henry agreed reluctantly. 'But if you ever need help, Celia, you must see PC Niven or at the very least talk to me.'

'I will . . . and thank you, you're very kind.' She gave Henry a nice smile.

She selected drive, but before she managed to set off, Henry said, 'Oh, we owe you some change. Your husband left far too much last night when he threw down that cash, even accounting for a ten per cent service charge.'

'Put it in the charity box.'

'If you want,' Henry said, but then had a quick idea. 'Or I could drop it over at your house, put it in your husband's hand?' he suggested.

Even though he could not see her eyes behind the sunglasses, Henry knew she had given him a chilling look.

'Charity box,' she reiterated, closing him down, then put her foot down on the accelerator and set off quickly.

As Henry watched the car drive into the distance, he was joined by Mrs Gough, who had kept a respectful distance but still managed to earwig the conversation.

Henry felt very uncomfortable as he gave Mrs Gough a thin smile, but he was also angry because any form of domestic abuse never sat easily with him. It never had. Once, early in his career as a young PC, when he'd tried to get his bosses to take action in a domestic rape situation, it had ended with the victim being murdered by her boyfriend; even now, in the deep recesses of his mind, that failure to protect someone vulnerable still lingered like a bad smell.

'So Mr Unpopular beats up his wife, eh?' Mrs Gough commented from the sidelines.

Henry just arched his eyebrows.

'I wonder if it's about all the affairs,' she added mischievously, then smiled innocently as Henry turned to look at her. 'And I'm not talking about business affairs . . . or have I said too much?' She put a finger on her lips like a naughty schoolkid. 'Maybe I'll be cheeky and ask him this afternoon.'

'This afternoon?'

'Yes – or have you forgotten, Mr Christie? It's our fortnightly meeting of SONAG from eleven thirty onwards at Th'Owl.'

'I hadn't forgotten.' He had.

'Well, Mr Unpopular – sorry, Mr Twain – has been asked along to do a Q and A with us about his frankly outrageous plan for The Swan's Neck . . . didn't I mention?'

'No.'

'Perhaps you could give him his change then and maybe arrange for PC Niven to "have a word in his lughole" as you so poetically put it? In the meantime . . . don't you have a meeting room to prepare for us?'

'Already done,' Henry said, confident that Ginny would have remembered. He checked his watch and was surprised to see it was almost eleven fifteen.

'And Lancashire hotpot?'

'Ditto,' Henry said, still relying on Ginny.

For a pub that had been on its last legs for many years, closed completely for the last few, then burned down, there was certainly a lot of ill-feeling that someone was going to demolish The Swan's Neck and turn it into something nicer, whatever that turned out to be.

Henry was thinking this as he watched the members of the Save

Our Neck Action Group file into The Tawny Owl and wondered what they could realistically hope to achieve.

He knew The Swan's Neck well enough from when he'd been a detective superintendent investigating the disappearance of a lone policewoman who'd last been seen attending a disturbance at the pub. Henry had discovered there had been a dangerous, predatory male at large, with links to the publican, and had finally unearthed the man's underground lair and the fate of the officer and other missing young women.

Not so long after that, The Swan's Neck had finally closed, never to reopen.

'Good morning.' Henry nodded amiably to the first SONAG member to come through the doors for the meeting. Eric Grundy was a hundred years old, wheelchair-bound, and was being pushed by his son, Ben, who was seventy-five. They were followed a short time later by an elderly couple, Mr and Mrs Williams (though rumour had it they were not actually married but had been living as husband and wife for almost fifty years now).

Next to arrive was Tom Derrick. Henry knew Tom because they had both been in the police. However, Tom had been a civilian crime scene investigator and was probably ten years younger than Henry, although he was also retired, or had finished early – Henry wasn't certain. Henry didn't know him well, other than to chat to occasionally, but he was aware that Tom had a good reputation as a CSI.

'Tom.' Henry nodded as he came in through the revolving doors as opposed to the side door which was open, as always, to facilitate wheelchair access.

'Henry.' Derrick nodded back as he passed.

More continued to arrive. Some Henry knew, others he didn't. They assembled in a function room behind the dining room in order to get down to their business of disrupting – as far as Henry was concerned – quite legal plans to do something nice to the dilapidated, burnt-out shell of a building that was an eyesore.

Mrs Gough was already in the room, having set up her laptop, linking it to a pull-down screen at the front of the room.

When Henry thought everyone had arrived, he popped his head around the door and got the nod from Mrs Gough, though he felt a chill run through him when he glimpsed the words projected on to the screen. He backed out quickly.

His job (and Ginny's) was simply to provide food and drink over the next two hours and hope that he never did anything to upset this bunch of people, who, although they had an old demographic, seemed ruthless in their approach. What he'd seen on the screen had somewhat shocked him.

It had read:

SONAG – THE STRATEGY.
Lawful/unlawful.
Lawful: tactics such as adopted by XR & Insulate Britain – demonstrations, gluing self to roads, chaining to each other, etc.
Peaceful protests such as letters to MPs, councils, etc.
Unlawful: consider murder.

One hour later, hoping the older generation wasn't sharpening machetes or polishing handguns, Henry announced his arrival and then backed a heated trolley into the function room and wheeled it across to tables at the back.

He was aware that all eyes were on him. He wasn't sure if they were pleased or annoyed to see him, and he wondered if he had just interrupted a murder plot.

However, Mrs Gough, who was still at the front, armed with her laptop, announced delightedly, 'Oh good, Ginny's homemade hotpot, unless I'm very much mistaken . . . meeting hereby adjourned for lunch and I recommend you all get a whopping helping, with the exception of Miss Withers who, of course, has just gone vegan' – Mrs Gough looked sadly at a thin old lady on the front row, then continued – 'in order that we will all have the necessary strength and energy to deal with the shameless shenanigans of James Twain when, or if, he deigns to come and face our wrath this afternoon.'

Henry rolled his eyes and heaved the trays of hotpot across to one of the tables, set out plates and cutlery, plus Miss Withers' specially plated-up bean and tofu salad.

As he peeled the foil covers from the hotpot, he inhaled and revelled in the aroma and knew it would taste amazing. Then he put out jars of pickled onions and red cabbage and stood back.

Real northern grub.

Henry turned to find Tom Derrick, the former CSI, behind him, also inhaling approvingly, the first in the self-service queue.

'Smells very, very good,' Tom said.

'Tastes that way, too,' Henry assured him, then stood aside and allowed the members of SONAG to dive into the food like a pack of ageing hyenas.

Which reminded him of how hungry he was. He'd been up at six that morning, eaten then but not since. He thought he might help himself to a portion when the queue thinned out.

He never got the opportunity.

The door to the function room opened, and Ginny stood there, ashen-faced, looking terrified. She beckoned Henry over urgently.

Instantly picking up on her body language, he strode over. 'What's up?'

He expected nothing more than something to be wrong with the gas supply, which had been playing silly buggers recently, even though her face definitely said something else.

She gasped. 'Henry . . . Dad . . . I think there's been a murder.'

FOUR

Her words were garbled, hurried, desperate. 'I didn't know what to do, I didn't know where to go, who to tell . . . I didn't know anything . . . I just, just . . . panicked . . . all that blood! Covered in it, all over the floor of the workshop . . . puddles . . . and there he was, dead, lying in the middle of it . . . his head, I don't know, smashed in, horrible . . . Oh God!'

Celia Twain's eyes seemed focused somewhere in the distance, beyond Henry's shoulder, as she relived those terrible moments, but then she refocused, came back to the present and to him.

'I just thought of you. I'm really sorry. I hope you don't mind,' she said in a staccato way. 'But I knew you were a police officer. A detective. Once.'

Celia had turned up on the doorstep of The Tawny Owl covered in blood all the way down the front of her blouse, the pretty one she'd been wearing when she'd driven by earlier and spoken to Henry near the memorial; blood was also on her hands and arms . . . and also, in her right hand, she had been carrying a large spanner. The murder weapon.

Henry had not seen any of this as he'd been hovering around the hotpot queue, and by the time Ginny had beckoned him out of the function room, Celia had been manoeuvred into the snug bar which was unoccupied at that time, unlike the main bar in which about half a dozen customers were already lunchtime drinking, rubbernecking and discussing Celia's dramatic, bloodstained arrival.

Ginny had breathlessly told Henry what had happened: that she had been the one who had come face to face with Celia as she stumbled up the front steps from her car, the door still open, still clasping the spanner. Ginny had then managed to head the hysterical Celia into the snug and hurried to fetch Henry.

And now, after listening to Celia's outpouring, Henry glanced around at the spanner, which Ginny had managed to gently pry from Celia's grip and place on a brass-topped table in one corner of the snug.

It was a heavy-looking piece of kit, bigger than most, capable of doing serious damage if used as a weapon to smash someone's head in. Henry had been to a few murders where similar tools had been used, and they were very messy deaths.

He looked back at Celia.

She was sitting, leaning forwards with her elbows on her knees, still gasping for air, sucking it in desperately.

Even then, Henry thought, *Suspect number one.*

He said, 'You did right. I get it, you panicked.'

Ginny came in with a mug of sweet tea and a glass of water, placing them on a table within Celia's reach.

'Oh God,' Celia moaned to the floor, 'he was just there . . . dead . . . next to the plane . . . oh God.'

'OK, OK,' Henry said softly. 'Take your time, Celia . . . take a deep breath and tell me what happened from the beginning. Just try to keep calm,' he encouraged, leaning towards her.

In his ear, Ginny whispered, 'Police? Jake Niven?'

Henry nodded, keeping his eyes on Celia. 'Slow breath. Have a sip of water or tea.'

Celia locked eyes ferociously with him, then seemed to brace herself. 'Right, right, right,' she intoned – then suddenly lost control again, slumped and sobbed. 'I can't get the image out of my brain.'

Henry laid a hand on her shoulder, trying to avoid touching any of the blood. 'It's OK, it's understandable.'

Celia exhaled, then breathed in and said a determined, 'Right.' She sat up, wiping her eyes with the balls of her hands, making them squelch.

Henry was reluctant to touch her at all. Not that he didn't want to offer comfort, but he was already thinking forensically, even though that wasn't his job any more. Treating people like evidence was no longer his concern, and maybe he should have given her a reassuring hug. But a pat on the shoulder would have to suffice as thirty ingrained years of conditioning as a cop found his mind screaming, *Get her clothing bagged up and get her into a forensic suit!*

'What happened after you left me at the memorial?' he asked, instead of requesting her to strip off, trying to ease her into a narrative she could pick up on. 'As I recall, you mentioned your husband was in his workshop and you hadn't seen him this morning.'

'Yeah, yeah, that's right.' She was still trying hard to get a grip and took a shaky sip of tea. 'After I saw you, I went to Lancaster . . . just had some things to buy, and when I came back, I went straight home . . . but there was no sign of James in the house. His car was in the drive so I assumed he was still in the workshop, tinkering with the plane.'

'Plane?' Henry recalled her having mentioned this and assumed it was perhaps something like a Cessna.

'He . . . he was restoring a Spitfire.'

'Oooh!' Henry said, unable to disguise his surprise, at the same time realizing she was already referring to her husband in the past tense. 'Oh, OK.'

'Anyway, I left it a while, then went into the workshop with some sandwiches I'd bought in town and a brew, just to make peace . . .'

'Which is when you found him?' Henry prompted.

Her eyes glazed over at the memory, and she nodded dully.

Ginny reappeared at the door of the snug with a cordless phone in her hand. 'Henry.'

He looked over at her and saw a few people clustered behind her, including a few members of SONAG. Mrs Gough was at her elbow, trying to get a peek past, and Tom Derrick was bouncing like Tigger to try to look over Ginny's shoulder.

Henry said to Celia, 'Give me a second.'

Her expression was still far away as she fiercely chewed her bottom lip.

She seemed not to hear him, seemed to be sinking further into shock.

He went to Ginny, who said quietly, 'Jake was on a job in Lancaster. He's on his way but could be twenty minutes.' She indicated the phone. 'No one else is closer, but CID are turning out from Lancaster, too.'

Feeling a little squirt of adrenaline rush into his system, Henry realized then how much he missed moments like this.

Then his mobile phone rang: Jake Niven.

Jake was Kendleton's local bobby, one of the few remaining dedicated rural beat cops actually living in the villages they policed, although his position now hung by a thread. Not because he was inefficient or ineffective – he was quite the opposite – but because, in modern policing terms, the local bobby living on the beat was deemed an expensive extravagance. He was still only in place because of the vociferous nature of the parish council; even so, he was spending more and more time being drafted in to cover Lancaster, which, to be fair, was ludicrously short of staff. It would not be long before Jake disappeared altogether.

'Jake,' Henry said, answering the call.

'I'm on my way, blues and twos,' the cop said. 'Tell me.'

Even though Henry knew Ginny would have given a good outline on her emergency call, Jake still wanted Henry's ex-cop take, which he gave succinctly.

Henry backed away from everyone's earshot as he spoke. 'We need an ambulance to The Tawny Owl, I would suggest,' he concluded after briefing Jake. 'And one to get up to Twain's house out at Thornwell, just in case James is still breathing, though if what I've been told is correct, he won't be.'

'I'll see what I can do,' Jake promised.

'Look, Jake,' Henry said, already beginning to regret what he was about to suggest, even though he was somehow unable to prevent himself, as if some sort of demon had taken possession of him. 'Celia's in good hands here for the moment; there's even a retired CSI on hand who might keep an eye on her evidence-wise . . . she's covered in blood . . . but I'm thinking I should go to the scene and check it out. What d'you say, mate?'

Henry sensed uncertainty in Jake's lack of immediate enthusiastic response.

'I won't touch anything, but if James is still alive, then he might just need a hand to survive . . . and if the offender is still present . . .' Henry said in an attempt to elicit a yes from Jake.

'Yes, go,' Jake said. 'I'll be fifteen minutes max behind you. CID are on the way plus a section patrol . . . oh, and FMIT are also on the way.'

'FMIT? Already? That was quick.'

'Uh, yeah, they were at Lancaster nick dealing with something else, and hearing the kerfuffle over the radio, they turned out, too.'

'Anyone I know?'

'Diane,' Jake almost whispered.

Henry swallowed and an eyelid twitched.

'And Debbie Blackstone,' Jake added.

'Jeez . . . the "A" Team,' Henry uttered. 'OK, whatev, I'm making my way to the scene now.'

'Take care, pal. I won't be far behind,' Jake said. In the background, Henry could hear Jake's two-tone horns and the scream of the engine in the beat-up old Land Rover that was Jake's transport.

Henry hurried through to the owner's accommodation, grabbed a jacket and his car keys.

To Ginny, he said, 'Try to keep her in the snug if possible.' He had considered moving Celia into the private area but decided against it, again thinking about preserving evidence; keeping Celia in one spot would be better than having to explain any further blood traces through the pub. 'There's at least one ambulance coming and hopefully a shitload of cops. I'm going up to Twain's place now.'

'Is that wise? Suppose the killer's still lurking there?' Ginny said.

'I'll be fine . . . just need a quick word with Celia before I go.'

Henry went back into the snug. Celia was still seated, trying to sip the tea, holding the mug with both hands wrapped around it to prevent it shaking and spilling. She watched Henry approach over the rim of the mug.

He sat across from her. 'Celia, the police are on their way, OK? Some officers will come here; others will go straight up to your house. I'm going up there now just to see if there's anything I can do for James.'

'Do you think he's still alive?' she asked.

'Let's hope so. Do I need a key to get into the workshop?'

'I think I left it open . . . I'm not sure, but my keys are in my car outside, the house key and the keys to the outbuildings including the workshop.'

'OK. Do you mind if I take them?'

'No, go ahead . . . it's fine.'

'OK, look, Ginny's going to look after you now.'

'Thank you. I knew you'd know what to do.'

'But you must stay here until the police arrive. Don't move. And don't touch that spanner again. You got that?' Henry told her.

'Why?' She pulled the mug away from her face and looked very worried.

'Because the evidence trail is important. You've got blood on you and, I'll be honest, the police will want to seize your clothing.'

'Oh my God, does that mean I'm a suspect?'

'It's routine,' he assured her, even though he knew she would be the starting point for the investigation. 'They have to gather all evidence in a case like this.'

She nodded, understanding the logic.

'Did you see anyone else in the workshop or around your home?' he asked quickly.

'No, no one.'

'Right, I'm going to go now. You stay here with Ginny,' he reiterated, casting a brief, critical eye over her and wondering if she was capable of murdering her husband.

But he already knew the answer to that one: given the right set of circumstances, anyone was capable of killing. And then he couldn't help himself and asked, 'Did you kill him, Celia?'

He hurried out of The Tawny Owl, down the front steps from the terrace to the car park where Celia's Mercedes had been abandoned with the driver's door still wide open. There were smears of blood on the driver's seat and inside the door panel. Careful to avoid touching any of these marks, Henry reached in and slid the ignition key out of its slot; using his knuckles, he closed the door and turned to go to his car, dropping Celia's keys into a sealable, clear plastic bag of the type used to store food in a fridge or freezer that he'd grabbed from the kitchens. He knew he probably shouldn't have taken the keys, but if it turned out that Celia's property was open, he would have no need to use them, and in the overall scheme of the already expanding evidence trail, this was a minor, justifiable transgression.

'Henry!' a voice called as he reached his car: Maude Crichton, the nice local woman, worth millions, who he was unenthusiastically seeing.

His heart sank just a tad.

No doubt about it, she was lovely and loaded, but for some unaccountable reason, the relationship wasn't quite gelling for him.

'Hi, Maude . . . I'm sorry, but I need to be somewhere, quickly.'

She looked crestfallen for a moment but then pulled herself together. 'Oh, that's OK, darling . . . you haven't forgotten about tonight, though, have you?'

Henry blinked. *Of course he had.*

Then it came flooding back. 'Course not . . . seven p.m. at yours . . . to meet your family.' The last four words came out very weakly indeed.

'Yes, but could you get to mine at six to help out? That would be great.'

'Yeah, yeah, course I will.'

'Anyway, where are you off to in such a rush, darling?'

'No time to explain.' He pointed to the front door of Th'Owl. 'Go and see Ginny; she'll fill you in.'

By this time, Maude was up close and she kissed him on the cheek.

'See you later,' he said and got into his car, moments later speeding out of the car park, purging all thoughts of Maude and a family get-together from his mind and focusing on what the next twenty minutes might bring.

Tempting though it was to steam up the driveway, screech to a halt and leap out, Henry's recently retired cop conditioning came into play as he sped along the country lanes towards Twain's home. He switched his engine off and came to a silent stop about one hundred metres short of the track that led up to the renovated farmhouse. Although there was perhaps some argument in rushing to the scene – the possibility James Twain was still alive (although if Celia was to be believed, he was very dead) – the thing that slowed Henry right down was the possibility that the offender or offenders (if Celia wasn't the murderer) might still be on the scene. Should that be the case, screeching up would alert them and make them flee.

By approaching in silent mode, he might be able to surprise and catch them.

He also balanced this with the fact that dumping his car a short distance away would only add a couple of minutes at most to his arrival time, which would probably not make any difference to James Twain's fate.

On top of that, Henry always preferred not to rush up to a crime scene – unless he knew the crime was in progress there and then;

it gave him a little extra time to take everything in, and he knew
there were never any second chances at crime scenes.

All these things went through his mind automatically – almost
without thinking, because he had applied such thoughts many, many
times in the past – as he got out of his Audi, closed the door gently
with a bump of his arse and started a slow jog towards the track
up to the house which was tarmacked on either side with grass
running up the centre. Straight ahead was the Twain's farmhouse.

Henry had never had cause to visit it before, although he did
know of it.

He maintained his gentle pace until he reached the turning circle
at the front, in which James Twain's big four-wheel-drive vehicle was
parked, but then veered left and went towards the rear where he
guessed the workshop was situated.

It was.

Henry had half expected to find a renovated barn or cowshed,
but it was actually a modern, prefabricated warehouse-type unit, the
bottom section being breeze block and the upper section a corrugated
metal of some sort.

There was a large shutter door in the centre of the front elevation,
which was closed, with a personal door on the right to which he
headed.

He listened hard as he approached, all his senses now jangling
on full alert.

In his earlier conversation with Celia when she had been on her
way to Lancaster, she had said that the engine of the plane James
was rebuilding had been on and loud. Henry could not hear anything
like that now and he knew from watching stuff on TV and seeing
Spitfires on occasional flypasts that they had noisy engines. He
would have been able to hear it from outside the unit, even if the
building had been soundproofed.

He could hear nothing. Just birds twittering.

He paused at the personal door and listened further: nothing.

He tried the handle. The door opened into a short corridor. Straight
ahead was another door and there were two doors on the right. He
guessed the one ahead led into the workshop and the ones on the
right opened into offices.

Time to find out.

He walked into the corridor and knuckled open the first door on
the right, which was ajar. It was a storeroom of some sort, shelves

stacked with box files, and he saw that several of the files had been tipped out, the contents scattered.

'Uh-huh,' he thought. 'Intruder . . . burglar . . . maybe killer?'

He did not enter the room but carried on the few steps to the next door, which was also slightly ajar. He nudged it fully open. This was an office – desk, chairs, shelves – and this too was a complete mess, with papers strewn around, files emptied, drawers open and contents flung around.

Henry was working mentally through everything.

If Celia was telling the truth (and if he had been the senior investigating officer on the case, every thought he would have, every hypothesis he came up with until proved differently, would be preceded by that statement: *If Celia is telling the truth*), and if the mess in these two rooms was caused by an unknown intruder, it would appear that person had carried out these searches after a confrontation with James, not before, and this would put a whole different interpretation on the chain of events.

He knew he was jumping ahead here, though, and the first thing to find out was whether or not James was in fact dead, then start working back from there.

He raised his eyebrows, turned slightly and walked slowly, quietly to the door at the end of the corridor.

He paused. This door was closed. He glanced up and saw it was controlled by a pneumatic strut.

He pulled down the handle, put his shoulder to the door and opened it.

Beyond was a large workshop.

Henry sidled through the door, which began to close slowly with a pneumatic hiss. He was holding his breath now, feeling his heart hammering inside his chest, his mouth going dry.

This was one of those things that never got any easier with time, age or experience: entering a property with the expectation of finding a dead body. Even now, so many years on, he could still recall every thought and feeling when doing it for the first time as a nineteen-year-old rookie cop, how that felt . . . and now, that slight feeling of nausea was with him again.

The Spitfire was in pride of place, more or less in the centre of the workshop, with the huge engine on a stand to one side of the fighter.

But Henry didn't have time to be impressed because the body of a man he believed to be James Twain was lying almost underneath the wing closest to him, face down in a pool of blood, with the back of his head stove in.

Except that was not all.

Squatting down close to Twain's battered head, but not in the blood, was a figure clad in a head-to-toe forensic suit, facing away from Henry.

Henry froze, his whole being tightening up as he took in this tableau. He emitted a long, slow breath through pursed lips as the person stood up. In their right hand he saw a gun, possibly a revolver, but he wasn't certain in those opening moments.

Then, just as Henry had done, the person seemed to freeze: had he or she sensed someone entering the workshop?

Henry still did not move. He was calculating distances, angles, routes, mainly in terms of beating a hasty retreat as there was no way he was even considering tackling this person physically, not least because he could not move anywhere as quickly as he could have done ten years ago and there was little chance of covering a distance of twenty feet or so before the person pivoted and shot him.

Maybe, in his more reckless days, he would have given it a go. That was once upon a time.

The figure did not move, still faced away from Henry.

For a few moments, nothing happened.

Until that fucking door on its pneumatic strut clicked shut behind him.

The figure spun. Henry had expected to see a face but instead saw a full-face hockey goalkeeper mask – but he did not have time to think about that because as the figure turned, the gun came up.

Henry's survival instinct kicked in like an explosive charge, and he suddenly discovered he could move a lot more quickly than he thought possible.

Hurling himself sideways, he went down behind a red-coloured reinforced steel tool chest on castors which provided a very effective, if temporary, bulletproof barrier between him and the shooter.

As he thumped down on to one knee on the concrete floor, jarring his whole body via his patella, two bullets clanged into the back of the tool chest, loud and scary as they ricocheted off the steel.

Henry knew he didn't have much time.

Hardly any, in fact.

All the intruder had to do was sprint across the workshop, lean

around and shoot the crouching ex-detective, which meant Henry
had to do an immediate reappraisal of his situation: he realized that
the only way to survive this encounter if the shooter was intent on
killing him was to take the initiative without hesitation and not to
ponder the pros and cons of anything.

He had to go on the offensive. *Just do!*

An upright tool chest on castors might well be ideal to hide
behind while under fire but it was also, he realized, perfect to use
as an assault weapon in its own right, rather like a mini-tank or
battering ram.

Hoping that the castors weren't locked in place, he spread both
hands, placed his palms against the chest and gave a mighty shove.

Much to his relief, the wheels turned and the chest began to roll.
He pushed hard, making it gather momentum quickly in spite of its
weight.

And as it sped up, Henry emitted a howl of rage like a battle
cry.

He fully expected to meet some resistance – more shots being
fired or the appearance of the shooter to one side – and he thought
he would somehow have to change the direction of the tool chest
in order to keep the barrier up, but nothing came at him – no shots,
no attack, zilch.

Puzzled, he gave one mighty heave, sending the chest rolling
across the workshop floor, but instead of going with it, keeping his
head down, he stood up – just in time to see the shooter run out of
the workshop by way of an outward-opening galvanized steel fire
door in the side wall, closing the door behind as they left.

Keeping to a crouch, Henry ran across, slammed down the panic
bar, then slowed down as he pivoted out.

By this time the shooter was a good forty metres in the distance,
running across James Twain's well-tended lawn and heading towards
a door set into a brick wall surrounding what Henry assumed
was a hidden garden or an orchard.

The shooter stopped at this door, turned, saw Henry, and once
more the gun came up and took aim.

Although the gap between the two of them was of a distance that
would make it difficult for anyone, however skilled with a firearm,
to be accurate with a handgun, Henry wasn't about to take a chance.

Whoever was behind that mask, dressed in a full-body forensic
suit, looked to have got over the surprise of being discovered at the

scene of a murder that they may well have committed and was now confident enough to take a breath and drop into a shooting stance.

Henry did a twirl, not willing to find out if this person was a brilliant sharpshooter or just dead lucky.

He twisted back through the fire door into the workshop, closed it behind him, leaned back in relief against the door and almost had heart failure when two bullets slammed into the door either side of his head, not coming through the steel but causing indentations.

Henry sagged instantly to a squat and rolled sideways as a further two bullets hit the door a couple of feet below the first two where his back had been resting. Neither of these bullets penetrated the steel.

He held his position then, wondering if the intruder was going to return, but a few moments later he heard the sound of a motor-cycle engine being revved up and then disappearing into the distance.

The breath he exhaled then was long and stuttering.

He was lying on his back, looking up towards the roof of the workshop. He turned his head and looked along the floor at the body of James Twain whose face, distorted and misshapen from the horrific blunt force trauma the back of his head had suffered, was twisted towards Henry. Only one of Twain's eyes was open, and it seemed, even in death, to be glaring accusingly at Henry.

FIVE

Even though Henry was now back home, sitting in his favourite armchair in the living room of the owner's accommodation at The Tawny Owl, no matter how hard he tried, he could not erase the image of a dead man's eye from his own, inner, mind's eye.

Whether or not his own eyes were wide open or tightly shut, he was struggling to rub out the way in which James Twain's single eyeball seemed to stare malevolently at him across the blood-soaked floor of the workshop, as though blaming Henry for his horrific demise.

Henry now had his eyes shut and was kneading his eyelids with a finger and thumb as though attempting to massage away that one-eyed accusing glare, but also to try to ease the storming headache that had come thundering on since returning home.

'Here, old guy.'

He'd been so deep in his own world that he hadn't even heard the living-room door open and close and someone come in.

His eyes snapped open.

Standing in front of him, in what Henry would have fairly recently dismissed as clothing entirely inappropriate for a detective or any other plain-clothes cop – unless undercover and the role demanded it – was Detective Sergeant Debbie Blackstone. Even though Henry had learned not to judge, sometimes her appearance still had the power to make him blink twice. Today: pink, punk-like spiked hair, a face full of studs including one, he knew from previously, affixed to her tongue and one looped through her nose, plus the others in her ears and lips; clothing consisting of a short denim jacket with *Ban the Bomb* patches over a Sex Pistols T-shirt, a tartan mini-skirt, deliberately laddered black tights and pink Doc Marten boots.

She was out of control but in a good way, Henry had learned.

She was holding a mug of steaming tea which she proffered to him. 'Here,' she said again, 'we need to look after our ageing population even if they have desecrated the future of planet Earth.'

Henry shook his head – not a debate he wanted to rise to, ever. He took the brew.

'Just as you like it,' Blackstone said. 'Full-cream milk, strong as fuck and eight heaped sugars – just that energy boost you clearly need after the shock you've had.'

She blubbed her bottom lip with her first and second fingers, indicating he was a cry baby.

Henry took a sip and ignored the jibe. The tea was exactly right – middling strong, a drop of skimmed milk, no sugar, exactly how he liked it, as Blackstone knew.

'Tastes good,' he said genuinely, looking at her.

DS Debbie Blackstone had been his immediate boss and running partner during his tenure as a civilian investigator on the Cold Case Unit, and despite her appearance and often grating personality, her unrelenting piss-taking of him about his age and what she called his 'Gammon views' (he had no idea what that meant), he found her to be one of the best, most committed detectives he had ever known and now, although he didn't let it be widely known, a good friend.

'We're going to need to talk to you good and proper now, you know that, don't you?' Blackstone told him. '"We" being the real cops, that is.'

He nodded, curling both hands around the mug. 'I'm just having a bit of difficulty purging the moment that three eyes met across a blood-soaked workshop floor . . . his eye and my two.'

'Really?'

Henry shrugged.

'Whatever, I'm just forewarning you that Diane will be around to talk to you shortly,' Blackstone said.

'I've already given her my story.'

'We know. We need more detail now, apparently, and a written statement.'

Henry shrugged again and sighed, and it was his turn to say, 'Whatever,' even though he knew this was coming . . . it had to.

He had already spoken to the police at the scene of James Twain's murder.

Half an hour ago, as Henry started to get slowly to his feet in the workshop, Jake Niven had arrived and blundered into the crime scene in his size elevens. Henry shouted a warning as he came through the door from the corridor to stop where he was while Henry went over to meet him. Before he'd had the chance to explain anything to Jake, Diane Daniels, Blackstone and another detective turned up, and Diane instructed Jake to sit Henry down in the police Land Rover once Henry had quickly filled them in on the scene, what had happened and his encounters with Celia Twain.

It seemed that somewhere wires had been crossed. No cops had split off to go to The Tawny Owl and all had converged on the murder scene.

Henry suggested it might be a good idea to get someone there ASAP and take Celia to a police station, either voluntarily or under arrest on suspicion of murder if necessary, so she could be dealt with forensically, her clothing bagged, samples and photographs taken.

Henry then sat like a good boy in Jake's Land Rover for about twenty minutes while the cops were busy at the scene; he watched further arrivals, including a dog patrol and the police helicopter, the latter taking up noisy station over the Twain's house, presumably awaiting instructions.

Finally Jake appeared, rolling his eyes and shaking his head.

'It's like Fred Karno's circus in there,' he said, adding nothing more. Except, 'I've been told to get Celia to Blackpool nick and book her in.'

'Better late than never,' Henry said caustically. He was now bored and irritable.

'Agreed,' Jake said. 'There's some big argy-bargy going on about who should have gone to deal with her . . . obviously, I'm in the firing line, but I know I told comms to send a patrol or a detective to Th'Owl and sort her out, but it got lost in all the excitement.'

'It'll be on the log if necessary.'

'I know,' Jake muttered, vexed. 'Anyway, it's my job now, apparently.'

'And what about me?' Henry asked.

'They'll see you back there in due course – but you mustn't come into contact with Celia, and we want your clothing bagged up, too.'

'OK,' Henry said wearily. 'Do you want me to strip here and now?'

'Let's split the difference. I'll grab a couple of evidence bags and you do it at Th'Owl, under my supervision, obviously.'

'OK.' Henry didn't have the inclination to argue. He slid out of the Land Rover, got into his Audi and they met back at the pub.

Celia was still in the snug being quietly supervised by Ginny and also Maude, who had volunteered to help. As Henry came up the front steps, Ginny ran out to meet him and he quickly explained what was happening and that he could not come into contact with Celia now that he'd been embroiled in the actual crime scene, and that Jake, who had pulled up on the car park, was going to deal with her.

'Was it bad?' Ginny asked. 'Was it like she described?'

'And more,' Henry said grimly but didn't elucidate.

'Bloody hell!'

'Mmm . . . has she said anything more?'

'No, hardly a word since you left, other than she wants to change her clothes, and I don't blame her – she's covered in blood.'

'She'll have to do that down at the station under supervision,' Henry said. 'They'll want all her clothes for analysis and they'll want to question her. They'll probably stick her in a forensic suit.'

Henry went through to the living quarters where he stripped and dropped his outer clothes into evidence bags being held open by Jake, who then sealed the bags. He put them in the front passenger seat of his vehicle and returned to deal with Celia.

Henry, changed into his jogging bottoms and an old hoodie, stood and watched as Jake spoke to Celia, who seemed numb and unresponsive at first, but when Jake told her she was under arrest on suspicion of murder, cautioned and cuffed her, she sagged down to her knees, completely devastated and verging on hysterical. Jake had to catch her and heft her gently through the pub and into the back of the Land Rover.

Henry retreated to the living room where he slumped into his armchair and began reviewing things, but he kept getting stuck on James Twain's single, accusing, eyeball.

'There is one thing I might just mention to you, Henry,' Blackstone began in a hushed, confidential tone of voice as Henry sipped on his mug of tea. 'A heads-up, you might say.'

'And that is?'

'It's a bit awks,' she said, using the shortened version of 'awkward' often utilized by younger people and applied to problematic social situations.

'Tell me, I'm a grown man.'

'Well,' she said, about to impart some rocket-fuelled news. She was forced to stop abruptly when the living-room door opened and Diane Daniels hustled in, followed by the male detective who had arrived at the murder scene with her. Blackstone's mouth clamped shut. She looked at Henry wide-eyed and quickly said, 'Can't say.'

'Can't say what?' Diane asked, overhearing this.

'Oh, nothing, nothing at all,' Blackstone said delicately.

'OK, good,' Diane said, all business. To Blackstone, she said, 'OK, DS Blackstone, I think we can take it from here. I want you to get back to the scene, please. I'm appointing you as crime scene manager for the time being at least.' She spoke politely, firmly, but with a hint of chill.

Puzzled, Henry watched the exchange and the furrows on his brow grew even deeper when Blackstone answered, 'OK, boss, on my way.' He was confused on two fronts. The first was Blackstone's presence to begin with, because as a cold case operative she did not turn out to murders. Henry was going to ask her earlier but hadn't had the chance. His secondary confusion was about Blackstone's subservience to Diane, calling her 'boss'.

He shrugged inwardly. No doubt the questions would be answered in due course.

Blackstone gave Henry a quick, surreptitious wink and turned to leave as Diane and the detective she'd arrived with moved to stand in front of him. Blackstone stopped at the door and looked at Henry between the two detectives, gave an *Eek!* expression and left.

Henry looked at Diane and the guy.

'Mind if we sit?' Diane asked rather formally.

Henry gestured to the settee and the other armchair. Diane perched on the edge of the settee at an angle to Henry, and the male detective sat in the armchair across the room, directly opposite, and looked appraisingly at Henry as if trying to weigh him up. Henry wondered if he knew of his bad-boy reputation.

He smiled at him, then looked at Diane, who squirmed on the cushion.

'How are you feeling?' she enquired.

'I'll be honest. I'm a bit shook up.'

'Only to be expected. Anyone would be – finding a murder victim, then having someone shoot at you.'

Henry knew just how empathetic Diane would be because she had been shot and badly wounded not so long ago; Henry had saved her life, and she had been on the critical list for a long time, could have died, had first-hand experience of it.

Henry just nodded. His head was really beginning to throb now.

'We need you to go through everything step by step, Mr Christie,' the male detective said from across the room.

'I think I already told you,' Henry said, although he knew it hadn't been in the detail required.

'Tell us again,' the male detective said, and in three patronizing words managed to wind Henry right up.

'So,' Henry said, just to wind him up in turn, 'I think we've yet to be formally introduced. You know who I am . . . you are—?'

'Uh, this is DCI Wellhaven,' Diane interrupted. 'Mark Wellhaven, my new boss on FMIT.'

'Ah,' Henry said, as though the name meant something to him, which it did. Now he understood what Blackstone had meant by 'awks'.

Wellhaven smirked.

And Henry swallowed a chill pill. 'We haven't met before, have we?' he said.

Wellhaven continued with the smirk. 'Nope.'

'You're a transferee from another force, I believe?'

'West Yorkshire,' he confirmed, eyes narrowing.

Henry's eyes went sideways to Diane. 'And I'm assuming you're Detective Inspector Daniels now? Are congratulations in order?'

'I'm substantive, yes,' she confirmed.

Their eyes held each other's for a moment longer than necessary, and Henry could not help but feel a steel blade of hurt penetrating his heart as he looked ever so briefly into the eyes of the woman who had publicly, if accidentally, dumped him not so very long ago – and yes, it still riled him – and who had now turned up with her new boss who, Henry had heard on the gossip grapevine, was also her new boyfriend. Or lover. Or whatever.

And the mischievous devil on Henry's left shoulder urged him to look at Wellhaven, hold up his right hand, cross his fingers and say, with arched eyebrows, 'You two, huh?' with a nod and a wink.

Wellhaven stiffened, and Henry regretted his childishness immediately, but his little red friend danced a jig.

Diane said frostily, 'Can we just get on, children?'

With a very false smile affixed to his face, Henry said, 'It would be a pleasure to further assist the police.'

'We will need a written statement, but this will do for now.' Diane had voice-recorded Henry's 'version of events', as she liked to call it, on her mobile phone, followed by a short question-and-answer session to clear up some points.

She picked up her phone from the coffee table and switched off the record function, at which moment the phone rang. She checked the screen. 'It's the boss,' she said to Wellhaven, which Henry understood to mean Rik Dean. 'I need to take this. Excuse me.'

She stood up and left the room, closing the door behind her, leaving Henry and Wellhaven alone.

There was a period of tense silence, broken when Wellhaven said, 'I hear you were a good detective back in the day.'

Henry snorted a laugh.

'That probably didn't come out as I intended,' Wellhaven said quickly. 'I just meant you have a good reputation.'

'I did OK,' Henry said vaguely.

More tense silence.

'Look . . . mate . . . we didn't mean this to happen.' Wellhaven crossed his fingers. 'You know. This. Me. Diane.'

'You don't have to explain anything.'

'I love her,' Wellhaven blurted, then fidgeted and reddened up.

'Best of luck with that,' Henry said sourly.

'What's that supposed to mean?'

Before Henry could formulate an answer that would have

prevented this uncomfortable exchange – he hesitated to call it a conversation or discussion – from going tits up, Diane came back in and hurriedly announced, 'We need to go, Mark – another murder's come in, a shooting.'

Wellhaven shot out of the armchair, and Henry could tell the guy was relieved at having to attend a murder rather than spend any more time with Henry. *Typical bloke*, Henry thought, *would rather see a dead body than talk feelings.*

'Got a name?' Henry asked.

Diane hesitated, obviously wondering if she should tell Henry, then relented. 'Marcus Durham. Ring any bells?'

It did, but Henry didn't get the chance to say anything as Diane's phone rang again, and she and Wellhaven left without waiting for an answer.

SIX

'M y, my, you look the part . . . ladykiller or what?' Blackstone said to Henry, evaluating him critically.

He returned the look. 'At least I know how to get dolled-up.'

'Oooh – right back at me,' she said, pretending to be offended but clearly not caring one jot about what people thought of her and also enjoying the exchange with Henry: both gave as good as they got.

It was just before seven p.m., and Blackstone had bumped into Henry just as he was about to leave The Tawny Owl and make his way on foot across the village to Maude's house, where he was due to put in an appearance at the family meal at which he would meet her offspring for the first time. He was dreading the encounter, was now running late and wished he had the courage to say no, both to the meal and to Maude . . . and for both those things he did not like himself an awful lot.

However, he had agreed to go – after all, it might just turn out to be a pleasant evening – and had made the effort to look half decent. After a long soapy bath to wash and warm away the stress of the James Twain murder scene and the day in general, he'd dressed in a jacket, chinos and brogues, and was fairly pleased with the end result.

'If you were thirty years younger – no, forty – I'd drop everything for you,' Blackstone said lewdly. 'I'd be all over you like a rash.'

'You really are a piece of work, aren't you?'

'You know that, I know that and the world knows it.'

Henry sighed. Over the course of the last few months working with her on the CCU, he had discovered a lot of depth under the brash veneer and a damaged person who thought that her only defence was to rail against the world. But Henry had seen another side to her, one he liked a lot, so he forgave her many trespasses.

Blackstone had called into Th'Owl on her way home from the murder scene, which she was now managing, hoping to have a chance to speak to Henry, and had been disappointed to find him venturing out.

That said, Henry was eager to have a quick catch-up with her about the Twains and whether or not she knew anything about Marcus Durham's murder, although Henry suspected a day as crime scene manager had kept her very focused on the task in hand.

'How has it gone?' he asked first.

'OK . . . CSM's just a process and I've got the hang of it . . .'

'Oh, I forgot to ask – how come you are here in the first place?' Henry enquired, going slightly off topic.

'Turning out to a murder, you mean?'

He nodded.

'Because I'm now off CCU and full-time on FMIT, where I've been CSM all day . . . Jeez, my life is full of fuckin' abbreviations and acronyms,' she moaned.

'Oh, I didn't know about the move.'

'Rikky Boy thought I should be given the chance. Says I'm wasted on cold cases.' She was referring, less than affectionately, to the current head of FMIT, Detective Superintendent Rik Dean, who happened to be Henry's brother-in-law, a very old friend and colleague.

'Not wasted, I'd argue,' Henry said, 'but FMIT is definitely a better use of your talents.'

'Well, at least it gets me back into the mainstream as opposed to the backwaters,' she said, alluding to the fact that for a long time she had been passed from department to department within the force like a hot potato. No one had known how to deal with her after her return to work following an acid attack when she'd gone off the rails and proved a challenge to supervise.

'That's good, congratulations.'

'Thank you.' She curtsied. 'I'm a real detective now.'

Henry came back to the subject in hand. 'I assume the mystery gunman or woman who escaped on a motorbike wasn't found?'

'Nah.' Then Blackstone picked up on what Henry had said. 'What do you mean, gunman *or woman*?'

'Well, it all happened so quickly, and I keep running it through my mind, and I only saw the person in flashes . . .'

'Get to the point,' Blackstone said irritably.

'What I'm saying is whoever it was – male, female or otherwise – had a fairly small build. Obviously, the forensic suit billowed a bit, so it's not like I could make out boobs or anything . . . I dunno . . . small man or a woman . . . wouldn't want to put all my eggs in one basket if I was the SIO,' he concluded.

'Helpful.'

Henry eyed her again. 'Anything of interest at the crime scene?'

'Other than a dead body? Some bullet holes? That sort of thing?'

'Anything.'

'Twain's filing system in his offices has been ransacked, but it'll be some time before we find out if anything is missing. Hopefully Mrs Twain will be able to help on that score.'

'Unless, of course, she's the culprit.'

'That what you think?'

'It's definitely where the trail should start,' Henry said. 'Anyway, not my problem.'

'Do you actually think she could have spannered him to death like that?' Blackstone pushed him. 'Bit brutal.'

'Murders often are . . . best get used to it now you're on FMIT,' Henry said with a wink. Then added, 'She did have a knife to his throat last night.'

'I didn't know that.'

'Ask DI Daniels and her lover, DCI Wellhaven,' Henry said acidly. 'That said, they got sidetracked to another murder. Have you heard anything about that?'

'Oh yeah, and no, haven't heard a thing . . . I imagine Rikky Boy's running round like a blue-arsed fly just about now, trying to find enough people to staff two murders with everyone and his wife coming down with Covid.'

'Murderers are just so thoughtless. Fancy having the temerity to kill someone during a pandemic,' Henry quipped. 'Anyway' – he checked his watch – 'I need to get going. I'm an hour late already.' He paused and looked at Blackstone. She looked pretty tired, and he knew she had a fair distance to get home to her apartment on Preston Docks. He also knew that, like all good detectives, she carried a change of clothing and a toothbrush in the boot of her car. 'Hey, if you want, you can grab a meal here, you know? And if you're going to be working nearby tomorrow, you can crash in the guest bedroom.'

Blackstone's eyes lit up. 'Seriously?'

'Ginny's in the kitchen . . . go and seek her out.'

Henry gave her a nod, then ducked past to make his way out but looked over his shoulder and called, 'Thanks for trying to give me the heads-up about Diane and lover-boy – it was "awks", as you say.'

Then he was out on to the front terrace of Th'Owl where he stopped for a moment and caught a breath. The evening was still relatively warm but just starting to turn dark.

He was amused and surprised to see Mrs Gough trundling down the road towards the village centre in her wheelchair, powerful torches sellotaped to each arm of it, both on, illuminating her way like a pair of headlights. She spotted Henry, stopped, niftily spun the wheelchair on the spot and drove towards him as he descended the terrace steps on to the car park, where they met up.

'Mrs Gough, out on patrol, I see.' Henry smiled.

'In my book, crime prevention only works when you go out and prevent crime,' she stated firmly. 'And I'm going around putting an end to these bloody youths who are causing distress to everyone.'

Henry warned her, 'Leave it to Jake. Don't get mixed up with these kids. They're a nasty bunch, from what I can gather, and they'll think nothing of tipping you out of your wheelchair.'

'They wouldn't dare . . . anyway, that's not what I wanted to talk to you about. What do you know about James Twain's death? Did the wife do it? What's happening with The Swan's Neck now he's gone? Or is someone else in the frame?'

'Questions, questions, questions – the answers to which I do not have.'

'Surely you must have the inside track to the cops, eh? Being an ex-one.'

'Even if I did, I'm not that interested, Mrs Gough. And as far as

The Swan's Neck is concerned, I guess that's a dead duck now.' He smirked at his cutting-edge humour, but added, 'Obviously, I can't say for sure, though, but no doubt it's a win for SONAG. Now, you be careful of those yobs, OK?'

'I hear you're at Maude's tonight?' Mrs Gough said cheekily, ignoring him.

Henry wasn't surprised by her knowledge. 'You hear right.' He gave her a mock salute and continued on his way.

Mrs Gough expertly spun the wheelchair and powered off on her quest to hunt down felons in the village.

Maude greeted Henry with a peck on the cheek and a worried look on her face, which Henry could not quite fathom. He was quickly distracted by Maude's dog, an energetic Bichon Frise, which he disliked intensely and who, in turn, seemed to sense this and harass him mercilessly because of it.

The dog grabbed his right leg and began humping his calf muscle. Henry peeled the brute off as delicately as possible without actually kicking it across the hallway.

Maude apologized for the dog's behaviour, and he apologized for being late, but he could tell she wasn't really with it as she handed him a glass of red wine and led him through to the lounge where her children, with partners, awaited. Henry could tell from the atmosphere that he'd walked into a tense situation, though he'd no reason to suspect it was anything to do with him.

Maude introduced him to her son Will (and his wife, Tessa) and daughter Eva (and her husband or boyfriend – Henry wasn't completely certain – David) – and they all shook hands because it was the right thing to do.

Henry felt he was intruding into some family disagreement, but when he glanced at Maude, she smiled at him reassuringly.

There was small talk during which Henry knew he was under intense scrutiny from Will in particular, although when Henry tried to hold the man's gaze, he always lowered his eyes, making Henry highly suspicious of him.

Eventually, the food was ready – a chicken and seafood paella prepared by Maude in a huge pan, plus salad and lots of warm crusty bread. Henry thought it was an unusual dish to serve, but it was delicious and did seem to ease some of the tension as they dug into it and steam rose from the rice.

Finally the whole dish was empty, everyone had eaten at least two portions and they were all sitting back replete, sipping Spanish wine and beer.

As they moved back into the lounge, Henry offered to take the paella pan back into the kitchen to soak it.

Maude looked upon the gesture with gratitude as none of the others had so far lent a hand, so Henry picked up the big dish, carried it through and began to run the hot tap. As he did this, he became aware of someone stepping into the kitchen behind him and closing the door with a firm click.

He didn't even need to turn his head to know who it was, but he did anyway, and he was right: Will Crichton, Maude's only son and heir. Mid-thirties, an entrepreneur, as he'd described himself, though he was vague about which field. Henry had already pinned him as a smarmy bullshitter, but now the way in which he leaned against the door to stop anyone else entering, plus the way he looked at Henry through snake-like eyes, made Henry wary.

'Henry Christie,' Will stated unpleasantly, not easy to do in two short words.

'That's me.' Henry smiled.

He angled the paella pan under the stream of hot water to rinse the rice away and added a squirt of detergent.

'Ex-cop, landlord of the local hostelry.'

'Guilty,' Henry admitted, already wondering how Maude would feel about her son being smashed in the face with a cast-iron paella pan.

'What is it with you and my mum?'

Straight to the point.

'In what way?'

'You – her – what is it all about?'

Henry lay the pan down on the draining board and picked up a tea towel. As he dried his hands, he turned to Will, feeling the hairs on the back of his neck rising into a hackle. The thing was, of course, at least from Henry's side, there wasn't really anything between him and Maude. He did wonder whether Maude might have said something different to her family, and if she had, it was urgent that Henry put her right on that score . . . put *her* right, not put *Will* right, because he was feeling pretty annoyed with the self-styled entrepreneur's attitude.

'Why, what has your mum said?'

'That you're just good friends and it's nothing to do with me.'

That relieved Henry, who said, 'Well, there you go, right on both counts.'

'Except I don't buy it.'

'Which bit, Will?'

'Both bits.'

'Hang on, hang on,' Henry said, patting fresh air in a calming gesture. 'Whatever you believe or don't believe is your problem.'

'You're sleeping with her, aren't you?'

'Nothing to do with you. You know, when you came in here, I thought you were going to get straight to the point, but you're actually fannying around, Will, and pissing me off.'

'Do you know how much my mum's worth?'

'I'm not interested in that,' Henry said.

'Eighteen million, give or take. My dad's legacy.'

Henry didn't show anything. He'd heard ten million rumoured; even at eighteen, he wasn't interested. He sighed down his nose.

'And that's what you're after, isn't it?' Will accused. 'You're just some ageing, beer-bellied, lothario gold-digger and you're after my mum's fortune, which is money that rightly belongs to me and my sister. You're a poor, retired cop running a local pub that's probably on the brink of collapse and you see my mum as a cash cow. Get into her knickers, get into her fortune.'

'You have a dirty mouth, Will.'

'And what are you going to do about it, old guy?' Will stood upright, literally puffed out his chest and bunched his hands into fists. Henry thought he probably hadn't thrown a punch in his entire life.

Henry wasn't a puncher, either – more a grappler, an over-powerer – and although he was certain he could get the better of Will despite their age difference, he did not want this evening to go completely down the pan for Maude's sake and the sake of his own dignity.

'Will, you believe what you want to believe. But the truth is that whatever the relationship is between me and your mum, it's nothing to do with you . . . you're a big boy now, so deal with it.'

'You need to leave and don't come back and don't see my mum again.'

'Simply because I don't want to upset your mum – though you don't seem to have that problem – I'll go, OK?' Henry said. 'But this is the one and only time I'll back off from you – do you understand?'

Henry jerked a finger at him, which made him jump. 'And by the way, just for your information, I happen to know your mum's left her fortune to Water Aid,' he lied on the hoof.

Henry stepped towards him, and Will edged aside to let him back into the lounge where Henry made a pathetic excuse about being called back to Th'Owl, grabbed his coat and said his goodbyes.

Maude followed him out on to the front step, closing the door behind her.

'It's Will, isn't it?' she said.

Henry shrugged. 'I don't want trouble.'

'He's terrified of losing his inheritance.'

'I kinda don't blame him in a way.'

'But you don't want my money, do you, Henry?' She looked pleadingly at him. 'All we want is a bit of fun. Both of us deserve it, don't we?'

Henry nodded. 'Yeah, I suppose we do.'

They hugged briefly, and Henry set off home.

Maude's house was situated on the opposite side of the stream that trickled through Kendleton, on the same road as Jake Niven's police house. Henry had to walk down past Jake's, then into the dip and over the narrow road bridge spanning the stream.

He paused halfway across the bridge and leaned on it with his elbows, looking towards the village, wondering about Maude and her family.

That she was a very nice, unpretentious woman was not in dispute, nor was the fact she was extremely wealthy – far richer than the rumours apparently – but she never flaunted it. It had been left to her by her husband.

She had grown fond of Henry over the last couple of years, and he'd succumbed to her charms a few times but just didn't see anything beyond it, which would be good news for nasty, money-grabbing Will, but Henry had baited him because one thing Henry despised was being told what to think or do.

So he was in a bit of a quandary.

He looked up into the clear sky for some inspiration and put the question to Kate, his dead wife who had been taken far too soon by aggressive cancer. She was his first and second wife, having seen fit to remarry him following a silly divorce of his own making. Generally speaking, he asked Kate the tough questions.

'Well, Kate, my love,' he asked out loud. 'What's the way forward here, babe? I know I don't love Maude. I like her. She's great company, but I'm not sure that's enough for her, despite what she says. Yet I don't want to hurt her.'

He opened his arms wide.

'Or what about you, Alison? What do you have to say on the subject?'

Alison was Ginny's stepmother, who Henry had been on course to marry before her tragic death. Henry knew how fortunate he had been to meet and fall in love with her, and he hadn't planned on letting her go . . . Now he liked to imagine that Kate and Alison, the two women who'd been the keys to his life, were both up there laughing heartily down at him.

'Aye, thought so,' he said and began to trudge towards The Tawny Owl.

As he did, he caught the faintest whiff of cannabis smoke on the breeze coming from the woodland glade at the far side of the village green, the spot where the gang of kids who were on Mrs Gough's radar mustered to share a spliff or two as well as inhale from nitrous oxide capsules. He heard laughter too and some shouting, and although he never wanted to spoil anyone's fun, he could not stop his top lip from sneering.

At least they were out of harm's way.

Until he heard a cackle of laughter followed by the sound of a woman's scream.

Henry stopped to listen, wondering if it was just the kids being loud and unpleasant as usual. He knew there were three or four teenage girls among their number who were as rowdy as the lads, but there was something different about these screams because they did not come with laughter, they came with distress, fear and terror. And they sounded like an older person.

As Henry came off the bridge, he turned sharp left to walk along the footpath that hugged the stream, about six feet above water level. It was a well-trodden, unlit path, one he'd strolled along many times, so although it was now dark, he was pretty sure of his footing; also, the ambient light from the spotlights that lit up the front of The Tawny Owl several hundred metres away and some streetlights on the road helped him to see.

Even so, he took out his mobile phone and switched on the torch app, angling the beam down to light up his feet as he knew that his brogues were probably not the best footwear for this sort of journey.

There was another scream.

Definitely female, definitely older.

Henry upped his pace.

Ahead of him, the stream ran parallel with the village green, then the water veered away left and it was on this section, protected by a semi-circle of trees, that the kids tended to congregate, out of sight, out of mind, but not necessarily out of hearing or smell, on a pebble-strewn bank of the stream.

Henry reached the turn and had to beat his way through several metres of shoulder-high bushes before eventually breaking out into the opening where, as he suspected, a gang had gathered, all without exception wearing dark-coloured jogging outfits, all standing around what at first looked like a bunch of rags by the water's edge.

Except it wasn't – and Veronica Gough's overturned wheelchair made that plain.

The 'rags' in the water were actually Mrs Gough's writhing body, and one of the lads had a foot on her head, pushing her face under the water, half drowning her, then releasing her to breathe again, as though waterboarding a prisoner. Each time she came up for air, the kids surrounding this cruel act let out a cheer.

Henry was immediately consumed by ferocious rage.

'You utter bastards!' he shouted as he emerged from the bushes and raced towards them, jostling roughly through them until he was inside their circle where he hurled himself at the main tormentor who was the one carrying out the torture.

Henry barrelled into him and sent him staggering knee-deep into the stream, ordering him, 'You stay there and don't move, lad.'

The boy had tripped up and gone on to his hands and knees.

Henry was aware some of the kids were backing off, some sprinting away into the darkness, petrified by his ire.

Henry knelt down by Mrs Gough, gently raising her into a sitting position.

She coughed, spluttered and sobbed, completely drenched, shivering and, most of all, terrified. She clung desperately to Henry, clawing at him, saying, 'Oh God, thank you, thank you.'

'You're all right now, I'm here,' he promised her. He slid a hand under her armpit and heaved her up. She was lighter and frailer than he anticipated, and it was easy to get her upright. He looked around at the circle of youths. Some had scattered but a few remained, which part of him found rather worrying.

'You!' he barked at one of the lads and flashed his phone torch beam into his face. 'Get that wheelchair upright now.'

The lad hesitated.

'Yes, you,' Henry clarified, glaring at him.

'Don't do a fucking thing!' the voice of the lad Henry had drenched shouted from behind.

Henry went rigid with even more fury.

The lad went on. 'Are you going to let him do this to me? Are you going to let him get away with this?' he demanded, pleading to his mates.

Henry looked back at the one he'd chosen to right the wheelchair. Coldly he said, 'Upright, now.'

The lad hesitated. His eyes flickered from his mate to Henry and back again.

'I won't tell you again,' Henry said.

'Are you? Are you going to let him do this?' the lad in the water screamed almost hysterically.

Still supporting Mrs Gough, Henry rotated towards this lad who was obviously the ringleader. He put the torch beam on his face. 'I'm going to kick your arse in a minute, laddie – right across the village green.'

'Did you hear him? He can't say that. He can't do that. I'll fuckin' sue you if you touch me.'

Henry turned to the others, glad to see another couple had scarpered into the darkness. They were losing their bravado. He played the torch over the one he'd chosen for wheelchair duty. 'If you don't sort the wheelchair out, you're in deep shit – understand?'

A realization seemed to dawn on the lad – maybe his adrenaline had left his system – and he did the right thing as the other lad in the water stumbled out and said, 'Come on, let's go.'

Henry manoeuvred Mrs Gough into the wheelchair, giving himself a free hand with which he grabbed the lad's bicep, which felt thin and weedy. 'You're going nowhere, mate,' he growled and jerked the youth towards him. To the other lad, he said, 'You push this lady up out of here and across the green . . .'

'I . . . I . . .' he began to protest.

'Do it,' Henry said darkly.

Some of the others were still there, watching on like jackals around a kill. Henry was glad to see none were filming with their mobile phones. To them, he said, 'Unless you want further trouble with me, you'd better scatter, but if you want it, you can have it.'

Henry gave the lad he was gripping a shake. The others got the message and fled.

'Now then, boyo, who have we got here?' Henry said, twisting the lad's face towards his.

The lad sneered. 'You're in trouble for even touching me,' he warned.

'Really?' He winked. 'Like I said, I'm going to kick your weedy little arse across the village green or drag you if I have to.'

Henry managed to get Mrs Gough in her wheelchair up from the stream, through the trees and on to the flat village green, at which point the lad Henry had been trying to keep hold of wrenched free and both young lads made a run for it, swearing threats at Henry and flashing V-signs at him.

By this time, his anger had slightly subsided, and he wasn't of a mind to go in pursuit; Mrs Gough was safe and looking after her was his priority. Despite her protestations, Henry called a woman he knew in the village who was a first responder and asked her to meet him at The Tawny Owl so she could give Mrs Gough the once-over.

Henry placed his jacket around Mrs Gough's shoulders and pushed her across the green. The wheelchair had been damaged and all the electrical power had ceased for the moment, making it big, bulky and unwieldy, especially on the grass.

'Thank you, Henry,' Mrs Gough said weakly. 'I think they would have killed me.'

'How on earth did you end up in that predicament?'

'I was following them . . . I thought I was being sneaky.'

'What? In your wheelchair? Hardly conducive for sneaking about, is it?'

'I think they were actually luring me. I think they knew I was watching them, and I fell into a trap.'

'Mmm,' Henry muttered.

'Don't you dare say I told you so.'

'I won't, but you can't stop me thinking it.'

'I know. I'm a silly old fool.'

'You won't find me disagreeing with that,' he teased her. 'Anyway, how do you feel?'

'Cold and stupid.'

'Well, let's go and get a mug of tea and a few blankets for the cold, but fixing stupid is beyond my powers.'

By this time they'd reached The Tawny Owl, and with a big effort, Henry pushed the wheelchair up the slope by the terrace, in through the side door, into the foyer and towards the private accommodation.

Ginny walked out of the kitchen and saw the dishevelled pair. 'What's going on?'

He explained, and Ginny immediately took over care of Mrs Gough. Henry, though he needed to get out of his wet things, decided to call Jake Niven first. One thing he knew was that the lad who'd had his foot on Veronica Gough's head needed to be locked up and put before a court.

'Attempted murder.'

'Pushing it a bit.'

Henry gave Jake a hard stare. 'The lad had his foot on the side of her face and was holding her head under the water. I saw it happening. And if she didn't drown, we're lucky she didn't have heart failure. Thankfully she's made of stern stuff.'

Jake sighed. He had been summoned from his warm home at Henry's insistence, even though he wasn't officially on duty, and the prospect of turning out was a wrench, but because it was Henry, he did.

'Do you know the lad's name?' Jake asked.

Henry shook his head. After a quick, warm shower and a change of clothes – back into jeans and T-shirt – he was rubbing his short-cropped hair dry with a towel as he spoke to Jake in the living room.

'He seems to be the head honcho of the gang that is currently running around the village, causing mayhem.' Henry gave Jake a pointed look. 'He has a Manchester accent.'

'I obviously know of 'em. I know a few names and I've warned them a couple of times, but I'm hardly ever here these days, so I admit things are slipping a bit.'

'Well, this lot need nipping in the bud.'

'I'll find him,' Jake promised.

Henry finished towelling his hair. 'Let's go back into the bar.'

*   *   *

Mrs Gough recovered remarkably well and quickly from her ordeal. Someone had done a quick repair to her wheelchair, and now she was sitting on it with several other customers around one of the tables. It was the sleuthing group, including Dr Lott, who were interested in reopening the investigation into the very cold murder case in Thornwell.

Alongside Mrs Gough and now with the group was Debbie Blackstone, who appeared to be just as interested in the murder as the rest of them, eagerly sifting through old newspaper reports and other paperwork.

When Henry had got back to the pub with Mrs Gough, Blackstone had been in the spare bedroom, showering and changing, and she and Henry had missed each other until now. She spotted him, rose and approached.

'You were back early from your tryst,' she commented.

'Good job, too; otherwise, you might be investigating another murder and Rik would really be pulling his hair out.'

'Yeah, good job you ambled along. I assume Jake is dealing with it now?'

'He is.' Henry looked up and spotted Jake leaving the pub after having had a quick word with Mrs Gough.

'Nasty bunch of gits,' Blackstone said. 'Anyway, as I said, you were back early? I take it things didn't go swimmingly at the merry widow's?'

Henry pulled his face. 'Family ructions.'

'In that they don't like you pawing Mummy?' Blackstone guessed.

'Correct. It got uncomfortable, so I beat a hasty retreat. Pretty unpleasant being trapped in the kitchen with a son who thinks I'm after his inheritance.'

'And you're not?'

'I might be now,' Henry joshed with a wink, then nodded towards the murder investigation table. 'Are you now embroiled in an unsolvable murder mystery?'

'Yes, fascinating stuff. I never knew of it. They've asked if I can fish out the murder file.'

'Save me doing it.'

'Of course, you're not a real cop any more, so you don't have access. I presume you told them?'

'No. I said I'd try to get the file but that I wasn't interested. It's been investigated so many times . . .'

'Perhaps it needs looking at again. Maybe someone missed something glaringly obvious,' Blackstone reasoned. 'The police have been known to miss clues.'

'Or maybe it is unsolvable and old ghosts should be put to rest,' Henry suggested. 'One dead guy and no witnesses make it pretty tough going, plus the fact it's eighty bloody years old. They won't let it slide, you know? You're caught in a trap now.' Having said that, Henry knew that if anyone could solve a WWII murder case, it would be Blackstone. 'However, I think I should take Mrs Gough home now, don't you?'

'Depends on whether you can separate her from her double whisky or not,' Blackstone commented. 'She seems settled for the night now.'

Both looked over to where the amateur investigators were in deep discussion, analyzing clues, re-drawing hypotheses and, Henry guessed, getting nowhere. As much as he might have liked to lend a helping hand, together with what bit of waning expertise he had, he was sure the murder would remain a mystery unless someone still living and breathing revealed something they had never revealed before.

That was the only way to solve it, and because of the date of the murder, there were very few people remaining who might know anything.

He and Blackstone walked over. Henry stood next to Mrs Gough and asked her how she was feeling.

'Much better.'

Henry knew the first responder and Dr Lott had checked her over and found all was in order as much as it could be. Mrs Gough now had a car rug from somewhere wrapped around her shoulders, a double Scotch in her hand and colour back in her cheeks. Her hair, normally well coiffured, was plastered to her head and her make-up was now non-existent. She might have survived the experience, but she did look like a cat dragged backwards through a hedge.

'Are you solving crime now?' he asked.

'I wouldn't go as far as to say that, but I'm fascinated. It's something that has haunted this area all my life, so it would be nice to get some closure on it.'

'It would . . . I don't want to be a killjoy, but would you mind if I ran you home now?'

She glugged the remainder of her whisky and rose unsteadily to her feet, using the table for support. Henry prepared to catch her if she toppled, but she set off towards the door. Henry followed, pushing the wheelchair as Blackstone stepped in and linked arms with the old lady.

'You can walk a bit, then, love?' Blackstone asked.

'A bit,' she confirmed. 'But two toes removed from my left foot by gangrene after a bypass operation on that leg, plus a whole mess of other stuff gives me about fifteen yards at most.'

'Well, tell you what, then' – Blackstone looked cheekily at Henry – 'I'll give you a lift home in my car and Henry can push the wheelchair. How about that?'

Henry opened his mouth to protest.

'That would be lovely, Debs.'

Blackstone continued to grin at Henry who mouthed, *Debs?* and shook his head.

Blackstone assisted Mrs Gough into her car, a restored sixties Mini Cooper, much to the old lady's delight. With a quick wave and a spin of the wheels on the gravel, Blackstone skidded off the car park, leaving Henry pushing the empty wheelchair along the road, whistling tunelessly but accepting his fate with equanimity.

Mrs Gough's house was on the other side of the village, in a small estate just off the Thornwell Road. It was a big detached Victorian house in grounds encased by wrought-iron fencing. It took Henry almost twenty minutes to reach it, by which time Blackstone was reversing out of the driveway on to the road, having deposited Mrs Gough home and seen her in safely.

Blackstone wound her window down as she came alongside Henry. 'She says to leave it by the front door,' she said, pointing at the wheelchair.

'I'd feel better if it was inside and out of sight.'

'Up to you.' Blackstone slammed the Mini into first gear and surged away with a wail of the engine, leaving Henry open-mouthed. He had expected a ride back at the very least, but he wasn't surprised. Blackstone rarely did what was expected.

He pushed the wheelchair through the high gateposts to the front door and knocked. The door creaked open, and Mrs Gough peered out with one eye. Before she could complain, Henry said, 'I think this should be inside.' He kicked the wheelchair.

'OK.' She opened the door. She was already in her night attire of a long fleecy nightdress covered by a candlewick dressing gown. A hairnet covered her head.

Henry manoeuvred the wheelchair into the vestibule. 'I know someone at the pub has slotted it all back together, but if you want, just to make sure it's safe, I could probably get someone round tomorrow to check it over. It has had a bit of a bashing,' he said.

'I have a contract with the wheelchair providers, and someone will come out, but thanks.'

As she spoke, Henry noticed there were no teeth in her mouth. She was all gums and spittle.

'OK, goodnight, Mrs Gough. Will you be all right?'

She gave him a gummy smile. 'I've been alone twenty years since my Barry passed. I'll be fine, thanks to you, Henry.'

'Right. I'm sure PC Niven will be around to see you in the morning, and he'll get those yobs sorted once and for all,' he reassured her. He turned to leave but spun back as a thought struck him. 'Sorry. Quick question. Have you lived in the village all your life, Mrs Gough?'

'Born, raised, married and going to be buried here, too,' she said proudly. 'At St Andrew's.'

'In which case, you'll know folk pretty well.'

'All but the newbies who seem to have invaded the place – present company excepted. Why do you ask?'

'Just musing . . . Are you going to get involved in investigating that old murder case with the others in The Tawny Owl?'

'I might. Something to do. The nights will start drawing in soon.'

'In that case, you might want to see how far back you can remember – names of families, those who were in Thornwell and Kendleton pre- and post-war.'

'Why? I was just a kid.'

'Because it might just give the old people's investigation team something to get their teeth into,' he said, knowing he'd used the wrong metaphor completely. 'They could go and chat to families still in the village who were around in the thirties and forties. Time's a funny thing,' he said. 'Sometimes it clouds things, sometimes it clarifies things . . . it's probably what I'd do if I was involved in it.'

'I'll see what I can dredge up in here.' She tapped her temple, gave him another gummy smile, then closed the door. He heard a key turn and two bolts slide across on the inside. He sauntered down the drive, looking at the metal gates which were wide open and looked as though they hadn't been shut for many years.

As he stepped on to the road, he heard a car revving, and a

moment later, swerving in reverse along the street, travelling far too quickly for safety, came Blackstone in her Mini Cooper, which slithered to a halt just three feet away from him. Blackstone shoved her head out of the driver's window and shouted, 'Get in!'

Henry dropped into the low-slung front passenger bucket seat, and Blackstone immediately slammed on, throwing him back against the leather, cricking his neck.

'You came back for me!'

Blackstone selected second and aimed the fast little car through the deserted streets.

Then she reached down between her thighs and pulled out her mobile phone which was jammed in there.

'Here.' She handed it to Henry, who frowned. 'Redial the last incoming number.'

Henry tapped the screen, then tapped the telephone icon which came up with the last number received only a couple of minutes earlier.

The contact was *Rikky Boy*.

Henry's narrowed eyes looked at her. 'Rik Dean – why?'

'Because he's suddenly on bended knee and wants to make you a rich man again.'

'No, no, no, no,' Henry babbled and tried to hand the phone back. 'He wants me to run a job, doesn't he?' he said wearily.

'You'll be able to name your price – again,' Blackstone promised him, referring to a previous occasion when Rik had lured a very reluctant Henry back into the fold, and Henry had asked for, and received, an outrageous daily rate of pay.

'I won't do it, whatever it is.' Henry was adamant.

'I think you might.'

It was at that point that Henry gave her a dirty look and simultaneously the phone in his hand began to vibrate and ring, a distorted, jangly ringtone that somehow seemed to fit Blackstone's personality.

The screen showed *Rikky Boy* and also a headshot of Rik with his mouth opening and closing like a fish in synch with the ringtone.

'Press his face,' Blackstone said.

Half-heartedly, Henry did and said, 'Me.'

'Henry, Henry, Henry,' Detective Superintendent Rik Dean said as though he was attempting to hypnotize him like a snake.

Henry said, 'No!' and ended the call straight away.

He held the phone back in Blackstone's direction, but she didn't take it. Instead, she swerved around the next bend, throwing Henry sideways against the door, making him reach for the seatbelt he hadn't put on.

The phone rang again.

Henry thumbed Rik Dean's robotic face again. 'I said no.'

By this time Blackstone had slowed and was pulling into The Tawny Owl car park, stopping with a deliberate jerk that threw Henry forwards, almost headbutting the windscreen, through which he looked and saw Rik Dean standing at the top of the steps, his image caught in the headlights like a malevolent, backlit king.

Henry eased the phone away from his ear and growled, 'Did you know about this?' as he firmly gave the phone back.

'On my mother's grave,' she said, placing the palm of her right hand on her chest, over her beating heart, 'I didn't actually know he was *here*!'

'That would be your mother's empty grave,' Henry said. 'She's still a living, breathing, sentient being as far as I know.'

'Be that as it may, it's the thought that counts.'

Wearily, Henry got out and trudged up to Rik, but then walked straight past him into Th'Owl, went to the public side of the main bar and ordered a pint of Stella which he took to a seat in an empty alcove. He sat down and waited for some foreplay.

'Henry, Henry, Henry,' Rik Dean cooed again like a needle stuck on vinyl. He had a pint in his hand and sat down opposite Henry.

Blackstone had resumed her position with the old murder investigation team, having been greeted with a loud cheer when she sat down. She did, however, keep one eye on Henry's predicament.

Henry had known Rik for many years. Way back, when Henry had been a DI on the CID at Blackpool and Rik had been a PC in uniform, he'd spotted the younger lad's potential as a thief-taker and managed to get him into the department. Rik's subsequent rise through the ranks had been all his own doing: he was as good a manager as a detective, a rare combination, but the fact that he'd eagerly stepped into Henry's shoes on his retirement left a bit of a sour taste in Henry's mouth, even though Rik was his brother-in-law and good friend.

'Spit it out,' Henry said, then sipped his Stella.

Rik looked uneasy. 'I've got two murders running now, the locations not a million miles from each other. James Twain and Marcus Durham.'

'Are they linked?'

Rik shrugged. 'Not sure yet. Possibly, but who knows? Early days, though the two are sort of business partners.'

'Oh, I didn't know that.'

'Anyhow, we have an obvious suspect in custody for Twain's brutal murder: his wife.'

'So why do you need me? Which is what I assume this ambush is all about?'

Rik's mouth twisted and his body writhed uncomfortably: bad body language. 'Because,' he said finally, 'we've hit a slight brick wall with the Twain thing.'

Henry waited. Sipped his cold lager. 'How so?'

'Celia Twain point-blank refuses to speak to any of my detectives,' Rik said.

'How is that a problem? Most people locked up for murder won't say a dickie-bird. Par for the course, innit?'

'However' – Rik waggled his finger at Henry – 'she says she'll speak to one person and one person only, and that person is you.'

'But I'm not a cop any more.'

'But you are still technically on our books as a civilian investigator. I know you're not active as such, but everything is still current – your DBS check, et cetera,' Rik said, referring to Henry's criminal background check.

'I understand that, but why does she want to speak to me?'

'She hasn't said, but I'm thinking if you come in for a day, say, like tomorrow, and interview her with DS Blackstone as second jockey' – he glanced across at her – 'get the woman's confession – because, I mean, she clearly did it – then it's all boxed off and I can concentrate resources, which are dropping like flies because of this Covid shit, on the other murder.'

'But what if she denies it? What if she isn't actually guilty and admits nothing?' Henry said with a dose of reality.

'Henry, she turned up here, covered in blood, brandishing the bloody murder weapon. Come on,' Rik whined. 'She came to you, Henry.'

'But she might not have done it, and if she tells a good, plausible tale, then the investigation is far from over and you're back to square one.'

'She did it, Henry. You know she did. Look, for me, eh? Pretty please. Go in, smooch and shimmy like I know you can and then prove the murdering bitch guilty,' Rik pleaded. 'Five hundred quid in your hand. One day's work. I mean, c'mon – one single, solitary day.'

Henry took a thoughtful sip of the Stella.

SEVEN

I t was familiar territory. Too comfortable, even.

Henry Christie had been a raw nineteen-year-old when he joined the police, and the years that followed had been spent in and around police stations, from the big old Victorian ones, now very rare, to the newer ones that seemed to be designed and built by people who had never set foot in a cop shop and never considered asking those who did for their input. Most of the older stations were never even replaced, other than by a pop-up counter in a post office or empty shop in a town centre. Henry often thought he'd served in a golden age of policing in the seventies and eighties, although he admitted that perspective was through rose-tinted specs; after the eighties, he had witnessed much change in the service as money grew tight, resources were squeezed, more was expected from fewer staff, and there was a move away from basic coppering which, he remained convinced, was what the public wanted but rarely got.

With a pint or two down him, he could have prattled on about such things until the cows came home, but he tried not to because it dispirited him . . . The point was that police stations, old or new, were familiar territory to him, and as he walked, not for the first time, into the very newly built (and impressive, he had to grudgingly admit) Blackpool police station, he felt at home.

Saddo, he thought.

It was seven a.m. He had driven down from Kendleton to Blackpool behind Debbie Blackstone because Blackpool was the custody centre for much of the north-western section of Lancashire, a situation Henry considered ridiculous, but one of those decisions that, once implemented and no matter how stupid, would never be reversed.

But, as he was wont to say these days, 'Not my problem.'

Other than the fact he had to trail all the way from Kendleton because Celia Twain was being held in custody there.

Henry was given a visitor's pass at the front desk to clip on to his jacket while Blackstone simply breezed in.

'Let's have a peek at her first, then have a look through the custody record, see where we're up to, have a quick skim through the interview tapes too,' Henry said.

The pair walked towards the custody office and were buzzed through to the prisoner reception area where, even at this time of day, two prisoners were in the holding cage, one of them vomiting spectacularly across the tiled floor, the other sitting on the bench, feet up with his arms wrapped around his shins, rocking gently and wailing like a baby.

Again, familiar territory to Henry: the custody office, the beating heart of the station.

Another prisoner, held upright by two arresting officers, was being frisked at the desk.

Henry looked around, taking it all in, thinking that maybe he was an oddball to feel so at home in an environment that most people passing through regard as hostile in the extreme. However, many were regulars, and although they might have hated it, it was their own doings and choices that brought them back time and again; the police just facilitated their journeys.

He and Blackstone lounged to one side, watching the booking-in process, until the prisoner was finally led away to the cells by a gaoler and the arresting officers had a quick conflab with the custody sergeant before leaving. The sergeant then beckoned them over.

Blackstone explained why they were there and that they wanted to have a quick look at Celia through the cell-door hatch but not disturb her for the moment. Then they would read the custody record and make arrangements for the duty solicitor to be present when they interviewed Celia later.

The slightly harassed sergeant tossed a set of keys at them. 'Female cell corridor, cell two. As long as you don't speak to her, you can go down unsupervised.'

They thanked him, let themselves through the first locked gate and went down the female leg of the complex to Celia's cell.

Henry quietly lowered the hatch and bent his knees slightly to bring his face down to peer in. Celia was awake, still in a forensic suit, and she immediately recognized Henry's face in the opening. She shot up off the bench and ran to the door.

'Henry, you came!' she breathed in relief.

'I did, Celia.'

'Thank God, I'm so glad you're here.'

'Why do you want to speak to me?'

'Because you know the truth.'

Henry sighed and shook his head. 'I know what I saw, Celia, but if you think you'll get an easy ride off me, you're wrong. I will search for the truth because that's what I do, and if it's a different truth to yours, don't be surprised. You need to know that.'

'I do know. And I know I'm innocent and *that* is the truth, Henry.'

'OK . . . look, we can't talk here and now. I have some preparation work to do, but we'll be with you in an hour or so, OK? We'll fix up a duty solicitor for you, too.'

'I don't need a solicitor,' she said adamantly.

'Well, you're having one.'

'If you say so.'

'Other than that, are you OK? Are you being treated well?'

'Yes to both.'

Henry thought she looked exhausted and guessed she wouldn't have had much sleep. He nodded and shut the hatch with a metallic clunk.

He and Blackstone had managed to snaffle a desk in the CID office after having nipped to the Tesco Superstore at the back of the nick to get some sustenance in the form of take-out sausage sandwiches and coffee, which they consumed while going through the paperwork.

They followed the trail from the moment Celia had arrived in the back of Jake's Land Rover the previous afternoon. She was presented to the custody sergeant and detention was authorized. She signed all the forms, indicated she understood everything but said she did not want a solicitor, although Henry was glad to see the custody sergeant requested one anyway. There was no way anyone accused of murder would not be given legal representation.

Following the authorization of detention, Celia was wheeled into a room in the custody suite and joined by a female police constable and female crime scene investigator. After being photographed in detail, her bloodstained clothing was taken from her and bagged up. She was swabbed and photographed from a crime scene perspective and given a forensic suit and slippers. Then she was photographed for a mugshot and fingerprinted, and a DNA sample was taken from her inner cheek before she was returned to the custody desk and the sergeant authorized her to be taken to a cell to await interview.

Henry was impressed by the attention to detail on the paperwork, but even though there was some reference to Celia's condition – upset, tearful, maybe in shock – it didn't really tell him much. To get a more rounded idea of that and because it could be useful when interviewed – a murder suspect's state of mind told a half-decent detective a lot about the person – he also watched the CCTV footage of her arrival at the station, including Jake helping her out of the Land Rover, having to keep her upright and from falling over as he led her inside.

'Thoughts?' Blackstone asked Henry.

They'd been watching the CCTV footage on the desktop computer of the desk they had commandeered.

'Clearly upset.'

'Or bulling us?' Blackstone ventured.

Henry shrugged. He had dealt with plenty of murder suspects who were, on the face of it, deeply upset, but underneath they had been playing the sympathy card. 'Could be,' he admitted. He started to riffle though the paperwork.

'Lost something?' Blackstone asked.

'The number of the Blood Guy.'

They Skyped him. The Blood Guy.

His name was Rostamian. He was a forensic scientist experienced in interpreting bloodstains. From his own offices and laboratory near Warrington, he ran a very lucrative and in-demand service for police forces across the north of England.

Henry had used this service on many occasions, and he quite liked the idea of someone obsessed with blood. He knew Rostamian had attended the scene at Twain's workshop.

When the connection was made, Rostamian had his face close up to the camera lens on his computer, so close as to distort his features.

'Henry Christie, I thought you'd retired?' Rostamian said as he settled back and adjusted his thick-framed spectacles.

'Morning, Kav . . . I've been lassoed back into the fold like a stray sheep.'

'Good for you. What can I do for you?'

'I'm helping out with the James Twain murder. I know you went to the scene yesterday and I also know you've been sent clothing worn by the suspect, plus photographs. Have you got around to analysing anything yet?'

'Only briefly.'

'And?' Henry urged him. 'What about time of death for a start?'

'I'm informed the deceased was possibly last seen alive around eight thirty a.m.,' Rostamian said, 'which, according to the suspect – his wife – was when he went, alone, into the workshop to work on his Spitfire. I know his body was "officially" discovered at about one fifteen the same day.'

By me, Henry thought, but he did not enlighten him.

'So, my best estimate so far, and don't quote me, is between that initial time and eleven a.m.'

Henry saw him shrug.

'What about the suspect's clothing?' Henry asked.

Rostamian frowned deeply. 'I have had a quick look.' He jerked his thumb sideways. 'It's all currently laid out in what I call the clothes room.'

'First impressions?' Henry probed.

'First impressions? Not consistent with the blood splatter I would expect on clothing worn by an attacker who had bludgeoned someone to death with a spanner – a murderous assault in a blind passion.'

'How so?' Blackstone asked.

'The clothing is heavily bloodstained but it does not show splashing of blood on the material. It does, however, support a story whereby the suspect says she found the body, went to help and cradled the already dead, or dying person, in her arms. The clothing is stained around the groin area of the slacks and the lower section of the blouse. There are no actual splash marks around the shoulders or lower legs which you would expect from a frenzied attack. But' – Rostamian held up a finger – 'I recommend caution because I have not yet fully investigated or reached firm conclusions.'

'Still think she's guilty?' Blackstone asked Henry as they stood outside Celia's cell.

'I suppose you have to go with the evidence as it is, which at the moment suggests she didn't do it, but that doesn't mean she didn't. Could be an elaborate ruse, a set-up to put us off the scent.'

'And there was also that gunman or woman?'

'That certainly skews it, but whoever that was, he or she wasn't covered in blood and may have been there for a whole different reason. Or was part and parcel of the plot.'

'Or came to kill Twain, only to find someone else got there first?' Blackstone mused.

'I'll make a detective out of you yet,' Henry said.

'Not much chance of that.' Blackstone slotted the key into the cell door.

'An innocent person does not need legal representation,' Celia Twain stated for the benefit of the tape recording.

Sitting alongside her was a duty solicitor. Opposite were Henry and Blackstone.

'Everyone should opt for it, innocent or guilty, Celia,' Henry advised. 'Especially when we're talking murder.'

'I am not a suspect,' she insisted.

'I'm afraid you are,' Henry insisted back. 'And I need to question you in detail about your husband's death. Surely you must understand that?'

Celia nodded wearily, and after being cautioned and the usual pre-interview formalities, Henry and Blackstone began an interview designed to set up all the subsequent ones. It covered her marriage to James, where they lived, what they did for a living, how wealthy they were, who benefitted from inheritance; from that, they moved to questions about the evening before the murder, which included the incidents at The Tawny Owl – James being assaulted by another customer and Celia almost sticking a knife into James's throat over a nicely chilled bottle of the most expensive champagne on the wine list.

'You want to know why that guy Renshaw attacked James? I'll tell you why,' Celia said, leaning forward earnestly. 'Because my husband was fucking Mrs Renshaw – that's why!' She sat back and folded her arms. 'And that's one of the reasons why I nearly slit his throat with a steak knife.'

'James was a philanderer, then?' Henry asked.

Celia looked puzzled.

Blackstone clarified the question. 'He means shagger.'

'He was, and I'd say that at least four husbands in the area should be on your list of suspects. I get why I'm under the spotlight and, yes, I did lose it a bit in the pub . . . it all got too much for me . . .

the humiliation, the secrets . . . all that, and yep, I put a knife to his throat and maybe I would have stuck it in if you hadn't come along.'

'What happened when you got home?' Henry asked.

'We had a blazing row.'

'And he assaulted you, didn't he? I saw the bruises on your arms. If I ask you to roll up your sleeves, they'll still be there,' Henry said with certainty. He also knew that photographs of those injuries had been taken. He pointed at her face. 'Plus the black eye.' Her cheek was swollen and bruised around her left eye, turning a sickly shade of brownish purple.

'Another reason for me to kill him,' Celia said bitterly.

'It's all stacking up,' Blackstone said.

'Well, I didn't. He got up before me, went into his workshop to mess with his plane . . . We weren't speaking, so I didn't go in and say bye-bye when I left, but to the best of my knowledge he was still alive and the plane's engine was running.'

'What time did you leave the house?' Henry asked.

'Say ten minutes or so before I saw you at the war memorial and apologized. That's how long it takes to drive from our house into Kendleton on a regular journey.'

Henry nodded. 'So, a bevy of aggrieved husbands might want him dead? Anyone else?'

She snorted. 'A queue of people. Aggrieved wives who couldn't get him to divorce me, even though I wish he would have done. Business rivals – he upset a lot of folk in that world, too.'

'We need names, Celia,' Blackstone said.

'I'll give them to you.'

Henry leaned back, critically surveying the prisoner . . . wondering if he believed her or not.

All he was doing here was a favour for Rik Dean. This wasn't his job, but if it had been he would have had to have a long series of interviews with Celia over the next few hours and ruthlessly check out her story, pick on inconsistencies, challenge her relentlessly. Mobile phone records needed to be checked properly, property and vehicles had to be forensically searched, CCTV footage had to be found and watched, house-to-house enquiries were needed – all routine but crucial stuff.

Next would come visits to anyone she named as having a grievance against James Twain and his wandering todger. He'd been a busy boy, had upset folk around the village, and his dalliances seemingly common knowledge as Henry recalled Mrs Gough's quip about 'the affairs'.

And then there was the mystery gunperson who may or may not be linked to Celia.

A lot of things to investigate.

Plus, despite the initial findings of the Blood Guy, which backed up Celia's version of events, Henry remained sceptical. He did realize this was his default position from years as a cop, during which most people lied to him or at least gave 'their version' of the truth – which was usually a lie.

He sighed. 'Do you have any security cameras at your house, Celia?'

'No, we've never had them.'

'OK. This is what we'll do . . . you'll have to remain in custody for another few hours while we continue our investigations, and then we'll make a decision.'

'But I thought you'd be on my side!' she said vehemently.

'This might sound lofty, Mrs Twain, but I'm on the side of truth and justice, a concept that seems to get a good kicking these days.'

'We have to break her. We have to get into her ribs,' Blackstone said grimly. 'She'll crack. I know she will.'

'I almost expect you to say, "Lemme at her,"' Henry said.

'You took the words right out of my mouth.'

Celia had been put back in her cell, weeping, but as her first twenty-four hours in custody were on the horizon, Henry thought the best course of action would be to release her pending further enquiries and not worry about getting the necessary authorizations required to extend her detention. She could always be arrested again, if and when necessary.

'At the moment, there's no evidence against her as such,' Henry said.

'I know what you're going to say – sorry, *bleat*,' Blackstone responded. 'Let's get all our ducks in a row and then go for her, blah, blah, blah!'

'Something like that,' he admitted. 'Then if what we get stacks up, let's give her a broadside . . . although I'll bet nothing turns up.'

Blackstone sighed dramatically.

'Why don't we go and have a brainstorming session, decide what needs doing and then I'll leave it with you as I'm only being paid for a day.'

Henry grinned, not knowing how wrong he was.

They were ten minutes into the brain-dump session, sitting at their commandeered desk in the CID office across from each other, when something caught Blackstone's eye. She looked up beyond Henry's shoulder towards the door. Her face dropped, and, without moving her lips, she said, 'Oh, shit, this doesn't look good.'

Henry looked at her, then over his shoulder to see what could have brought on such a reaction.

And there it was: Rik Dean with a crooked, mock-amiable smile, negotiating his way through the desks; behind him, with faces set like grim scree slopes, were Diane Daniels and DCI Mark Wellhaven.

Without moving his lips, Henry replied, 'You could be right.'

'Henry, Henry, Henry,' Rik said – again – like treacle, as he sat down next to Blackstone so he could face Henry.

Henry's throat clammed up, particularly as he glanced behind Rik at Diane and Wellhaven, who stood there, arms folded, their eyes hooded like snakes, regarding Henry. Their expressions reminded Henry of kids who'd had their toys taken away by a big boy.

'I never liked that opener,' Henry said, focusing on Rik. 'It's like a precursor of doom, some evil spell being incanted.'

Rik tittered nervously.

'Spit it out, Rikky Boy,' Blackstone said bravely.

Rik's head swivelled towards her. 'If you ever call me that again, I'll have your guts for garters and you will be on school-crossing patrol duty in Bacup.'

'Meh!' Blackstone said.

Rik snarled. To Henry, he said, 'Do you know a man called Marcus Durham?'

Henry nodded. 'Yep . . . bit of a roughneck, tough guy, kidnapped a work rival maybe ten, twelve years ago . . . got eight years, I think. Not the brightest button in the drawer, but nasty . . . a builder . . . I led the kidnap job but handed it over when he was arrested.'

'His body was found floating in his swimming pool by one of his employees yesterday afternoon,' Rik said.

'I'd heard.'

'Murdered, shot to death.'

Henry shrugged. 'The news doesn't surprise me.'

'It was like a gangland hit,' Rik said.

'He was one of those people who annoyed a lot of others. A bully . . . and while this is interesting, why are you telling me?' Henry glanced at Diane and Wellhaven. 'These two guys have it in hand, don't they?'

'There's a complication,' Rik said.

'Fuck me,' Blackstone uttered, 'I've heard about beating around the bush, boss, but this takes the biscuit.'

'Don't push me, Sergeant. There are plenty of custody officer vacancies that need filling around the county,' he warned her. Then he looked at Henry again and dropped the bombshell. 'The complication, as I mentioned, is that Marcus Durham was James Twain's business partner.'

Henry sat back at the news and let it sink in properly, which he hadn't done before when Rik had mentioned this. 'I don't recall that being the case when he was arrested for that kidnapping.'

'It wasn't. They linked up after Durham came out of prison.'

'OK, interesting.' He tilted his head questioningly. 'And?'

Rik seemed to brace himself for an unpleasant bit of news. 'Two business partners murdered on the same day – bit too much of a coincidence, wouldn't you say?'

'Certainly a coincidence, yeah,' Henry agreed.

'As I recall, you taught me everything about coincidences. "Coincidences is clues" – isn't that your mantra?'

Henry glanced at Blackstone, who rolled her eyes, then he said to Rik, 'Get to the point, or I'll *volunteer* for traffic duty.'

'The point is that this is too much of a coincidence, even though the causes of their deaths are very different and it seems likely that they were murdered by different offenders . . . but what I intend to do is open a double murder enquiry to investigate both deaths simultaneously so that any cross-overs won't be missed.'

Henry nodded. 'Half-decent plan.'

Rik swallowed, his Adam's apple making an audible click as it rose and fell in his throat. He seemed to be suddenly in pain. A lot of it. Like trapped wind.

Then he blurted, 'I want you to head it.'

Behind him, there was a double groan of disbelief and possibly the utterance of an obscenity, and if rolling eyeballs could have made a sound, they would have been heard as Diane and Wellhaven reacted with disgust.

Next to Rik, Blackstone gave a jubilant air-dig with a fist and said, 'Yay!'

Henry said, 'No.'

'You want me to run a double murder investigation?' Henry asked, trying not to laugh out loud. He and Rik had decamped to an empty office to discuss the delicate matter between themselves. 'Not only am I not a cop, but I have a business to run; I'm also as rusty as hell and, above all, the answer is no. Today, interviewing Celia was a favour, and you can have it on the house, buckshee, save you five hundred quid. You've got eager, talented detectives who should be given the chance—'

'What? To screw up a double murder?' Rik pinched the bridge of his nose as if a migraine had replaced the trapped wind. 'Please . . . I've already run it past the chief, and if you say yes, it's a yes from him, too.'

'Whoa! The chief has already been told?'

'Henry, despite what you say, I don't have anyone with the requisite experience to run this. John Egerton' – he named a detective superintendent on FMIT – 'is on gardening leave . . .'

Henry perked up at that. 'Why, what's he been up to?'

'You don't want to know,' Rik said bleakly. 'And I seriously do not have anyone else capable of juggling this. I've got four ongoing jobs across the county and a big armed robbery committed this morning in Skelmersdale, so I am fucking spinning plates here!'

'What's wrong with Wellhaven?'

'I won't be allowed to write this actual phrase on his appraisal, but he's an imbecile,' Rik said.

It was Henry's turn to pinch the bridge of his own nose.

EIGHT

The remainder of that day had been a whirlwind, hectic, non-stop, Henry rushing round like the proverbial blue-arsed fly. After being browbeaten and squeezed (it felt) into accepting the role of Civilian Senior Investigating Officer (CSIO), a job title made up on the spot because it hadn't actually existed minutes before, Rik did a little circular dance of victory in the office. Henry quickly chose his deputy (Debbie Blackstone) and decided it would be wise for him to do a quick visit to the scene of Marcus Durham's swimming-pool murder where he met up with Diane Daniels and Wellhaven, who had both acquired master's degrees in grumpiness.

They were waiting for him at the bottom of the drive leading up to Durham's immaculately restored farmhouse. The name of the property – Chipping View – was etched on a brass plate on one of the gate pillars. However, Henry did notice a square piece of stone inset into the brickwork that looked as if it once had the original name of the property carved into it. It had been covered over with a layer of concrete filler, but it was still possible to make out what the place once had been called: Nine Elms.

Henry looked at it and knew it meant something to him in the deep recesses of his brain cells, wasn't quite sure what. He didn't sweat on it, not least because Diane Daniels stood in his path and shoved a plastic bag containing a full forensic suit into his chest. Wellhaven kept his distance.

'Still an active crime scene,' she said bluntly. 'Put this on.'

'Thank you.'

He went across to his car and used it to keep balance while he pulled on the suit, including elasticated overshoes and nitrile gloves.

The get-up of a killer, he thought.

Diane watched him critically, then sidled up to him. 'This should have been Mark's job, his first proper one since transferring, his chance to make a good impression.'

'I don't disagree,' Henry said, tugging the gloves on, 'but not my shout, so let's stay professional about it, eh?' He knew he sounded supercilious.

'You could have turned it down.'

'True. But I didn't, and we are where we are.' He leaned against the car and slid the shoes on over his own.

'I'm livid with you, Henry.'

Henry shrugged. 'It's what Rik wants so take it out on him if you must . . . mine is not to reason why,' he said philosophically and did not believe it was his business to tell her what Rik thought about Wellhaven.

He could see Diane was smitten with Wellhaven and was perhaps under the impression that, because he was a new boy, so to speak, she had to fight his corner for some reason. This had obviously badly tainted her feelings towards Henry in the extreme, which he was actually fine with now. All was fair in love and war, he believed, having got over his humiliation of being dumped by her; God knows he'd been in both of those types of conflict in his life to be able to see the many sides of the arguments. However, while he was content to be philosophical about Diane's outrage towards him, he had a job to do and he had no intention of allowing bitter feelings to derail the catching of a killer or two.

Diane had changed. So be it, that was her prerogative, not that he was necessarily going to give her an easy ride.

'Just show me around the crime scene and let's leave our anger at the gates,' he said, knowing he now sounded like a lifestyle guru.

'Fuck you, Henry.'

Diane spun towards the police cordon tape stretched across the gateposts. Henry smiled at Wellhaven and followed Diane, all three ducking under the tape and signing into the scene on the clipboard held by the young PC at the gate who was logging the comings and goings. Henry wrote his name, then *CSIO*, knowing it would rile Diane and Wellhaven when they signed in after him.

'Can you believe it?' he heard Diane remark. 'CSIO? What's that when it's at home?'

Wellhaven grunted. Henry guessed he probably wasn't too bothered and would be more inclined to toe the line and not fall out with Rik Dean, who would have a big say in his career.

Henry took his time wandering around the house and the pool area, impressed by it, though not too enamoured by the sight of the blood which still hung like a cloud in the pool.

'We turned the filters off when we got here yesterday,' Wellhaven said, 'if you're wondering why the blood's still visible.'

'Good shout,' Henry said.

'Here.' Wellhaven handed him an album of crime scene photographs. Although everything was digital these days, it was always useful to have what Henry called 'analogue' copies. There was nothing better than leafing through an album of printed photographs; somehow they gave him more time for actual thought and reflection than scrolling through photos on a phone or an iPad.

Henry started to look through the ring-binder photos which

consisted mainly of Durham's body floating face down in the water followed by a series of photos of him being pulled out by officers (which he knew would have been videoed) and finally the body laid out, naked, by the pool.

'Tell me what you think happened,' Henry asked Wellhaven as he looked at the album.

'Who, me?' Wellhaven asked in surprise.

'Yes. You were the first senior detective on the scene; presumably, you must have some hypothesis?'

'Well, yeah . . . but I didn't think . . .'

'Think what? That I'd want your thoughts?'

'Kinda,' he said awkwardly.

'Well, I do.' He closed the book and turned to the DCI. Diane was close by, in earshot. 'I know I've pissed you off by being asked to head this investigation, and I get that, but I know it's teams that catch murderers, not individuals, so yeah, I want and value your input, Mark.'

'Oh, OK.' Wellhaven seemed to brighten up. Diane still rolled her eyes. 'Looks like the victim – Durham – was having an early morning swim when he was shot, and piecing it together, it looks as though he may have been shot while standing on the edge of the pool. As you can see from the photos, he was shot in the chest – although we have recovered two bullets from the bottom of the pool itself.'

Henry flipped back through the album and looked at a photo of two bullets, laid next to each other alongside a twelve-inch ruler for size and context. They were undamaged and would provide good evidence if the gun was ever found.

Wellhaven went on, 'So he might have been shot at the poolside, then dived in to evade the attacker, or possibly shot at while in the pool, ordered out, then executed and fell back in.'

'Either way, there are bullets in his body and two pristine ones found under water.'

'Correct, boss,' Wellhaven said.

'But no shell casings?'

'Nope.'

'Which suggests either a revolver or a semi-automatic pistol, and if it's the latter, then the casings were somehow collected, either picked up by the shooter or caught in a bag around the hand as they ejected, rather like the shooter I stumbled across in James Twain's workshop who had a plastic bag around the gun. So, one thing we need to do urgently is to dig out the bullets that person fired at me and get them compared to those found here and in Durham's body. Can you fast-track that, Mark? That would be a crucial lead.'

'Yes, sure, boss.'

'Did Durham live alone here?'

Wellhaven nodded. 'He had girlfriends, but we're pretty sure he was living alone – according to the woman who found him, who seems to have some knowledge of his private life, though not much.'

'In that case, we need to talk to her in some depth, I'd suggest, get as much as she knows out of her about Durham.' Henry said, finding he was getting back into the swing of things as his brain started to line up the various elements – location, victims, offenders, forensics and post-mortems – that constituted the two crimes he was now investigating and any possible links between them.

Standing by the blood-clouded swimming pool, he started to think about the location, wondering what choices and decisions the attacker had made. Was the location significant? How did the attacker get here? How did he or she escape? Is it a familiar location (ex-girlfriend, maybe)? Was the meeting engineered or was it an ambush? How well planned was it? What was the relationship between the dead man and the killer? And was there any link to Twain in all this?

Henry felt a surge of excitement course through him.

Oh God, he loved this sort of thing – it felt so good. He knew he could have walked away from it – the choice was his, and he was strong enough to have said no to Rik Dean – but he was suddenly now overwhelmingly glad he had accepted it. He realized that his being drafted in had already and would probably continue to cause ripples of discontent among the ranks, but he was prepared for that. He knew that even as a 'real' cop he hadn't been the most popular kid on the block, but he also knew that people liked working for him because they saw someone who led from the front, would never ask anyone to do something he wouldn't do himself and who would also have their backs if things went shit-shaped. The fact he didn't now have a rank didn't worry him too much.

I have charisma, he thought wryly – then kicked his ego mentally up the backside.

'Penny for those deep and meaningful thoughts tumbling through your head.' Diane interrupted his reflections.

He came back to reality. 'I'm going to have a close look at two dead bodies,' he declared. 'In the meantime, Diane, can you get the major incident room set up at Lancaster, plus I want intranet access to be arranged from The Tawny Owl because I want to be able to look at the force's databases from there, and get a HOLMES terminal installed there as well. It's been done before,' he said, quickly cutting off her open-mouthed protestation. He then went through a list of personnel he wanted to be brought in, using his fingers to tick them off. She didn't make any notes, but he knew she would easily remember everything.

He concluded, 'And I'd like you to run the MIR, please.'

'OK.' She didn't sound impressed.

'What about me, boss?' Wellhaven asked, getting a dirty look from Diane at his brown-nosing.

'Obviously, that ballistic link to start with,' Henry said, referring to the fast-tracking of the bullets, 'but also the main fast-track menu and how we're going to implement that.'

Wellhaven took this on board.

'With both murders, we're getting into and beyond the twenty-four-hour mark, so time is of the essence.' Henry checked his watch. It was getting late. 'I want to hit the ground running tomorrow morning, so that means you two need to sort a briefing for eight a.m., but all of us guys' – he pointed to them both and him – 'will be in for a pre-briefing at six thirty at Lancaster nick . . . oh, Diane, see if you can get me a swipe card so I can gain entry to every nick this side of the Pennines, please. Right . . . bodies!'

Wellhaven and Diane watched him walk away. Without actually looking at Wellhaven, Diane said, 'You called him "boss", for fuck's sake!'

'He didn't seem all that bad, to be fair.'

Henry was too far away to hear the exchange, but he didn't let it worry him.

As he signed out, ducked under the cordon tape, he glanced back at the name of the property that had been erased on the gate post: Nine Elms.

He knew that it meant something to him; he just wasn't sure what.

'Did Celia say anything to you? Did she admit the murder?' Henry asked Blackstone.

They were in the car park adjacent to Lancaster public mortuary behind the main complex of buildings that was Royal Lancaster

Infirmary. Henry had asked Blackstone to run Celia Twain home once she had been released still under investigation enquiries, because Henry had thought giving her a lift was the right thing to do in the circumstances, rather than tip her out on to the streets of Blackpool, the better part of forty miles away from home, and somehow expect her to get there under her own steam.

'Naff all,' Blackstone said. 'Quiet as a mouse. I didn't press it, didn't want to complicate anything.'

'Understood.' An interview in a moving car would be hard to explain or justify to a court and wasn't worth the hassle.

Henry and Blackstone entered the mortuary and went through to the room containing the bank of fridges in which bodies were stored, then to the actual post-mortem room to find two stripped bodies laid out on separate slabs divided by a plastic screen: James Twain and Marcus Durham.

Two CSIs were setting up a video camera rig next to Twain's body, which was first in line for the knife.

At the stainless-steel sink, the Home Office pathologist was busy arranging the tools of the trade while whistling tunelessly.

His female assistant hovered close by.

Even from behind, Henry recognized the pathologist, a thin, lanky man, with big FA Cup ears. Having also clocked a classic E-Type Jaguar parked outside, Henry already knew who this was.

Henry sauntered across. 'Professor Baines.'

The man in the green hospital smock turned with a wide smile on his face, which made his ears rise. 'You, Henry, are like a bad penny,' Baines said. 'Can't you just retire?'

'All down to the queen's shilling,' Henry replied, rubbing his thumb and forefinger tips together. It was a lie, obviously.

'But you must have oodles of money stashed away?'

'He's a paper millionaire,' Blackstone cut in. 'The pub's worth a mint.'

Baines looked at her and grinned – he knew her, too – and said, 'Our Henry is a dark horse, that's for sure.'

'So, Professor, what are your first impressions?' Henry indicated the bodies on the slabs.

'I can probably tell you now how each man died.' He pointed to James Twain. 'Bludgeoned, traumatic brain injury consistent with the heavy spanner I've been shown.' Next, he pointed to Marcus Durham. 'Four gunshot wounds to the chest causing massive injuries to the heart, lungs, liver, aorta. Obviously I have to complete a full post-mortem on each.' He smiled at Henry, his ears rising again. 'Are you staying? I need an update on your love life, which has kept me, a one-woman man, highly entertained for so many years.'

The two men had known each other for almost thirty years and had developed a friendship that had evolved at the conclusion of many a post-mortem usually in a pub or café, where the findings could be mulled over, speculated upon, and Baines could then quiz Henry about his once roller-coaster love life which fascinated the scientist; more recently, however, it wasn't so much a roller coaster as an old banger race.

As a senior investigating officer, Henry had always preferred to stay to observe post-mortems for the deep insights they provided into death, but that decision was always weighed against all the other issues vying for his attention.

'How long do you think you'll be?' Henry asked Baines.

'Give it five hours.'

Henry turned to Blackstone. 'Will you stay, then give me a call when they're being wrapped up and I'll come back for a debrief?'

Blackstone nodded unenthusiastically.

'I'm going to the MIR to make a few phone calls and perhaps start to kick butt.'

Henry abandoned his car on the upper car park at Lancaster nick after writing his mobile number on a scrap of paper and slipping it under a wiper blade because he had blocked a couple of cars in.

He still hadn't got his swipe card, so he followed a couple of uniformed constables in and made his way up to the top floor of the station where the MIR was located.

As it was already set up and on standby in terms of phone lines and computer terminals, all it needed was staff and someone to press the 'Go' button.

Diane Daniels was there on the phone, making the calls to get the ball rolling, bring people in and kickstart the investigation. She was at a desk at the front of the room, talking on a landline but watching Henry walk the full length of the MIR towards her.

She concluded the call as he reached her.

'Two HOLMES operators sorted,' she said, referring to the phone call and the personnel who would be brought in to run and input information and intelligence into the computer system. 'I've sorted an intelligence cell – a DC and a civvie from the intel unit. They're already on the job but will be working in here from tomorrow.'

'Great stuff,' Henry said genuinely, knowing how much skill and schmoozing it took to get the right people into an MIR. He realized that only a few years out of the job meant relationships he had built up before were not necessarily there any more, and he now had to rely on people like Diane to do what he might have done easily in the past. 'Has Mark gone over to speak to Durham's admin person?'

'Yes.'

'Good, good.'

There was an uncomfortable pause between them.

Then Diane said, 'It is wrong you're running this, you know? Mark is well qualified.'

'I think Rik needs to see him in action first,' Henry said. 'I'll make sure he gets chances as they arise . . . plus John Egerton might be back,' Henry said, referring to the detective superintendent who was on gardening leave.

'I doubt that,' Diane spluttered.

'Why? What's he done that's so awful?'

'What hasn't he done?' she said. She did not elaborate. 'Look, all I'm asking is that you treat Mark fairly.'

'Fairly is my middle name,' Henry promised. His mobile phone rang. 'Speak of the devil.' He answered it while looking at Diane. 'Hi, Mark.' He arched his eyebrows at Diane. 'You managed to speak to her . . . excellent . . . anything?' Henry listened hard. 'Right, get the details and get back over here and we'll get moving with it . . . yep, while the iron's hot.' He ended the call. 'Mark in action,' he said to Diane. 'Already struck gold.'

It was after nine p.m. by the time Henry got back to The Tawny Owl. He'd spent the last few hours sorting out the MIR with Diane – a very frigid few hours – discussing Wellhaven's findings and planning a route forward with them; then he returned to the mortuary when he got the call from Blackstone that Professor Baines was winding up the post-mortems. The results only confirmed what Henry had expected to hear – a bludgeoning and a shooting – with no apparent connections in terms of how they'd met their deaths.

The men had been business partners in life. But even that connection seemed tenuous.

From Wellhaven's visit to the still very shocked woman who

worked as Durham's admin person and general gofer, it was ascertained that while the murdered men did work with each other on various projects, it was only on an ad-hoc basis, and their business relationship wasn't enshrined in any form of partnership agreement or limited company. That did not surprise Henry unduly. From what he'd gleaned from Celia Twain when she was in custody talking about James, Henry saw him as a well-off rogue; when he spoke to Wellhaven, the picture of Marcus Durham was that he was also a rogue, which, of course, fitted in with what Henry knew about him from the half-baked kidnap escapade.

Wellhaven had brought back as much office documentation as he could carry. Durham's admin assistant had been glad to hand it over.

Henry met up with Blackstone at Th'Owl. He'd told her that if she wanted to, she could camp out in the guest bedroom for as long as she liked if it was more convenient for her, living so far away. She liked the idea, so after the post-mortems she'd dashed back to her flat in Preston, grabbed a few changes of clothing, stuffed them into a holdall and hared back up to Kendleton which would be her operating base for the foreseeable future.

She was already in the bar, heads down with the guys who were still fixated on solving the long-ago murder in Thornwell.

Foolishly, Henry poured himself a lager and sauntered over to the cluster of men, plus the newest members of the gang, Blackstone and Veronica Gough.

'Henry! Everyone finds it fascinating that you've been drafted in to run a local murder enquiry,' Dr Lott said. 'So' – he indicated the paperwork, consisting mainly of the newspaper cuttings the group had accumulated, once more spread out on the table between and under drinks glasses – 'maybe now you're switched on again, you'll be able to look through this lot – when you have time, obviously – and with your detective head on, maybe you'll see something we've missed.'

Unsurprisingly Blackstone gave a derisive snort and muttered something scathing under her breath.

Henry shot her a hard look, then to the group he said, 'Or not!'

As he turned to leave, Mrs Gough grabbed his arm. 'Henry! Quick word.'

She was in her wheelchair which, like her, seemed to have suffered no lasting damage from the distressing incident in the stream; she also appeared to be back on form.

Henry sat on a chair to come down to her eye level.

'I'd just like to thank you again for saving me.'

'You're welcome.'

'And also to apologize for my dismissive comments about your skills of detection. Clearly you have some; otherwise, you wouldn't have been asked back into the fold.'

A few chairs away, Blackstone snorted again.

'Apology accepted. Do you know if there has been any progress on *your* incident?'

'Only that I know Jake Niven's been trying to identify the youths responsible, but he's not having much luck: a wall of silence, apparently – a bit like this,' she said, jerking her thumb towards the unsolved murder investigation table.

'I'm pretty sure *they'll* get nowhere,' Henry said, 'but I'm sure Jake will.'

'Me, too, but it's something to do, isn't it? And you never know.'

'Good luck with it. Fortunately my murder victims are a bit fresher.'

Mrs Gough held him with a steely gaze. 'Did she do it? Celia?'

Henry smiled inscrutably. 'I couldn't possibly comment.'

'Well, if she didn't, you've got plenty of other suspects to go at.'

After detaching himself from the bar, Henry returned to his living room.

He'd brought a pile of paperwork home, including the files Wellhaven had brought back from Durham's office and a large stack of other files seized from James Twain's ransacked offices, although he did keep them apart.

As he sat down on the settee and all the energy fizzled out of him, he had more moments of doubt about taking on this job far too readily.

It was clear to him that even though he'd enjoyed the buzz of the day and his brain was in gear, he was still very rusty. He knew he had to be on top form for the morning's briefing, which meant he needed a decent night's sleep – the days of powering through, assisted only by caffeine and adrenaline, were long gone.

Yet he realized he also had some homework to do before then.

He forced himself to move over to the desk on which he'd stacked the files for both cases. He pushed them aside, opened a brand new A4-sized notebook, drew a line down the centre of the first page from top to bottom, headed one column *TWAIN* and the other *DURHAM* and began to jot down in bullet points what he knew so far about both murders. On the next page, he started making further notes about where the details crossed from victim to victim.

Partway through this process – which he always found useful – Blackstone crashed into the room and came to look over his shoulder. She peered at what he was writing, and Henry leaned back to allow her.

'All ideas welcome,' he said.

'Nah – looks good,' she said, unusually complimentary, running her forefinger down the list. 'Blah, blah, blah.'

Henry chuckled at her.

'Oh, wait a minute,' she said. 'What's this all about?'

Henry looked at the point where her fingertip had stopped on the page beside her name. 'That is me giving you the job of going through these.' Henry patted the stacked files on his desk. 'I know you're good at this sort of stuff, analysis and all that; just want you to see if there's any overlap, anything that connects Twain and Durham business-wise, personal-wise, that could result in an action' – an action being a deployment of detectives in order to investigate information. 'These two were obviously Jack-the-lads and maybe somewhere in this lot there's a transaction worth following up.'

'So I'm going to spend all day reading?' Blackstone whined as if she hadn't heard a word.

'As well as being my lackey.'

'Great,' she said glumly. 'One minute I'm your boss; now I'm your bitch.'

Henry chuckled again and said, 'The true order.'

Blackstone scooped up the files and said, 'Bed. Reading. Night night.'

After she'd gone, Henry stretched, yawned and stood up. He was about to hit the sack when Ginny came in, looking just as whacked as he felt. She'd been up before him that day and worked just as hard throughout. Henry had kept her informed of developments – in that he'd accepted the job of running two murders – which would mean he wouldn't be spending much time in the pub for a while. This didn't faze or annoy her, mainly because it kept him from under her feet.

She kissed him on the cheek. 'Busy boy,' she said.

'For a few days at least.'

'Maude's been in a few times, hoping to catch you. She seems very upset,' Ginny told him.

'I'll pop round and see her when I've got time,' he said.

'You need to sort things out with her properly, you know? I hate to say it, but neither of you are getting any younger.'

'I will, I promise,' he said weakly.

Then he went to bed. Alone.

His mobile phone vibrated and his dream dissolved, which annoyed him because whatever the dream happened to be, it had been complex yet enjoyable.

The phone continued to buzz softly on the bedside cabinet, doing a little circular dance. He reached blindly for it. His searching fingers eventually caught it and he rolled on to his side as he answered it.

He spoke thickly. 'Henry Chr—'

'Henry, Henry,' a whispering female voice interrupted him. Even then, still three-quarters asleep, Henry could hear fear and trepidation in a voice he didn't recognize immediately.

'Yuh . . . who?'

'It's me, Veronica . . . Mrs Gough.'

He pushed himself up on to an elbow. 'What's up?' Now he was awake.

'I didn't know who to ring.'

'That's all right . . . What's up?'

'They're here. In the house, I think.'

'Who? Who's there?' he asked. He sat up and swung his legs out of bed.

'Those boys, I think . . . I don't know . . . I can hear banging and laughing downstairs, as if the kitchen's being wrecked or some-thing . . . Oh God, Henry, I'm so sorry to bother you . . . I'm so scared.' She sounded terrified.

'It's fine.' He'd clamped the phone between his shoulder and cheek as he hobbled about trying to hitch up his jogging bottoms. 'Where are you in the house?'

'My bedroom.'

Henry threaded himself into a T-shirt, then forced his un-socked feet into his trainers. 'Front or back of the house?'

'Front . . . Oh my, something's smashed. Henry, I'm really scared.'

'Look, you're doing fine, Mrs Gough . . . I'm dressed now and I'll be there soon . . . keep on the line and keep talking to me, OK?'

'OK,' she whispered.

Henry scooped up his car keys and dashed out of the bedroom, keeping the phone clamped to his ear.

He noticed a light under the door of the guest bedroom in which Blackstone had taken up residency. Henry hesitated. He knew Blackstone's inner demons often meant sleepless nights for her, but he still wasn't sure if he should disturb her. She could have been fast asleep with the light on for all he knew.

In the end, he didn't have to make a decision because as he paused outside the door, it opened quickly, and Blackstone stood there looking ruffled but still fully clothed, just minus footwear.

'Henry! What are you doing creeping around?'

He waggled his phone. 'Intruders at Mrs Gough's.'

Blackstone's 'Gotcha!' was instant, and she was all business as she spun back into the room and slid her feet into her Doc Marten boots and grabbed her phone. She joined Henry as he went out into the pub and crossed to the front door. 'She's still on the line,' he said over his shoulder as he pushed the door open and exited.

'Henry . . . please hurry . . .'

'I'm running to my car now,' he assured Mrs Gough. To Blackstone, he said, 'Two things: call Jake now, then do a treble nine, see what response we can get.'

'On it,' Blackstone said. She'd already found Jake Niven's mobile number on her phone, and as she dropped into the front passenger seat of Henry's car, she was calling him.

Henry fired up his Audi, accelerated off the car park and sped towards the village with his phone still lodged between his shoulder and cheek, although an instant connection was made between the phone and the car by Bluetooth, which helped.

'Veronica, you still there?'

'I am.'

'You still hearing things?'

'Yes.' Her voice wavered. 'I think they're on the landing.'

'Does your bedroom door have a lock?

'No.'

'Right . . . we're only minutes away . . . keep calm, OK, and keep on the line.'

'The door handle's turning!'

'Shit!' Henry uttered as he careened through Kendleton, aware that Blackstone had connected to Jake and was talking urgently.

He negotiated the next two bends far too quickly and almost lost it, making Blackstone groan as she hurriedly explained the situation to a clearly groggy Jake who, in a very short space of time, she ended up shouting at.

'We're nearly there,' Henry told Mrs Gough, skidding on to the small estate off the main road on the other side of Kendleton. In his mind, he tried to weigh up the best approach. Full on, headlights blazing, skidding into the driveway, engine revving, in a move designed to scare the intruders away; or a more subtle approach, engine off, lights off, cruising to a silent stop a hundred metres short of the driveway, going the rest of the way on foot, creeping up to the house.

The fact was if Mrs Gough was right and intruders were now entering her bedroom, a subtle approach would give them time to attack or just scare the living crap out of her.

Henry did not want her molested in any way. And he didn't want her frightened to death, either. Her safety was the first consideration.

Blackstone ended her call to Jake and was now on the treble-nine emergency line.

Just to be on the safe side, out of the corner of his mouth, Henry said, 'Ambulance, too.' Into his phone, he said to Mrs Gough, 'Almost there.'

In response, she screamed a blood-curdling, terrifying scream.

The time for a subtle approach was long gone.

The entrance to her driveway was less than a hundred metres distant now. Henry braked at the last moment and swerved in between the gateposts, surging the last thirty-odd metres up the long driveway to the front of the house, skidding to a halt. Even before he'd stopped moving, he and Blackstone piled out of the car and were sprinting to the front door.

It was solid. Locked. Even a firm shoulder could not budge it.

'Round the back,' he said.

'I'll go that way,' Blackstone said, peeling off left. Henry went right, checking all the windows for breakages and signs of entry as he hurried around, finally coming to the back of the house and meeting up with Blackstone in a pincer movement.

And here was the obvious weak point of the house.

Across the back was a rickety lean-to conservatory which, in its day, would probably have been great and genteel. Now, its timber frame was clearly rotting; the windows were all single-glazed with the panes easy to smash, and the whole construction seemed to have a slight lean to it. It looked as though one concerted push could have toppled the whole thing.

It had double doors halfway along. They had been kicked open. Henry entered.

Another scream on the phone.

The next door facing Henry was the actual back door of the house. This was newer than the conservatory, made of UPVC. It had been jemmied open.

'Shit,' Henry said, stepping into the dining room beyond.

He went for the light switch and immediately the damage done by the invaders was clear. The dining-room table had been upturned, a sideboard pulled over and every plate once displayed on it was smashed to pieces on the floor. Several dining chairs had been stomped on and broken.

It was a rampage.

'More than one of them,' Henry said, then shouted, 'POLICE! We are police officers entering this building. Come down and show yourselves!'

He went into the lounge which had also been brutally trashed. He swerved sideways through a door into the entrance hallway to see the flash of two shadows hurtling down the stairs, which caught him off balance.

The racing shadows split. One ducked one way past him, one the other way, like fast-moving phantoms. He twisted and grabbed for one but missed.

Behind him, Blackstone was just emerging from the lounge and she too grasped and spun as she tried to grab what were obviously – now – two black-clad teenagers. But they were quick and lithe, and they shot past her, spinning her like a top.

'I'm going after them,' she shouted to Henry. 'You see to Veronica.'

'Take care,' he warned and contorted up the staircase, taking the steps three at a time, dinking around the chair of the stairlift at the top, coming up on to a wide landing. Several plant pots on stands had been kicked over, the plants and soil spilling everywhere.

'Veronica! It's me, Henry,' he called out as he made his way to the only open door on the landing, pocketing his phone.

All he heard was a muted, moaning sound.

He flicked the light switch on the landing, becoming more aware of the heartless damage done, and went towards the bedroom door.

He toed the door further open.

And as it swung back, a black-clad youth came at him, screaming and armed with a machete.

Henry hadn't been expecting this. Because two intruders had fled, he had stupidly assumed that was it, and his guard was down.

Seeing a curved blade slicing down at him was not what he expected, and somehow he had to recover from that millisecond of shock; otherwise (his brain calculated), his right arm would probably be hacked off at the shoulder.

He whirled away and actually felt the whoosh as the nasty blade sliced through the air, missing him by a fraction of an inch.

And in that moment he saw the snarling, feral face of the person attacking him under the shadow of the hoodie they were wearing.

There was no time to reflect on that because everything was now on a life-and-death footing. The blade was coming around again in an arc, and once more Henry had to take immediate, evasive action so as not to get slashed. The twist he had done in order to avoid the first attack was modified instantly into a kind of limbo-like backward sway, but it put him off balance, twisting on an ankle and tumbling away with a crash sideways just as the machete passed him a second time to be embedded into the door frame.

Henry rolled away as the youth tried to pull the knife out of the wood, but it had gone in too far, and after his first attempt to yank it free, he gave up, leapt over Henry's outstretched legs, sprinted down the landing and flew down the stairs using the bannister to help him.

By the time Henry was up on one knee, the lad had gone.

Henry felt himself sag, completely winded, slightly disorientated for a moment before everything came back into focus as he shook his head and, using the door frame as leverage, pulled himself up. His eyes came level with the embedded machete, at which point he exhaled unsteadily while looking wide-eyed at the rusting, deadly instrument. But there was no time to reflect on how fortunate he'd been – that would come later – because a groan from inside the bedroom brought him back, and he stepped in, just as he heard Blackstone calling from downstairs, 'Missed the bastards – couldn't catch 'em.'

Henry entered the bedroom. 'Christ!' he said, crossing the room and crouching down where Mrs Gough was on her back, lying half in, half out of her big old bed, entangled in flannelette sheets and a candlewick bedspread as if she had been dragged out and thrown down. She looked a pitiful sight.

Her mobile phone was about six feet away from her fingers on the old, worn carpet.

Henry dropped to one knee to look. She was unmoving, although her eyes were wide open, and for a fleeting moment Henry thought she might be dead, but a big gulp of air seemed to bring her round and her eyes began to focus on Henry.

'It's me, Henry,' he reassured her.

'Henry . . . I have such a sharp pain across my chest,' she gasped, and her right hand clamped down on her sternum. 'And up my arm.'

'There's an ambulance on the way,' Henry said, hoping this was true, knowing the reality of the pressure the ambulance service was currently under because of the ongoing pandemic. 'If I help you, do you think you can get back into bed?'

'Holy shit!' Blackstone appeared at the door, her face level with the machete in the frame.

'Give me a hand here, Debs,' Henry said, crawling around the half-prostrate figure of Mrs Gough and easing his hands under her bony back in order to get them under her armpits.

'Christ!' was Blackstone's next expletive as she swooped across. Between them, they gently raised Mrs Gough on to the bed where she seemed to sink into her pillows. Henry pulled a blanket over her, looking at her worriedly. He could hear her lungs rasping as she breathed.

'She might be having a heart attack,' Henry whispered to Blackstone. Then, 'Veronica?'

The old lady's eyes popped open.

'Can I get you anything?'

She pointed loosely towards the bedside cabinet. 'The spray. It might help me.'

There were several sprays and inhalers on top of the cabinet, plus pill bottles and blister packs, a bottle of water and a glass.

'Which one?'

'Nitro-glycerine, for my angina.'

Henry found it and handed it to her. She opened her mouth and sprayed a puff under her tongue. It had an immediate effect, helping her to breathe more easily as the medicinal explosive opened her veins and arteries, allowing the blood to flow. From a pasty grey pallor, her complexion quickly gathered some colour, making her look much healthier within seconds.

'Thank you.' She handed the spray back to Henry. 'That helps, but I've still got an awful lot of pain across my chest.'

Through the thin curtains, Henry saw the swish of rotating blue lights as Jake arrived, followed almost immediately by an ambulance.

Jake said, 'I've an idea now who some of the kids are, but no one's coming forward with names.'

He was responding to Henry's berating about not having identified the youths who had assaulted Veronica Gough by the stream, which had then led to an escalation in the form of a violent home invasion – which could have led to her death and possibly still might.

Both men were at Royal Lancaster Infirmary, having followed the ambulance in their respective vehicles. They were now standing outside the A&E unit under a canopy in an ambulance bay, banished outside by staff. Blackstone was still at Mrs Gough's house awaiting the arrival of an on-call joiner to secure the property.

'You're sure the lad with the machete was the same one that held her face under water?' Jake probed.

'Hundred per cent,' Henry said firmly. 'Saw his face, then I ducked out of the way to prevent my beheading. A nasty piece of work.'

'You were lucky.'

'She was luckier . . . so far,' Henry said bleakly.

Mrs Gough had been swiftly and expertly transferred from her bed into the back of the ambulance by paramedics in an NHS wheelchair, with Blackstone holding her hand on the precarious journey down the stairs, preferring not to use the slower chairlift as they were well experienced in this sort of manoeuvre. Fifteen minutes later, after a journey at breakneck speeds along virtually deserted roads, she'd arrived at A&E.

Henry had grabbed a terrible coffee from a dispensing machine and was sipping it and wincing at the taste as he talked to Jake.

'I'm not making excuses,' Jake said, 'but I spend less and less time on my own beat these days . . . and the two new estates that have sprung up in Thornwell, where I think these kids are from, are bloody huge, with folk coming in from all over the place to live in the county. I just don't know anyone any more. I know these kids need to be nipped in the bud, as you say, but as much as I whinge to my sergeant, Lancaster's problems outweigh Kendleton's and Thornwell's, unfortunately.'

'This incident racks it up a few notches, though,' Henry reasoned.

They stopped talking when the sliding doors to A&E opened and the two paramedics who'd arrived in the ambulance and conveyed Mrs Gough to casualty emerged and made back towards their transport.

'How is she?' Henry called. Mrs Gough had been in for about half an hour now.

The female paramedic peeled off to talk to them. 'Not brilliant. She did have a heart attack, a fairly mild one, but at her age even mild is serious. They're doing tests now.'

'Can I go and see her?'

'You can try.' The paramedic nodded and re-joined her colleague.

Backed by the authority of Jake's police uniform, Henry blagged his way past nurses acting like security guards and found Mrs Gough in a curtained cubicle. She was propped up and sipping a cup of tea. She looked much better but still sounded frail when she spoke in a low, scratchy voice.

'Thank you again, Henry,' she managed to say. 'I'm sorry I bothered you, caused so much trouble. I didn't know who else to call. I had you on speed dial.'

'Speed dial?'

She gave him a sheepish look.

'Anyway, the main thing is you're OK. But now we need to have a concerted effort to arrest these kids and get them into the justice system. What happened to you in the stream was bad enough, but this goes beyond, and I'm furious.' Henry looked at Jake and raised his eyebrows.

Taking the cue, Jake said, 'It's my number-one priority.'

'Thank you,' Mrs Gough said quietly. She looked at both men, and tears began to stream from her eyes. She reached out for Henry's hand, grasped it tightly and dug her nails into the back of his hand.

'What is it, Veronica?'

'The lad, the one with the knife or whatever you call it.'

'What about him?' Henry asked, instinctively knowing that what she was about to say would be very unpleasant.

'He screamed and screamed at me. Said he was going to hack

me to pieces . . .' She went quiet, then said, 'But only after he'd raped me first because he liked raping old women.' As she spoke, her words became more and more emotional, but then she suddenly clutched her chest as terrible agony coursed through her upper body. Henry shouted for a nurse.

NINE

It was almost six a.m. when Henry emerged, blinking like a salamander, from the depths of the infirmary into the dawn light of what looked like the start of a lovely day. He took stock of how he was feeling: gritty, tired, hungry and thirsty, and just a bit conscious he had a murder squad briefing coming up, comprising detectives and other cops and specialist support staff, all of which made him feel vulnerable and unprepared as well.

Once more, he questioned the wisdom of having accepted this job.

With that in mind, he made his way back to his car, which he'd left illegally parked on a nearby side street, hoping he hadn't got a ticket from an overenthusiastic, insomniac traffic warden.

He hadn't. He got in and called Blackstone. 'Hey!'

'Hey!' she reflected back. 'How're you doing, pal?'

For once, she sounded as drained as he was. Usually, she was the epitome of bubbly, and the fact she hadn't immediately insulted him made him wary.

'How is the old dear?' she asked.

'Stable now. She's going to be all right, hopefully.'

'And the other old dear?'

'That one,' he said, 'is unstable and knackered. You?'

'Back at Th'Owl. Mrs Gough's house is secure, and now I'm feeling enraged about what happened.'

'Me too, but I think we're going to have to leave it to Jake to sort.'

'Even though they were armed with a frickin' machete?'

'I'll speak to Rikky Boy – jeez, you've even got me calling him that – and see if I can hive off a couple of detectives to help out. I honestly can't see how hard this should be. They've got to be local kids.'

'Don't you remember? Nobody speaks to the cops these days, so everything we do is hard,' Blackstone told him, a sobering truth when the police force of today was struggling in so many ways, admittedly often through its own fault, to get communities to trust it.

'Good point. Anyway, I'm about to drive back, and you can call me a heathen, but I'm going to go to the McDonald's drive-through to get breakfast. You fancy one? The roads are empty, and if I put my foot down, I could be back in ten minutes so it'll still be warm and edible.'

'You silver-tongued old guy – get me one!'

Blackstone was waiting outside The Tawny Owl for Henry's arrival with the food parcel. As she drew up, she flew into the car and ripped open the bag containing her breakfast. Henry tore into his too, famished, and both devoured the food as in a scene from a medieval banquet, silently, ravenously.

They discussed Veronica Gough for a few minutes before moving on to the subject of the double murder investigation looming over them.

'I've never seen you in action,' Blackstone said.

'In what context?'

'Running a murder, leading a team.'

'Well, all I can say, Debbie Blackstone, is this: watch and learn. Now' – he screwed up his fast-food wrapper into a tight ball – 'shower, shave, change of clothing . . . the first lesson you need to learn is that' – here he looked deliberately at her – 'you need to look the part . . . it's a tradition of sorts.'

'Which arm did you have your booster vaccination in?'

'Why?'

'I'm going to punch it.'

Following breakfast and ablutions, he was raring to go for at least another eight hours, as long as he had access to coffee.

There was a full-length mirror in his bedroom in front of which he got dressed, deciding not to wear a suit – suspecting the two he owned would be too tight for him these days – but to go for the jacket-and-chinos look. When he'd finished tying his tie, he thought he looked pretty good: business-like but not overpowering.

He spun as a knock came at the door, and Blackstone swung in without waiting for him to invite her to enter. She stopped in her tracks and admired his look.

'Bit dull but half-decent,' she said. 'Here . . .' She came over and made a fuss of straightening his tie. 'You may not believe it, but I once dressed like a nerd, had bobbed hair and wore sensible shoes.'

Henry did know. He also knew what had changed her, the way she dressed, and understood why she was the way she was now.

Even so, he said, 'I couldn't even begin to imagine that . . . and just so you know, I like you the way you are.'

'You, too.' She stood back and admired her handiwork. 'Anyway, less of this mutual appreciation society . . . Give Rikky Boy a call – he's been trying to get hold of you and he doesn't sound happy.'

'I must've been in the shower.' Henry gave his short hair a pass with the palm of his hand and reached for his mobile phone.

'Unbelievable!'

Henry strode angrily through The Tawny Owl with Blackstone, files tucked under her arm, scurrying along in his slipstream, which was unusual because, more often than not, she led the charge with him in tow.

'What?'

'Bloody Covid . . . both Diane and Wellhaven have tested positive for eff's sake and won't be coming in for days, self-bloody-isolating . . . probably having a shagathon, more like!'

'That sounded very bitter.'

'It was,' Henry confirmed.

He burst out through the front door of the pub, heading for his car.

'So what does it mean?' Blackstone asked as they crossed the terrace.

'It means that all the tasks I was going to heap on him – sorry, allocate to him in order for him to shine – will probably now have to be done by yours truly – me, and you, of course, because' – he stopped suddenly and Blackstone crashed into him – 'it also sounds like Covid has decimated the murder squad and they're all dropping like flies.'

'Oh, bloody great!'

'My master plan was to let lover-boy have the Marcus Durham side while we tackled the Twain side and see, if you'll pardon the expression, if the twain should meet. I've been saving that one up for a while, by the way.'

'Eh?'

'Forget it.' He stomped to his car and, before he got in, said, 'Couldn't get any worse, could it?'

It did. With one fell swoop, the virus had annihilated the murder squad overnight. Detectives and specialists fell left, right and centre, and only a smattering of people rocked up as requested; had it been anything less than murder, Henry would have called the whole thing off and sent everyone home.

Just to be on the safe side, Henry and Blackstone took lateral flow tests, which both turned out to be negative.

Then things went from bad to worse, when Rik Dean called Henry just before eight a.m. and announced he too had tested positive and wouldn't be in work as such, but would remain contactable through all the other channels including Zoom.

'So, let me get this straight,' Henry said glumly, 'we've got two murders and no staff to investigate them. We are in the latter stages of the golden hours,' he said, referring to the critical first seventy-two hours of an investigation, which were often when an investigation was won or lost. Beyond those three days, everything got more difficult.

He and Blackstone were in the MIR, sitting opposite each other while Henry spoke to Rik on the phone, their eyes in constant, anxious contact. 'What exactly am I supposed to do with zero staff?'

'Do what I'm paying you to do,' Rik said harshly. To be fair, he sounded rough, having audibly deteriorated even since Henry had last spoken to him, suddenly full of sniffles and a croaky-sounding throat. 'Investigate a murder – sorry, two murders.'

Finally, the call ended, and Henry tossed his mobile phone contemptuously on the desk between him and Blackstone, who he looked at beseechingly for inspiration. When none was forthcoming, he said, 'Give me some inspiration!'

'How about a road trip and do what detectives are supposed to do – go and talk to people, ask questions and, if necessary, kick in some doors?'

'Love it!' Henry said, rocking forwards out of his chair and going through to the skeleton-crewed MIR which reminded him of the *Mary Celeste*, minus the half-eaten meals.

The phone on the allocator's desk (which was unoccupied) was ringing forlornly, no one to answer it. Henry snatched it up.

'Henry Christie, CSIO, can I help?' he answered, managing to get his tongue around his new job title and giving Blackstone a grin.

'Hello . . . is that the investigation into Marcus Durham's murder?' a quiet female voice asked tentatively.

'Yes, you've got the right number. I'm the lead investigator. Can I help?'

'Oh, good.' The woman sounded relieved.

'Can I ask who is calling?' Henry said, using his politest phone voice.

'I'm May Jones . . . I'm Marcus's admin person,' she said, sounding slightly flustered. 'A detective came to see me yesterday – DCI Wellhaven?'

'Yes, that's right. You gave him some of Mr Durham's files to look at.' Henry glanced at the desk on which the files had been abandoned.

'Well, he said if I found anything else I thought might be of interest, I should call him, which I did on his mobile, but it turns out he's got Covid, so he gave me this number.'

'OK,' Henry said.

'Well, I have found something.'

Henry drove. The files taken from Durham's and Twain's offices were now in the passenger footwell at Blackstone's feet and spread untidily across the back seat of the Audi. Henry thought it all looked a mess but Blackstone seemed to have it all under control as she pored through the paperwork with a pad resting on her lap, making notes and occasionally tossing a sheet of paper over her shoulder into the back seat, grunting now and then, continuing the process she had begun the night before in her room at Th'Owl.

Half an hour later, after traversing the Trough of Bowland and driving through Clitheroe, Henry pulled into Durham's building yard, recalling it well from the time he'd led the arrest of Durham for kidnapping all those years before. It didn't seem to have changed much. The office was a Portakabin, and there were several ships' containers at the back of the yard where Durham kept his equipment and in one of which he'd scared Josh Price shitless. Henry remembered the fast-moving investigation that was resolved in less than a day. He'd mentioned it to Blackstone on the way across from Lancaster, and she'd asked if there could be any link to that incident and Durham's murder.

Henry chewed it over and said he didn't think so, but nor did he want to discount it. At the back of his mind, something gnawed at him, but he could not quite place what.

May Jones was waiting for them at the office door. She was a small, plump, middle-aged woman in jeans and a flowery top, and to Henry she somehow seemed out of place working in a builder's yard, but he realized that was probably him making stereotypical assumptions.

Henry did not recall her from his previous encounter with Durham, which, to be fair, had not lasted long. Durham was in cuffs and away within minutes of Henry and a firearms team descending on the place and liberating Josh Price.

'Hi, I'm Henry Christie and this is DS Blackstone. You must be May?'

'I am. Come in.' She turned into the office, and the two detectives followed. The temporary structure was quite large, even having a shower room and loo, and a separate office at one end, with the remaining space having a small, muddy seating area and a desk for May. She seemed to have a tidy space, but the remainder was a shit-tip in Henry's eyes, a typical builder's space, all dirty-wellie footprints and mud smudges on the walls.

Once inside, May turned to them.

Henry said, 'I'm sorry about Marcus.'

'Me, too.' She sighed. 'And for me, too: job over, I reckon.'

'That's a shame,' Henry said genuinely. 'Look, May, I apologize for this, and I thank you for contacting us, but as you know, DCI Wellhaven has Covid and he didn't really get a chance to tell me very much about his visit yesterday, so if we go over things again, please bear with us.'

'It's all right. There wasn't that much to say, to be honest. Marcus employed me, paid half-decent money and let me get on with it – looking after invoices, contracts, banking and even doing his tax returns, although I must say the figures in them didn't usually match the cash I saw coming in, if you get my drift. He always made a loss on paper. I gave all the stuff I had to that DCI.'

'We know and we're very grateful. We're already studying it,' Henry said. 'What else have you found?'

She slid a hand into her jeans pocket and pulled out a key. 'One place I was never allowed – the safe! It's in Marcus's office, which is through there.' She pointed to the door at the end of the cabin.

'I suspect he thought I didn't know he even had a safe because it was always, and still is, under a stack of old clothes. But I did know, just never knew where the key was. Not that I was bothered, even though I was curious, as you would be. Anyway, I found the key Blu-Tacked under an old girlie calendar on the wall behind his desk, so I opened it.'

She paused dramatically. Henry encouraged her with a nod.

Less subtle, Blackstone demanded, 'And found what?'

May's fingers went back into her pocket and came out bearing an SD card between her finger and thumb. 'This, for one thing. We have a CCTV set-up in the yard and there's some footage on this from a Saturday a few weeks back, when I wasn't in. I don't do weekends, and before you ask, I don't religiously check what's on the camera, only when we've had a problem or damage caused, something like that, because there's mostly nothing to see. Follow me.'

She led them to Durham's office, which was a tip in progress.

May laughed nervously. 'He wasn't a good housekeeper, at least not in here, but up at his house it was a different matter, shall we say? Even though I've only been up there twice. Hell of a place. Anyway.' She pointed to an old, creased calendar on the wall behind the desk. Henry blinked at the image. Blackstone uttered an 'Ugh!' The photograph was of a hugely well-endowed man being sucked off by a hugely well-endowed woman.

'Bit more than a girlie calendar,' Blackstone muttered with distaste.

'Mmm,' May said. 'Anyway, the key was stuck on the wall behind it and the safe' – she heaved a pile of grubby builders' clothing away from one corner of the room to unveil a sturdy safe bolted on to the office floor and wall – 'is here.'

'And what else did you find?' Blackstone asked.

'See for yourself.' She bent over, unlocked it, pulled open the door and took a step away.

Henry gave a short, appreciative whistle.

Blackstone said, 'Bingo!'

They emptied the safe's contents on to May's tidy desk. There was a lot of cash in tight rolls, each with an elastic band around it.

Eighteen rolls, to be exact.

There was also a file containing more paperwork.

Blackstone filmed the treasure trove and the moments when Henry – now wearing disposable gloves – unravelled one of the rolls and slowly counted five hundred ten-pound notes. For the benefit of the recording, he said, 'Five thousand pounds in this roll, so if each roll, eighteen in total, contains that amount, we're looking at ninety thousand here approximately.'

'Any idea what this related to, May?' Blackstone asked, swivelling the camera to her.

She seemed to shrink away from the limelight and shook her head. 'No idea, honestly.'

'We'll need a statement from you,' Henry told her. 'I know you've already given one about discovering Marcus's body, but we will need more.'

'Yep, no worries.'

'Now then,' Henry said, picking up the SD card, 'shall we have a look at what's on this?'

'I'll copy it first,' Blackstone said. She held out her hand and took the card from Henry, then inserted it into a slot on the side of her phone.

'You can do that?' Henry asked.

'Duh!'

He sighed. He was always at least one step behind the technology curve and accepted he would never likely catch up.

'Done!' Blackstone pulled the card out and handed it to May who sat at her desk and slotted it into her laptop. The screen lit up into four equal squares. She said, 'We have four cameras, all outside, basically covering the yard and cabin from four different angles. Generally, not much goes on – deliveries, that sort of thing.'

Henry and Blackstone went to stand behind her and saw the date stamp on the screen, working it out to be three Saturdays ago.

'I'll jump to the interesting bits,' May said. The pictures began to jerk forward and Henry saw the time stamp move from nine a.m. to eleven thirty, when May lifted her finger off the key and everything went back to real time and showed a large motorbike stopping at the gates, the rider dismounting and unlocking the gates from the roadside and pushing them open. 'This is Marcus arriving. He's usually in his four-by-four, not on his bike.'

Henry watched Durham hop back on to the bike and ride to the front of the cabin where he got off again, removed his helmet and, rubbing his hair flat, entered the cabin.

May skipped forward again. Nothing happened until twelve thirteen when a car drove into the yard and circled to a stop in front of the cabin, alongside Durham's motorbike. It was a big off-roader of some sort – black, sporty, with greyed-out windows in the rear. The registration number was slightly blurred as the car had stopped in such a position that the cameras could not pick up on it. Henry didn't see that as a problem. He had faith that the tech team would be able to zoom in and get a reading.

It was hard to see how many people were in the vehicle.

Certainly a driver and front-seat passenger, both big males, but it was impossible to determine how many were in the rear.

The front passenger got out. A man, dark-skinned, but it was hard to say if he was tanned or of Asian origin; dark hair slicked back, wearing a black leather jacket and tight jeans that showed big thigh muscles and tapering legs. He was about five feet eight inches tall but looked a handy guy.

Henry glanced at Blackstone. She shook her head: didn't know him.

The man – Henry had already named him 'Slick' because of the hair – opened the rear door.

The angle of one of the cameras was such that it captured the person emerging one foot and one leg at a time.

A woman.

Who was wearing black, knee-high boots with high heels, Lycra leggings and a tight blouse, and carrying a handbag.

Her head was the last thing to come into view, followed by her face as she turned full-on for the camera to capture her image.

May pressed pause and the woman stopped moving.

This time, unlike the car registration numbers, her features were clear to see.

Henry gulped. His head twisted quickly to Blackstone who gave the faintest of nods.

May saw the exchange. 'You guys know her?'

'No,' Henry said, probably too quickly. 'Keep going.'

May pressed play, and the woman and Slick entered the cabin, closing the door behind them, leaving the driver in the car.

Nothing happened for the next twenty-eight minutes.

Glancing around the cabin, Henry asked May, 'No cameras in here, then?'

She shook her head.

The attention of all three returned to the computer screen. In that hiatus of twenty-eight minutes, all that happened was the driver of the four-by-four got out and leaned against the vehicle, having a smoke. He was older than Slick, probably late thirties, heavy-set, leather jacket, chinos, and a nasty-looking bruiser. Henry named him 'Nasty Man'.

May skipped on until she suddenly said, 'Here,' and took her finger off the keyboard. As the footage returned to normal speed, the cabin door flew open, and the two men who had been inside, Slick and Durham, tumbled out, grappling with each other, closely followed by the woman who was – silently because there was no sound on the video – screaming at the two men and laying her own punches and kicks on Durham as and when he came within reach.

Nasty Man scuttled around the car and launched himself into the fray to help his mate.

But Durham swung Slick around to become a shield between him and Nasty Man. Slick squirmed. The woman kicked out.

Durham fended her off, knocking her aside with his forearm. Then, with a superbly placed uppercut into Slick's jaw, he sent the smaller man staggering back into Nasty Man, who hooked his hands under Slick's armpits as he fell backwards into him. Slick looked stunned. Durham's punch must have addled his brain and everything south of it.

Durham shoved the woman away, then ran into the cabin, re-emerging almost immediately with a taped-up baseball bat in his hand, swivelling it menacingly though not quite hitting anyone.

There was some kind of verbal argument between him and the woman, while Nasty Man comically dragged Slick around the four-by-four and started to heave the semi-conscious guy into the back seat; having done that, he strode purposefully around the vehicle, seemingly with the intention of going for Durham, who brandished his bat forebodingly and looked likely to use it.

The woman raised her hands, trying to bring some peace to the proceedings, but Durham kept dancing towards them, step by step, forcing them backwards until they got the message. The woman got in the passenger seat, and Nasty Man ran back and scrambled behind the wheel.

Durham slammed the baseball bat down on the front wing and roof of the car, causing expensive-looking dents, as it skidded away with a lurch and sped out of the yard with the woman gesturing at him, flashing V-signs and a middle-finger through the open window, plus, Henry assumed, accompanying and appropriate words.

Then it was gone. Durham stood in the middle of his yard, panting heavily and leaning on his bat like a knight on his sword.

'Bit of a contretemps,' Blackstone said. 'So you don't know who the guys or the woman are?' she asked May.

'Never seen them before.'

'And this money?' Henry indicated the cash laid out on the desk. 'This appeared when?'

'I've no idea,' May said, sounding honest. 'It was just there when I unlocked the safe, I assure you.'

'Do you have any idea what it could be for? Any building jobs, cash in hand?' Henry asked.

'I don't know. Marcus did a lot of cash stuff, but I generally knew about it.'

Henry rubbed his hands together and looked at Blackstone. 'We need to get someone up here to seize this money, count it and give May a receipt. We'll take the SD card now as well as the documents in the folder. Is that OK with you, May?'

'Suppose it'll have to be.'

Blackstone contacted the MIR and arranged for a DC (one not laid up with Covid) to come out and seize the cash, even though Henry, if he was being honest, really did not have sufficient justification to take the money; as much as anything, it was for safekeeping and he would hand it over, if he had to, to Durham's estate when things reached that point. The thought of such a large amount of money lying around, unprotected, made him uncomfortable.

While waiting for the detective to arrive, May brewed a pot of tea, and they all chatted about Durham, but the conversation did not shed any light on anything for Henry.

When the DC finally landed from the MIR, he was given his instructions, and Henry and Blackstone got into Henry's car. For a few moments, they were silent, but there was a ripple of excitement between them. Henry started the engine, looked at Blackstone and said, 'Don't say a word until I've counted to three.'

Blackstone nodded eagerly.

Henry began. 'One . . . two . . . THREE!'

On the next beat, both simultaneously blurted the name, 'Sue Daggert!'

The next, unexpected, part of their road trip was relatively silent.

Blackstone sifted through the paperwork seized from Durham's safe.

Henry concentrated on the road, but his mind wandered back to the murder scene in James Twain's workshop, close to the Spitfire, and the gun figure clad in a forensic suit.

As was normal with such attire, it wasn't figure-hugging, so it was not obvious if the person was a man or a woman. It could have been either. Initially, he'd thought man, but perhaps he was wrong, and the more he reran the scenario through his mind on a continuous loop, the more he thought it could have been a woman. Or was he now trying to shoehorn what he had learned today into these circumstances? He knew for certain that Sue Daggert was more than capable of killing someone by shooting or bludgeoning.

He sighed and glanced at Blackstone reading the documents. 'Anything?'

She slid the paperwork back into the folder and yawned. 'Dunno. Need to sit at a desk and do some surfing. What's going on in your mind?'

'That it could have been a woman at Twain's murder. It was all pretty fast, but I immediately nailed the intruder as a bloke in my brain. I could be wrong.'

'Is this because of what we've just seen on the CCTV?'

'Yep, I admit that.' He drove on.

After leaving Clitheroe, he had gone on to the A59 and driven towards Preston, then dropped on to the M6 north before peeling off on to the M55 towards Blackpool.

Henry had slotted the mobile phone into the hands-free holder on his dashboard, where it automatically connected with Bluetooth. It rang; he answered.

From the display, he knew he was taking a call from the Blood Guy, Professor Rostamian. 'Hi, Prof.'

'Henry, hi . . . uh, you seem to be travelling?'

'Yep. You got something for me?'

'I do. Can we speak or should we reconnect later?'

'Is it something that could wait an hour, say?'

'I'll call you back,' the Blood Guy said.

They hung up.

Henry's fingers tightened around the steering wheel, a move noted by Blackstone.

'You OK, old guy? Do you need the toilet?'

That made him chuckle at least. 'Tell me what you know about Sue Daggert.'

'I know more about Jack Daggert, her hubby, to be honest.'

'Dangerous, dangerous man,' Henry said.

'One of the biggest drug dealers in the north-west, Blackpool-based; didn't he get sent down a while ago, four million worth of cocaine, three hundred grand cash in his possession?'

'You might be right, but I think he's out now.'

'And Sue is the wife, lives a life encrusted with diamonds and pearls, and drives a Bentley convertible, last I heard,' Blackstone said.

'Seen her mugshot, and Jack's, in the society pages of *Lancashire Life* and other such magazines, lord and lady-ing it, giving dosh to charity,' Henry said.

'Sounds about right.'

'But to be honest, I don't know what their current situation is . . . or do I?' Blackstone said mysteriously. She picked up her phone and logged on to the internet. 'I think I just remembered something.'

Henry drove on down the motorway, keeping one eye on Blackstone as she scrolled.

'NCA website,' she explained, referring to the National Crime Agency. She flicked through it and went, 'Yep.' She read for a moment, then said, 'Four men arrested in a twenty-million drugs bust in Birmingham . . . dah, dah, dah . . . Yep . . . Jack William Daggert, aged forty-five, from Lancashire, plus three other men whose names mean nothing to me, from various parts of the country . . . remanded to Birmingham Crown Court for trial. So he *is* locked up!' She looked sideways at Henry. 'Meaning that Mrs Sue Daggert is looking to be a drug dealer's widow if he gets the going rate for sentences, which are huge these days.'

'And she's possibly now stepped up to the mark and is now keeping the business going?' ventured Henry.

'I know it's all assumptions . . . but the ninety grand in Durham's safe could be linked to the drugs biz?' Blackstone shrugged.

'If Jack's in the clink, she may be resorting to desperate measures, and Durham's not averse to going over to the dark side, is he?' Henry agreed. 'Best thing we can do is go chat to her.'

Henry came off the motorway at Marton Circle and took that route into Blackpool, passing fairly close to the housing estate where

he used to live with Kate. He felt a pang of something at the proximity, remembering a house in which he'd raised his daughters,
Jenny and Leanne, and for a moment became almost breathless as
the memories gut-punched him. He pursed his lips and exhaled.

'You OK?' Blackstone asked, noticing this. She seemed to have
an eye for detail where he was concerned.

'Yep, yep.' He blinked, swallowed. 'Just memories.'

'Oh?'

'And guilt, as ever . . . damn!'

Blackstone knew what he was talking about. They'd shared their
rocky back stories before, and she touched his forearm gently in a
gesture that took Henry by surprise. He gave her a wan smile.

'We're a couple of soft twats,' she remarked.

'One way of putting it.' He sat up, pulled himself together and
said, 'South Shore, baby.'

Even in the few short years he had been retired, the South Shore
area of Blackpool had changed considerably. New road layouts,
houses flattened, new estates and shopping areas popping up,
although even this 'tarting up', as Henry called it, could not disguise
the widespread deprivation and poverty of the area he knew so well
and had regularly visited as a cop to knock down doors.

But no matter what changed at sea level, the place was still
dominated by the Big One, the huge roller coaster on the Pleasure
Beach, Blackpool's main amusement park.

Henry drove along Lytham Road, did a few left and right turns,
before entering a small, grotty industrial estate consisting of a few
dozen units of varying sizes.

'Their place was in here if I recall,' he said, slowing the car right
down and almost leaning his chin on the wheel as he navigated his
way along streets strewn with a variety of battered vehicles, stacked
pallets, discarded furniture and rusting white goods. 'The beating
heart of wholesale Britain,' he observed.

'I had another description in mind,' Blackstone muttered, her
eyes taking in everyone and everything they passed.

This was another of those places Henry had previously had cause
to visit, often accompanied by a strike team, over the course of his
tenure in Blackpool: basically, a backstreet estate on which most
businesses were above board, but several others were fronts for
more nefarious activities.

As he meandered along, the emotional feeling he'd had a short time earlier was now replaced by one of low-level excitement, coupled with a heightening of the senses. You never could tell just what you might stumble across; last time he was in a place similar to this, he'd been confronted and attacked by a gunman who had almost killed Diane Daniels.

He was in 'cruise-look' mode.

And he noticed a couple of vehicles which, at first glance, seemed to be part of the background of the estate, but which, on a double-check, were clearly not.

One was a Transit van.

What he noticed about it was an air vent on the back panel, which wasn't standard and, like a tiny Venetian blind, was angled open to allow a flow of fresh air into the van. There was also a short, stumpy aerial on the roof that didn't look standard.

The next vehicle ever so slightly out of place was a too-new Renault Clio, greyed-out windows with a similar roof aerial to the Transit but with two figures slouched low in the front seats.

Henry said, 'Cops. Surveillance.'

Blackstone, who had also noticed, said, 'Roger that.'

'Two may mean more we haven't seen,' Henry said. 'Does that make a difference to us?'

'Not in my book,' Blackstone said. 'We don't know what they're doing here.'

Henry crawled around the next corner into a short cul-de-sac with small units either side, including a carpet wholesaler and a garage workshop; but it was the one at the far end that was their target. Behind a high fence was a hairdressing wholesaler, and Henry knew this was the premises that constituted the legitimate business of the Daggert family, providing a cover for Jack Daggert's extensive drug-dealing activities.

Henry drove into the car park and pulled into a customer parking spot, noticing the four-by-four that had paid a visit to Marcus Durham's place (the indentations in the roof and bonnet courtesy of Durham's baseball bat attack) and a Bentley convertible in staff-only parking. A sign over the door read, *Daggert's Hair & Beauty Supplies*, and underneath, *Props: J. & J. Daggert*.

Henry sat at the wheel, engine idling.

'Is your Spidey sense tingling?' Blackstone asked. 'Because mine is going fucking berserk!'

Henry nodded. Just something in the air.

'Well, we're here now, so we might as well go knock on doors,' Blackstone said. 'That's what you like doing, isn't it?'

'That's what I *lurve* doing,' Henry corrected her, switching off the engine. Both started to get out at the moment the front door of the unit opened and Sue Daggert, no less, stepped out. She was dressed in tight jeans, high boots, a faux-fur coat, leopard-skin style. Her hair was silver-blonde, scraped tightly back, and her face was plastered in what Henry would have called 'big' make-up.

That said, she looked pretty good to him as she slung a handbag over her shoulder, saw and recognized him, put on a beaming smile and sashayed over, hips a-swaying.

'Jesus! Tart alert!' Blackstone said.

'Henry Fucking Christie! Well, I'll be damned!' Daggert chuckled in a hoarse, gravelly voice. 'You come to lock me up, put me in handcuffs?'

'Only if you've done something really bad,' he responded weakly, recalling and now experiencing how overpowering she could be, using her colossal personality and looks as weapons to overpower men and women.

Henry tried to imagine her in a forensic suit. Could she really have been the shooter at James Twain's workshop?

She came up to him. Close. Her head tilted cockily and yet she managed to look down her sharp nose at him. He could smell her. He might have said it was cheap perfume but he knew better. There was just a lot of it, and cheap it certainly wouldn't be.

She gave her hair a shake.

'Jeez,' he heard Blackstone mutter on the opposite side of the car.

Daggert gave her a contemptuous smirk and said to Henry, 'She with you, darl'?'

'Yep,' he said throatily.

'Too bad. Is this your motor, Henry?' Daggert pointed at his car with long, sharp, red-painted nails.

'Yep.'

'Wanna take me for a ride?'

Henry, refiling his hormones, said, 'So soon in our relationship?'

Daggert gave him the exact same grin she'd just given Blackstone, but then something unexpected happened that Henry wasn't prepared for.

Suddenly, there was a small, snub-nosed, two-inch-barrelled revolver in her right hand pointed down at his guts. Then she swung sideways, raised the gun and fired at Blackstone.

Twice.

Blackstone fell instantly.

Then, keeping the gun pointed at Henry, Daggert scuttled around the front of the car, screaming, 'Get in! Get in and drive me, you fucker! Do it or I'll shoot you too. DO IT!'

Stunned, and in a compliant trance, Henry did as he was told, as Daggert got in the opposite side, ramming the muzzle against his head. Now he whiffed gunsmoke mixed with her perfume.

'Drive, you fucking bastard! Get me out of here – now, fast!'

Henry put the car into reverse and slewed out of the parking space. 'You shot her! You fucking shot her!' he screamed.

'I shot *at* her – there's a fucking difference.' She tapped the gun against his head again and growled, 'I missed, but I won't miss you. Now, get me out of here.'

Henry aimed the car towards the open gate, glancing in his side mirror and seeing Blackstone's prostrate figure on the ground, seemingly unmoving.

'Just drive,' Daggert warned him. 'Nothing funny or I'll splat your brains.'

'What's going on?'

'I need to get out of here,' she began to explain.

Henry turned on to the cul-de-sac and things began to happen very quickly.

First, fifty metres ahead of him, a black-clad figure rose up between a roadside skip and a flat-back truck and hurled something that looked like a huge python across the road in front of the car.

A Stinger.

Henry recognized it immediately – the piece of kit used by police, usually in car chases, a tactical tyre-deflating device with hollow spikes designed to puncture tyres in slow deflation, allowing police to bring a target car to a controlled stop.

Instinctively, Henry swerved, but the narrowness of the cul-de-sac meant he could not avoid driving over the Stinger. Even though he hadn't reached any great speed, he felt the front of his car lurch uncomfortably as the spikes penetrated his tyres; in a parallel train of thought, he wondered how much two new tyres would cost him.

Alongside him, Daggert swore. 'Keep fucking driving; put your foot down.'

Wrestling with the steering wheel as the tyres went down, Henry did as he was told – and again in that parallel train of thought, he realized that if he carried on driving with two flat tyres, the car would be running on wheel rims very soon, which would cost even more and probably go on to damage the brakes, steering and front suspension. He was mortified.

But he didn't get the chance to go much further because some kind of chunky four-wheel-drive monstrosity, with huge bull bars attached to its front radiator grille and wrapped around the sides, appeared from a yard on his right and, in a screaming surge of noise and power, rammed mercilessly into the front wing of his car, forcing it sideways with a horrible metal-tearing, screeching noise that sounded like a Jurassic Park dinosaur, bringing Henry to a stop.

The impact threw Daggert against the passenger-door window, cracking her head, stunning her.

Henry was then aware of his car being surrounded by people in dark-blue overalls, ballistic vests and helmets, seeing the letters NCA stamped on their chests and backs, machine pistols in hands, his door being jemmied open (more expense) and him being dragged out by men and women screaming orders at him and flinging him roughly face down and his hands being forced behind his head. Glancing up through the corner of his eye, he saw the muzzle of another gun pointed directly at that eye.

He assumed the same scenario was being enacted on the other side of the car with Daggert being the centre of attention.

Although desperately worried about Blackstone, he knew he had to let the situation run its course for a few more seconds before pleading his case and his concern; in his experience, cops carrying out ops like this rarely listened to anything because of the adrenaline pumping through their brains with the volume of a garage rock band.

He rested his forehead on the tarmac.

Waited.

Then he felt a toecap inserted under his right shoulder, and he was rolled over to face the sky.

Blackstone looked down at him, not grinning for once.

'You're all right!' he gasped.

'I'm fine . . . your tart's a very bad shot, even at close range.'

Blackstone looked sideways at someone and said, 'He's one of us,' then back at him. 'You can get up now.'

He rolled to one side and began to get to his feet, bit by bit.

'I thought she'd shot you,' he said.

'Missed by a mile.'

Finally he was up, standing but unsteady.

On the other side of his car, he saw that a handcuffed Sue Daggert was being bundled into the back of a police van, squirming and spitting at the officers either side of her up to the moment a cop pulled a spit-mask over her head.

Henry then looked at his damaged car. 'Really?' he said. '*Really?*'

TEN

'Well, the fact is I didn't expect to be kidnapped, held at gunpoint, told to get into my car, have a gun shoved into my face and be told to *drive!*' The last word was emphasized on a rising inflection.

Henry got a grip of his brittle emotions, counted to ten, then said, 'So, yes, I'm making a claim. I am insured for business purposes and specifically for police business, and I require a courtesy car pretty damn quick. Get back to me on my mobile number when it's sorted.'

He slammed the phone down on the poor insurance agent at the other end of the line in the vain but passing hope that the guy's – he had to be called Scott, didn't he? – eardrum had burst.

Then he sighed and looked across the desk at Blackstone, who was, as usual, observing him with quivering lips, trying not to laugh out loud. Henry thought she was taking having been shot at far too well.

So he told her that.

'Still here, still in one piece, so can't complain too much,' she said philosophically.

'You really are a mystery to me,' Henry admitted with admiration.

They were sitting in a small office at Blackpool police station, which is where the snarling alley cat that was Sue Daggert had been brought and locked up. They were waiting for someone from the NCA to update them – and give them a chance to interview Daggert before they whisked her away to London. In that hiatus, Henry had taken the opportunity to phone his insurance company and get the ball rolling as regards his now undriveable and probably irreparable car. It hadn't been an easy conversation with Scott and it frustrated him to infinity.

As the office door opened, Henry's and Blackstone's heads swivelled to see Detective Superintendent Catherine Evans from the NCA enter. She was still wearing the ballistic vest from the operation she'd been running and into which Henry and Blackstone had unwittingly stumbled.

She perched on the edge of the table. 'If nothing else, we've got her for attempted murder and kidnapping,' Evans said. 'All grist to the mill. What were you two doing there?'

Between them, they explained. Henry then asked Evans why the NCA was running an op on Daggert.

'You probably know that hubby, Jack Daggert, was arrested in Birmingham a few months ago for importing and supplying a huge quantity of Class A drugs, probably destined for the north-west. He was caught bang to rights, and we seized a substantial amount of drugs and cash. It just seemed prudent to run a follow-up on Mrs D, who we assumed would be carrying on the family business after a period of keeping her head down . . . and she was, naughty little missus, which is why we stepped in.

'A substantial amount of cash and drugs have been found in the hairdressers' unit since her arrest. We think someone tipped her off about our op, which panicked her into taking a potshot or two at you, DS Blackstone, and getting you to drive her away at gunpoint, Henry. You're both very lucky.

'However, while it is very interesting that she paid a visit to a man who was subsequently murdered, you're on a bit of a wild goose chase here.'

Both asked, 'Why?' simultaneously.

'There's every chance that Marcus Durham is or has become part of the Daggert family drug distribution network, and perhaps he and Sue had a fall-out, or whatever . . . we may never know . . . and that ninety grand in his safe may well be connected to that relationship, but the fact of the matter is that Sue Daggert did not personally kill Marcus Durham. I'm not saying categorically she didn't have some connection to his death, but she definitely did not pull the trigger.'

Henry ended up calling his insurance company again, asking to speak to Scott, then meekly apologizing for the earbashing he'd given him, because as he and Blackstone walked out of Blackpool nick, a courtesy car was awaiting: a nice, small, Mercedes hatchback.

After making that call, Henry and Blackstone were in the car, speeding east along the M55, cutting north on to the M6 and going back to Lancaster to revisit the MIR.

By that time, it was almost six p.m., and Henry had been on the go for over twelve hours, more if the incident at Veronica Gough's house was included. They were both ravenous, necessitating a stop at Lancaster South motorway services to grab a sandwich and coffee to go.

Back in the car, Blackstone said, 'At least we have one suspect less to worry about,' as she ripped open Henry's triple bacon, lettuce and tomato pack for him and passed the first sandwich across.

'We will need to follow up the conspiracy side, though,' he said. 'With the aid of the NCA, in case she is involved in Durham's murder somewhere along the line.'

'True, but at least Sue is discounted from pulling the trigger.'

'Yep – handy for her that she'd been under twenty-four/seven surveillance by the NCA for the past week. A pretty iron-clad alibi.'

Henry ate, drove and drank, and said, 'I'll see if I can send a couple of detectives to London to get an interview with her.'

Blackstone nodded agreement.

Henry's phone rang, and Blackstone answered it for him. 'Mr Christie's phone.' She put it on speaker.

'Henry, it's Professor Rostamian, your go-to blood guy.'

'Hi, sorry for not getting back to you . . . one or two things sort of cropped up.'

'No problem.'

'You have something for us?'

'Only my thoughts and observations about the Twain murder scene. I've emailed you the full report, but I wanted to give you the salient points verbally.'

'Go on.'

Blackstone passed Henry sandwich number two.

'You said you thought the person you encountered at the scene was wearing a full forensic suit or similar?'

'Correct.'

'And that to the best of your recollection there was no blood on that person?'

'Also correct.'

'And when you say a full forensic suit, does that include overshoes?'

'Yes.'

'I ask because reviewing the photographs and videos of the crime scene, plus my own visit, I think there is a partial footprint – shoe print – in the blood on the floor.'

'Oh, is that good news? Do you have a partial sole print, maybe?'

'Yes and no. I've looked at the blood splatter on the workshop floor and seen this partial – it is only partial, I warn you – but as a result, I looked at forensic suit overshoes, and if I was pressed, I would say that the partial I can see is that of such an overshoe – featureless, flat – so I think whoever made it was probably wearing an overshoe of some sort.'

Henry allowed this to filter for a moment. 'I'm as certain as I can be that the person I disturbed at the scene did not have any blood on the soles of their shoes; otherwise, there would have been a trail to the fire exit – and there wasn't.' He paused. 'Are you saying that whoever killed Twain might have also been wearing a forensic suit, perhaps?'

'I'm saying it's a possibility,' the professor confirmed.

The call ended.

Henry said to Blackstone, 'So if that is the case, then it seems this was a very premeditated murder.'

'Which makes you wonder about Mrs Twain again. Still in the frame.'

'Very much so.'

Henry came off the motorway at the Lancaster North junction, and they were back at the police station five minutes later.

He spent the next two hours in the MIR, first liaising with the detective superintendent from the NCA in order to get a pair of detectives from Lancashire down to London to interview Sue Daggert, who was already en route to the capital to be held at a police station in north London. After that, she would be on remand

and, if all went well, unlikely to be released for the next ten or more years. The NCA had a lot of work to do with her, but Henry managed to wangle a provisional interview slot the next day, which meant getting two DCs down that evening for an overnighter.

Once that was sorted, Henry went through everything that had come in that day from all sources regarding Twain and Durham. There was a lot of background on the two men, some tittle-tattle from anonymous sources, all very interesting in building up a picture of the men but of no real evidential value.

Blackstone chased up the ballistic side of things. Although the bullets taken from Durham's body and the swimming pool had been fast-tracked into the system to make a comparison with the bullets fired at Henry, they were in a queue behind other fast-tracked ammunition from crime scenes across the country. Pandemic lock-downs, it seemed, hadn't reduced serious crimes very much. That said, a bit of sweet talking ensured she was promised a result late the next day.

Finally, Blackstone stretched, yawned and declared, 'Knackered.'

'Time to call it quits,' Henry agreed.

It was well after eight p.m. Too many hours on the go for anyone sane.

They rose from their chairs, Blackstone collecting the files she intended to look at later, just as Jake Niven came into the MIR.

'Hoping I might catch you,' he said. He had a witness statement from Veronica Gough in his hand, which he'd just taken from her up at the infirmary. He waved it at Henry.

'How is she?' Henry asked.

'Still very shocked, but OK otherwise.'

'Who wouldn't be?' Blackstone said.

'Where are you up to with it?' Henry asked, wincing internally as he had a flashback of the machete slicing its way towards him.

He shook his head. 'I think the silence might be down to the gang leader threatening others with consequences if they talk. That's the rumour so far.'

'I can't believe we can't nail a bunch of kids in a bloody village,' Henry said.

'A village in which nearly a thousand new houses have been chucked up in the last eighteen months,' Jake reminded him. 'Anyway, I'll keep on with it, when I get the chance. I'm down for

Lancaster patrol again tomorrow' – he looked pained – 'but I intend to go door-to-door in Thornwell for an hour before I set off.'

'Good man,' Henry said. 'Err . . .' He looked at Blackstone, then Jake. 'Are you going home now?'

Jake nodded.

'Do you mind jumping in with him?' he asked Blackstone. 'I'd like to go up and see Mrs Gough.'

She didn't mind.

Jake had some correspondence to collect, and Blackstone said she'd meet him at the Land Rover in a couple of minutes, then she and Henry made their way down through the nick and waited at Jake's car.

'How are you feeling?' Henry asked her. 'Now that you've had the chance to assimilate being shot at, savour the experience?'

She shrugged noncommittally. 'Like I said, I'm still here and I won't need counselling.'

Henry smiled at her in a way that made her say, 'Whaaaat?'

'Look, don't take this wrong, Debs, but I honestly thought she'd killed you and . . . and . . . I didn't like it. I know you're not Miss Touchy-Feely, at least not where I'm concerned, which is fine and I get it, but the thought of you being, well, dead scared me shitless. Like I said, don't take this the wrong way, but can I give you a hug? Nothing romantic or sexual . . .'

Before he could finish his little speech, she said, 'You big, soft lummox, come 'ere!'

Henry strolled up to the infirmary and charmed his way into the cardiac unit where Mrs Gough was still under observation. She was propped up on pillows, but her eyes were closed and she didn't notice his arrival until he pulled up a chair and was sitting by the bed.

'Henry!'

'Thought I'd pop in. That OK?'

'More than OK.' She reached out with a bony hand and took his. She felt cold and brittle to him. 'Very kind of you.' She exhaled a stuttering breath.

'I know Jake's just been to see you, but I thought I'd say hello before heading home. So, how are you doing?'

'As well as an eighty-nine-year-old whose house got broken into and then had a heart attack can be expected to be, I suppose.'

'We'll get 'em,' Henry said confidently. 'Promise.'

'I was terrified and completely overpowered,' she admitted. 'For the second time,' she added, referring to the incident at the stream.

'They are very scary kids. Like a new breed.'

'And the rape threat . . .' Her voice tailed off weakly. 'They can burgle me all they want, but that . . .'

'Horrible . . . Look, Mrs Gough, I forgot to look or ask if you have any sort of security camera system at your house. If you have, it might be useful for us to examine the footage.'

'I do, actually,' she said, then hesitated. 'One slight problem – I mean, I haven't checked it recently if I'm honest, but there was a bit of an accident with one of the cameras.'

'Go on.'

'Well, there's a camera on the front gatepost, one over the front door and two covering the back of the house . . . it's the one on the gatepost. I had a food delivery a few days ago, and the van driver reversed into the drive and knocked the camera skew-whiff with the corner of his van when he left. So I don't know if it's affected anything, but the other ones should be all right. They record on to my laptop in the study.'

'They might be very helpful. I'll get someone to collect the laptop if that's OK? If we could get some images of the offenders, we might be able to do a press and social media release, and someone might recognize them in such a tight-knit community. A job for Jake, I think.'

'Hmm, it's hardly a tight-knit community any more . . . not sure if Thornwell ever was, really, unlike Kendleton. They are very different animals, especially now. I mean, have you seen how many new houses have been built and how many more are in the pipeline?'

'I know. Jake was just saying the same thing.'

'I'll bet the kids are from the new houses,' she said.

'You could be right, but we will find them,' Henry said. Then asked, 'Is that part of the reason for the creation of SONAG? To stop further development?'

'SONAG? In part, I suppose. The council have ridden roughshod over what the people who live in the two villages want, and although we know there is no way of stopping the juggernaut that is the council's building strategy, we wanted to make our views felt and be as awkward as we could be.'

'I thought the plans for The Swan's Neck weren't linked to the council's?' Henry asked.

'No, but they won't say no to any plans to build houses. We just thought if we stopped the old pub from being knocked down and turned into a housing estate, it would at least be a victory for the little people, but it won't happen. All we'll be able to do is delay it.'

'You seem to be a very vocal lot.'

'Oh, we are, we are . . . and it's something for us oldies to do, annoy people.'

'I'd like to ask you a question about your members if that's OK?'

Mrs Gough eyed him suspiciously. 'So not just a welfare visit? Part of your murder enquiry?'

'Both, if you don't mind.'

'It's someone to talk to,' she said with a touch of sadness in her voice.

'Your family have been to see you, though?' Henry asked.

'I don't have any family.'

The news stunned Henry. 'Surely . . .'

She shook her head. 'My husband died twenty years ago, my son, Ron, two years ago, and that's it – all alone now. My sister lives in Newquay, but she's got dementia very badly, and her hubby died ten years ago.'

'I'm really sorry. You told me your husband had passed away. I assumed you had sons and daughters. I'm very sorry to hear about your son.'

'He was in his sixties, so he wasn't that young, and he was a widower with no children . . . but your child dying before you, that's not the order of things, is it?'

'No, it isn't.'

'You lost your wife, I heard?'

'Cancer.'

'And then Alison?'

'Murder.' Henry gulped as all those thoughts suddenly came tumbling through the closed doors in his mind again. Kate, then Alison. The two rocks of his existence.

Mrs Gough squeezed his hand tenderly. 'You have daughters, though?'

'Both married, living away. Don't see them much, but we are in touch and we're OK. That said, I've got Ginny, Alison's stepdaughter. We're close, and I've got the pub and all the crazies who frequent it, so I'm not exactly alone in the world.' He sat up, back to business. 'Anyway, SONAG,' he said, pulling himself together. 'I noticed at your meeting the other day you'd written the word *Murder* as an option for activism?'

Mrs Gough giggled, but then became serious. 'Are you suggesting . . .?'

'I have to follow every lead.'

She shook her head in disbelief. 'I'd say the average age of that group is eighty-four. Not one of them is capable of murder and certainly not whacking Twain with a spanner, smashing his head in and *then* coming to a SONAG meeting. They'd need the rest of the day off!'

'You can kill anyone, no matter how old you are,' Henry said, 'though I get your point. So, humour me, tell me about the members, tell me what you think about them, what motivates them . . . and are any of them capable of killing?'

She inhaled, exhaled deeply and winced.

'Are you all right?' Henry asked, concerned.

'Fine, just overwhelmingly tired.'

'Then this can wait. I can come back. You need rest, Mrs Gough.'

'No, it's fine.' She squeezed his hand again. 'And it's Veronica from now, OK?'

'I can come back, Veronica.'

'No, let's talk.'

She worked her way through the members of SONAG who regularly attended the meetings, giving a short pen picture of each. Henry asked her to allocate marks out of ten, one being least likely, ten being most likely, to have killed James Twain.

It became apparent that most of them were there for the company rather than activism and the cause. It was something to shout about, something to get embroiled in and hot under the collar about, not to actually dive under a digger to prove a point, and it was also apparent that Mrs Gough – Veronica – did not necessarily like each member.

Henry had taken notes and came back to a few of the names.

His finger rested on Tom Derrick. 'Always struck me as odd that Tom would be part of this group,' he said.

'Oh, your ex-colleague? He lives right opposite me, you know? Anyway, I suppose it's because he, like me, only lives a spit and a stride away from the proposed development, even though we're just off the main road on our nice estate. But increased traffic flow and more people knocking about will affect us – more disruption, new roundabouts, that sort of thing, so I understand him being there with us, though he is a bit younger than most.'

'Fair points,' Henry conceded.

He pointed out one or two more on the list and she dismissed them as being of no interest to his investigation.

Finally, he pointed to a man called Eric Grundy, the hundred-year-old guy in a wheelchair.

Henry knew he was quite a bit older than Veronica; being wheelchair-bound, he was very, very unlikely to have killed Twain. Henry recalled him arriving for the meeting on the day of Twain's murder, being pushed by his elderly son.

There was no immediate response from Veronica.

Henry glanced up from his notes to see a very strange, dark expression spread across her face.

'What is it? Are you OK?'

She swallowed. 'I wish he wasn't part of the group.'

'Eric Grundy?'

'Yes, Eric Grundy. Every time I hear or say that name, it's like a vampire has walked over my grave.'

'Why, Veronica?' Henry could see anguish etched across her face, adding to the physical pain in her chest.

'Perhaps I don't want to talk about this any more,' she whispered. 'I'm sorry I mentioned anything.'

Puzzled, Henry said, 'That's OK; you've given me lots of information I didn't have before, and you do need to rest.'

'It's time you left, please.' A nurse had sidled up behind him and spoken into his ear.

Henry checked the time, not realizing how long he had been there. 'No problem, just leaving,' he told the nurse. He patted Veronica's hand. 'I'll be off; it's been a long day.'

Underneath his, he felt the old woman's hand begin to tremble.

'What is it, Veronica?'

She looked desperately at him now. 'I don't know how to say this, Henry.'

He was struggling to understand the sudden problem. 'Erm,' he said unhelpfully.

'It's a secret,' she whispered. 'A secret I've kept for seventy-five years.'

'OK . . . do you want to tell me?' He was now intrigued.

'No.' She shook her head vehemently. 'No . . . no, I don't want to tell anyone, ever . . . but I think I have to. I think the time is right or I'll never forgive myself.' She took a breath to steady herself, then looked squarely at Henry with her old, milky eyes that seemed to be in so much pain. Henry didn't dare say anything. 'I thought I would go to my grave with this . . . this *thing* still trapped inside me . . . and now I absolutely realize that I can't.'

Henry was starting to have his own palpitations. 'What is it?' he asked hoarsely.

'Eric . . . Eric Grundy . . . He raped me when I was thirteen years old.'

She began to weep softly.

ELEVEN

A rriving back at The Tawny Owl and judiciously ignoring everyone in the bar by adopting tunnel vision, Henry made his way straight through to the owner's accommodation, into his bedroom, stripped and went directly into the shower.

Afterwards, dressed in jogging bottoms and an old Rolling Stones T-shirt with Charlie Watts' face on the front of it, he attacked his personal stash of Jack Daniel's, adding a handful of ice from the freezer, and tipped it back in one, the broken ice cubes crashing against his teeth. As the tentacles of the spirit spread through his chest and warmed him, he poured another, grabbed a stack of Pringles, flopped on to the settee and allowed every last remaining joule of energy to drain out of him.

'Fuck, fuck, fuck.'

He sipped the JD now, staring blankly at the wall above the fireplace, going over everything Veronica had revealed, at immense personal cost to her. He was only the second person she had ever told of this terrible thing that had happened to her at the age of thirteen.

This time, Henry had not needed his notebook because every word she had spoken was branded into his brain.

*   *   *

The year: 1945.

The place: Kendleton-with-Thornwell.

The event: VE Day celebrations, Tuesday 8 May.

The two villages had turned out following Churchill's historic radio message at three o'clock that afternoon, announcing that the war in Europe was over. Everyone in Thornwell gravitated to The Swan's Neck, then a thriving public house serving pickled eggs and ale, and through the course of the evening the adults all got drunker and drunker, and the kids got more and more excited as they danced frenetically around the village fuelled by sugary lemonade.

These kids included thirteen-year-old Veronica Arkholme who started off dancing with her mum, then found her friends and went bonkers around the village, little knowing that she was under the scrutiny of a sex offender.

'I can still see it,' Veronica had said to Henry. 'And hear it. And smell it. The singing and dancing, the bunting, the euphoria of a terrible war ending – and don't you believe it when they tell you youngsters don't understand anything. I knew exactly what it all meant.'

Henry, perched on the chair next to the hospital bed, continued to hold Veronica's hand between his own.

'We danced as though we were stupid. Stupid happy,' she said and swallowed dryly. A tear ran down her cheek from one eye. She dabbed it away with the scrunched-up tissue she had in her hand not being held by Henry's. 'It was my own fault.'

'I doubt that.'

'I knew him. I knew Eric. He was a gamekeeper up on the duke's estate – but that didn't make him a good man. He was an out-and-out wrong'un, no doubt. It was in his eyes, and if you look closely, you can still see the evil.'

Henry blinked, thought about the surname: *Grundy*. Familiar for some reason in another context.

'I'd seen him looking at me before, and he really gave me the creeps . . . and someone else told me he'd put his hand up a girl's skirt and another time got his willy out and flashed it around. And that he liked hitting people too, really hurting them.'

Henry opened his mouth to say something at that point, but Veronica held up her hand to stop him. 'I'm all right, Henry. Just a big moment for me, this.'

'I know,' he said softly.

'This sort of thing must have happened to you many times over the years, some girl or other telling you their deepest secrets.'

'Less often than you'd imagine,' he said.

Veronica closed her eyes, rested her head on the plumped-up pillows, remembering back many years.

'Then, at some point, I got a stone in my sandal and I stopped while the rest of my friends went running on. Within seconds, I was suddenly alone on an unlit road, hopping around, trying to shake the stone free, and there was a rush . . . and he came out of nowhere. In a flash, I had a dirty, smelly hand over my mouth and nose, and my feet were off the ground, and I was being lifted bodily across to the drainage channel by the side of the road.'

She stopped speaking then, collecting her thoughts again.

Then she began again, talking slowly but deliberately, covering every terrifying detail of the rape. Every touch, sensation, smell, feeling, pain, breath, terror until finally it was over.

Henry listened with a cold anger stoking up inside him. His teeth grated, his jaw clenched and his breathing was short.

'When he'd finished – I mean, it seemed like forever, but it was probably only a minute at most – he was still on top of me, and my skirt was pulled up to my waist, and he smelled of sweat and grit, and he said if I ever told anyone, he would kill me and rape and kill my mum, too. He said he knew how to kill. Said he'd done it before and it was easy, and he'd do it again in a flash. He whispered all those threats into my ear, and I could feel his unshaven face next to mine.'

Veronica shivered.

'And I didn't tell anyone, not even my husband when we got married years later.' She closed her eyes sadly at that point. 'He was a wonderful, loving man. He loved me, and though we did it now and again, and I fell pregnant, it . . . it never worked for me. I dreaded sex. Dreaded my husband's arm coming over me in bed. He was understanding, but then he also didn't understand because I couldn't let him into my mind about it. Eric Grundy ruined my marriage and my life,' she concluded. 'And he's still doing it every time I see him at SONAG, just by his presence.'

On the settee, back in The Tawny Owl, Henry ran this all through his mind time and again and said, 'Fuck!' again too, just as the door opened and Blackstone poked her head through and heard the expletive.

'Not glad to see me, then?' she said.

'Eh? Course I am. Come in, take a pew and grab a JD if you like.' He pointed to the bottle and the armchair.

She came in, helped herself, then flopped on the chair.

'I saw you sneak back in . . . I got collared by the amateur detectives for my sins and couldn't get free . . . oh, the merry widow's been in asking about you, BTW.'

'BTW?'

'By the way,' Blackstone explained. Henry just shook his head. 'Ginny fended her off.'

'I'll thank Ginny later,' he said, then the thought he'd been unable to pin down flipped through his mind, but again he failed to nail it down.

'Perhaps you should talk to her,' Blackstone suggested. 'Clear the air one way or the other, let her know where she stands. Not 'ard, is it?'

'Her son, Will, let me know exactly where I stand,' Henry snapped.

'He sounds like an arse, but she isn't her son,' Blackstone pointed out.

'I know, I know.' Henry fell silent.

'How was Mrs Gough?'

Henry blew out his cheeks and took a sip of his Tennessee sour mash whiskey.

'What is it?' Blackstone asked, noticing the wobble.

'Well, in terms of the heart attack, I think she's all right. Really scared by the thought of the break-in, obviously . . .'

'But?'

'In terms of her whole life, she's far from all right.' Henry downed the JD, rocked up to his feet, crossed to the sideboard and tipped another measure into his glass.

Blackstone waited like the experienced interviewer she was, letting the subject feel the need to fill in the gaps.

Henry told Blackstone all he knew.

'So she has spent her whole life in close proximity to him, terrified, avoiding him, seeing him at village functions, catching him looking at her.'

'Why not just move away?' Blackstone said reasonably, although she was horrified by the story.

'I thought that, but things are never that easy, and she shouldn't have been the one to go. Eric Grundy should have fucked off . . .

but her hubby was a local farmer, and they only sold up in the last years of his life when he became poorly and moved into her current house; by that time, he didn't want to leave, knew he didn't have a long time left and wanted to be in the community he'd spent his whole life in, not knowing the fear his wife had been living under. She couldn't bring herself to tell him.'

It was Blackstone's turn to blow out her cheeks and grab another JD. Before drinking it, she nipped across to her bedroom and changed out of her work clothes into pyjamas and a dressing gown. "Kin 'ell,' she said, sitting back down in the armchair. 'So she lived in his shadow all her life, letting it screw up her relationship with her hubby, God rest him.'

'Yup.'

'Bastard!'

'Yup. But for the last few years she has hardly seen anything of Grundy,' Henry said, recalling what Veronica had told him. 'He ended up in a wheelchair, virtually housebound until this SONAG action group got formed, and suddenly Grundy crawled out of his cesspit with his son pushing him and became an active participant for some reason – as much as a hundred-year-old guy can be with a seventy-five-year-old son.'

'So why do the plans for The Swan's Neck affect him?' Blackstone asked.

'Veronica doesn't know. He doesn't live in close proximity, so although she's curious to know, she hasn't been able to find out because she wants to keep her distance from him. Apparently, he leers at her every time he sees her. He seems to still have all his marbles in spite of his age.'

'What a bloody shame. Rape . . . all about power and dominance,' Blackstone said.

'I know. I get it.'

Blackstone faced him furiously. 'How the hell do you get it?' she demanded.

Henry's mouth dropped open at her sudden vitriol, but he didn't respond as she regarded him savagely and then, seeing the hurt on his face, with curiosity.

'Something you're not telling me?'

Henry swallowed. 'Let's not go there, eh?'

'Fine, whatev . . . but that doesn't answer the question of what we're going to do about it, does it?'

'You mean, what are the police going to do about it? That would be down to Veronica anyway, not anyone else,' Henry warned her. 'I'm not sure she could survive an investigation at her age, although I wouldn't be too bothered about Eric Grundy surviving.'

'You know he'll have got a hundredth-birthday message from the queen?'

'Depressing, isn't it?'

Ginny managed to herd everyone out of Th'Owl by eleven thirty, and Henry, though dead beat, went through to help her tidy up and clean the bar area and beer taps.

He asked her about Maude turning up.

'She looked pretty distraught if I'm honest,' Ginny said. 'Please speak to her; it's only fair, and if you don't want to have any sort of relationship with her, then she needs telling, Henry. I think she's confused.'

'I will,' he promised.

He had been behind the bar, wiping down the surfaces, then came around to the main area to clear and wipe the tables, one of which had been used that evening by the amateur sleuths. One of them had inadvertently left a notepad behind. Scrawled across the front of it in thick felt tip were the words UNSOLVED MURDER: THORNWELL, 1941. Underneath, in smaller letters, was a list of the names of the enthusiastic little group, names that included Dr Lott and now Debbie Blackstone and Veronica Gough, the latest recruits.

Henry picked up the notebook for safe keeping, and when he and Ginny had finished the cleaning-up tasks, he went back into the owner's accommodation and to his bedroom, passing the guest bedroom that Blackstone had commandeered. He didn't mind. He liked having her around. She brought a new energy to the place and to his life.

In his bedroom, he put the notebook on his bedside cabinet, stripped off and slithered under the cool quilt, planning the next day's activities in his brain. It was going to be another busy one.

He dropped off quickly.

Then woke with a jump-start.

Three thirty-three a.m.

He sat up, switched on the bedside lamp, blinking as he focused, and then reached for the unsolved murder notebook and flipped it open. The first few pages consisted mostly of folded-up newspaper cuttings printed from the internet and a few scribbled notes from various members of the group.

To be honest, Henry had never really closely read any of the stuff before, and if he'd been asked, he could not even recall the name of the victim who had been shot way back on that fateful night in 1941.

But now he did read the young man's name.

He flipped off the bedclothes and yanked on his tracksuit bottoms and T-shirt. Bearing the book, he went out into the hallway, which was in darkness, making it easy to see that the light was still on in Blackstone's bedroom.

He knocked gently. 'Debs?'

A moment later Blackstone ripped the door open. 'Hell d'you want, creeping about at this hour?' she demanded, a worried expression on her face.

'Can I come in?'

'No, you frickin' can't! What the . . .?'

'No, no, no . . . Jeepers . . . I'm not *that* guy, honestly!'

She burst into laughter. 'I know. Just pulling your cracker,' she joshed. Then added mock-seriously, 'Well, not your cracker.'

'Just let me in.'

She stood back and opened the door to allow him in. He saw the light was on because she was still reviewing the files taken from James Twain and Marcus Durham. They were strewn on the desk by the window and fanned out on the carpet. Henry wasn't particularly surprised she was working into the early hours.

'Busy?' he asked.

'Just about to crash for a couple of hours. What d'you want?' She stretched.

Henry held up the notebook.

'Seen it,' she said.

'And?'

'And, what?'

'And . . . have you actually read it?'

'Duh! Yeah.'

'OK . . . do you ever, say, see film stars with the same surname and go for years before reading that they're brother and sister, or father and son?'

'It has happened.'

'OK, tell me the name of the victim in this shooting.' Henry held up the notebook.

Blackstone blinked, then a dawning realization came over her face. In unison, they said, 'Lucas Grundy!'

There was a murder squad briefing scheduled for nine the next morning. Henry and Blackstone grabbed a quick breakfast at Th'Owl at seven thirty and were on the road ten minutes later. Henry was in his courtesy car, Blackstone in her Mini Cooper. She set off ahead, racing along the narrow roads away from Kendleton, putting the machine that she had rebuilt from scratch through its paces, leaving Henry to follow at a more sedate pace. He preferred it this way because he wasn't under any pressure from her tailgating him, as she would have done.

It was a very depleted team.

Diane and Wellhaven were still absent, still self-isolating, and a couple more had dropped out too, stricken by the virus. Henry wondered how the rest of the force was faring; there were minimal cop numbers to start with, and now they must be decimated, he guessed. It seemed like a bit of an extravagance to send a couple of detectives down to London to interview Sue Daggert, but it needed doing, not least because she had tried to kill Blackstone and kidnapped Henry at gunpoint.

Following the briefing, Henry had a Zoom meeting with Rik Dean, who looked and sounded miserable and was stressed up to his eyeballs. Henry brought him up to speed with the Sue Daggert situation and also the slight quandary he was now having with Veronica Gough's rape revelation.

'Wow, a hundred-year-old rapist!' Rik said.

'He was twenty-something when it happened,' Henry pointed out.

'Yeah, suppose. What are your thoughts?'

Ha! Henry thought. In the best traditions of police leadership, Rik Dean had Teflon-coated shoulders.

'Well, he's one of the members of SONAG who had a downer on James Twain, so as a matter of course I have to go and speak to him. At least that will give me a measure of him, his physical and mental state, although to be honest, even if he's not great – and I don't expect a hundred-year-old guy to be running marathons or doing *University Challenge* – if he did rape her, he should face the consequences. Plus,' Henry added, 'it doesn't necessarily stop there, does it? If he raped one, he could have raped others and got away with it. I've checked the criminal record archives, and he doesn't have any convictions, so this could be a whole can of worms . . . maybe.'

'I think it needs doing,' Rik said.

'The other thing, of course, is that I don't want to do anything without Mrs Gough's say-so. She might not want the hassle, which I understand.'

'Yet she opened the can,' Rik said.

'I know . . . but she had to for her own mental well-being . . . and there is other stuff concerning the old fella, too, including the unsolved murder of his brother in 1941.'

'Don't get too sidetracked, Henry,' Rik advised.

'I won't,' he said. *But probably will*, he didn't say.

The Zoom call ended, and Henry went to find Blackstone who was surfing the internet on a desktop computer in the MIR, looking for unsolved crimes in the Thornwell/Kendleton area from the forties and fifties.

She stood up as Henry came in. 'Pity our own bloody computer records don't go back that far,' she whined, knowing that historic crime recording was in a pretty poor state prior to the 1990s, almost non-existent prior to the 1970s, and if she wanted to find anything, it would mean sifting through a lot of paper files. 'Anyway, what's our plan for the day?'

'I've got someone looking more closely at Marcus Durham's background and unearthing any more possible suspects, so while that's going on, I'm thinking we nip up to the infirmary to see Veronica, then start trawling through the SONAG members as regards James Twain, see if any could be viable suspects. Plus we need to start to try to ID the husbands or partners of the women that Twain was allegedly sleeping with, beginning with Dale Renshaw, the guy Twain had a tussle with in The Tawny Owl the evening before he got his head smashed in. What say you?'

Blackstone screwed up her nose. 'Well, it's half a plan, I suppose.'

Veronica Gough looked drained, but she was bright and certainly with it, sitting up and reading a book on a Kindle.

'How are you doing?' asked Henry as he dragged a chair to one side of her bed and Blackstone sat on one the other side.

'I'm good. The doctor came on his rounds early and told me I'm now stabilized and I can go home, which is good.'

'Excellent news.'

'Only I've no one to take me home.'

'We can fix that,' Blackstone said, 'if you fancy another ride in my Mini.'

Veronica's eyes sparkled at the prospect. 'I'm told it may be this afternoon.'

'Well, when you get a time, either you or the hospital can ring me and I'll come for you,' Blackstone said.

'You're very kind.' Veronica turned to Henry.

'What you told me yesterday . . . I've let Debbie know, too.'

'I thought you would. It's not a problem.'

'The thing is, Veronica, what do we do about it now?'

'I'm not sure,' she said. 'It was good to tell someone at last. Like a boulder being lifted from my shoulders.'

'That is good,' Henry said. 'But if you want to take it forward, the reality is that unless we can somehow get more evidence against him, or another witness maybe, it would be your word against his, a stalemate.'

She pondered this. 'Agreed. It's a funny one.'

'That doesn't mean we don't pursue it. Just because he's a hundred years old doesn't mean we can't speak to him about it,' Blackstone said. 'In fact, I want to see the old bastard squirm. But your wishes are paramount here, Veronica.'

'You are sweet,' Veronica replied. 'And I understand the problems, but I think I'd like you to look into it, all things considered.'

Henry took a breath as he tried to find the right words. 'When you were describing to me what happened that night, you told me he warned you not to tell anyone, or he would come after you . . .' He saw her tighten up.

'Yes, he did; that's what he said.'

'You also said he boasted that he'd killed before.'

'He did.'

'Who do you think he was referring to?'

'I don't know.'

'I think you do.' Henry smiled.

She conceded immediately. 'I think he was talking about killing his own brother, Lucas, but . . .' She shrugged. 'Maybe he was just trying to scare me – which he did.'

'Can I take a guess here? Is that why you've joined our amateur sleuths who want to reopen Lucas Grundy's unsolved murder case?' Henry said.

'My, you really are a detective, Henry,' Veronica said and gave a little clap of her hands.

Henry bowed his head, basking in the adulation for a moment before asking, 'And? Was it worth it?'

Veronica's mouth twisted down. 'Nope. I've read everything they've found with the exception of the actual police file, and as far as I can tell there is no more evidence than there ever has been – and I've always kept an eye on newspaper reports and that. This lot of old fogies have found nothing new, no eyewitnesses, no scientific evidence, other than Lucas was shot with his own rifle.'

'His own rifle?'

'Yes, he was a gamekeeper like Eric was, on the duke's estate, and he was found with the weapon by his dead body. Tests proved it was definitely the one that killed him. It looks like he was disarmed and the rifle used against him. He was shot in the back of his head, so perhaps he was running away. I joined Doctor Lott and the rest of them wondering – *hoping* – there might be evidence that pointed to Eric, but there's nothing, just a rehash of old newspaper reports. It's unlikely ever to be solved.'

'Do you think Eric did it?' Henry asked her.

'It's more a hope than anything . . . and it did happen in 1941 when I was nine, so I was just a kid and not really that involved in it, but I do remember it happening . . . just after the bombing and the air crash on the moors.'

'Bombing and air crash?' Henry asked, startled.

'A German bomber on the moors.'

'I never knew that . . . Anyway' – Henry looked over at Blackstone – 'is that your take, too? Nothing new?'

'Pretty much. I haven't had time to unearth the actual file, but it looks like the news coverage has quite a lot of stuff from police sources, so I doubt there will be much more in the files themselves.'

'Mmm,' Henry said. He'd thought as much and guessed that over the years most of what had originally been in the police file would have been released to the press, but it would be worth looking at again if he got the chance. 'However, we do have a legitimate reason to go and talk to Eric to start with, and maybe we could broach his brother's death somehow, while we're there.' He raised his eyebrows at Blackstone, who nodded agreement. 'Right, we need to get on the move,' Henry said, slapping his thighs.

Blackstone rechecked that Veronica had her mobile number – she did.

'Call me when you are being discharged and I'll come for you,' she instructed Veronica.

'I will. That's very kind.'

The two detectives rose to leave, but Veronica grabbed Henry's hand and said, 'Could I have a word, just you and me?'

Henry looked at Blackstone who said, 'I'll set off back to Kendleton . . . bye, Veronica.'

She left.

Veronica said, 'I have something else to tell you, Henry.'

Henry came out of the hospital and began walking down the hill to the city centre, completely stunned and shaken by what Veronica had just revealed to him. He clamped his phone to his ear and called Blackstone.

'Old guy,' she answered, 'what?'

'Have you set off yet?'

'Not quite, why?'

'Hang fire.'

Henry upped his pace and found Blackstone on the lower-ground-floor car park at the nick, in her car, revving the engine impatiently. She did not get out but opened her window, forcing Henry to bend over in order to get his face down to her level. He was slightly breathless from the hurried walk.

'What?' Blackstone demanded again.

'She had an abortion.'

TWELVE

When Henry dropped this bombshell, it hit Blackstone like a gut punch. She stared at him, unblinking, until finally she said, 'Oh, God . . . my God.'

She switched the engine off and climbed out of the Mini and said, 'I know this isn't a good use of our time, Henry, but please can we go and get a coffee somewhere . . . not here.' She flicked a thumb at the police station.

Five minutes later, they'd found a small café in the city centre. Henry bought the drinks and took them to the window table where Blackstone was sitting. She took her coffee with the twitch of a smile, and Henry could see she'd been crying a little.

'You OK?'

She wiped her eyes with the back of her hand, spreading her make-up. 'I just don't know why it's affecting me so much,' she admitted.

Henry sat down opposite, certain it had affected him, too, though not to the same degree.

'I mean, I hardly know the woman,' Blackstone said. 'The offence happened a fucking hundred years before I was born . . .'

'Give or take a year.'

'Yeah, yeah . . . so I'm not invested in it. Nothing will probably come of what we do whenever we get to see the old bastard who . . . I was going to say impregnated her, but I'll stick with raped. It'll probably go nowhere. The CPS will do their usual cowardly shit.' She hung her head and said, 'What did she say?'

'It wasn't in great detail, but essentially she realized she'd become pregnant after the rape. She'd only just started her periods, and she had to tell her mother, but she refused to say who the father was. Fear, I guess, based on Eric's threats to kill. Anyway, less than a week later she went to a back street abortionist in Manchester and had' – Henry hesitated here, got a grip – 'had what she believed, and still believes, was a knitting needle inserted—'

'Jesus! Fucking horrific. Poor, poor girl. It's a miracle she even survived.'

'I know. She was poorly for a month, and they did think she was going to die, but she pulled through.'

'And lived her teenage years and the rest of her life in the shadow of that bastard.' Blackstone lifted her coffee to her mouth. Henry could see her shaking with rage and disgust. She wiped her lip. 'Did he ever know? About the pregnancy?'

Henry shook his head. 'Only her mother. It was kept a secret, and when she met her husband-to-be, he never found out either.'

'Hell of a secret.'

They drove separately back to Kendleton, got into Henry's courtesy car, then drove together into Thornwell on to one of the two new housing estates thrown up in the last eighteen months as part of the drive by the government to increase housing stock to meet the perceived shortage. What Henry hadn't realized before was just how big the estate was. Hundreds of houses ranging from 'affordable' up to luxury five-bedroomed ones, all clumped tightly together with hardly any space between them. They all looked nice and modern, but Henry found the overall tone quite depressing, and he could see why long-standing residents were putting up some resistance against more being built on the site currently occupied by The Swan's Neck. He was beginning to think it would at least be a nice victory for the small guy, as Veronica put it, although Henry guessed that, in the long run, the protest would not be successful when, not if, some new builder moved in and took over the project.

It was rare such protests were ever successful, he thought.

Years before, he had been part of the police operation in another part of the county, where people were protesting against the route of a new motorway that would entail the destruction of swathes of woodland. Several protesters had been living in trees due to be cut down, but finally the road went through and now those protests, once headline news, were now just vague memories, and most drivers now using the motorway were not even aware of the controversy and conflict it had once caused.

Henry himself was no tree-hugger, as the protesters were once sneeringly called, but the older he got, the more sympathetic he grew to such causes; even as a cop, he truly believed in the right to protest, but he also had an innate dislike of protesters' methods, particularly if they involved blocking highways and disrupting other people's daily lives.

The housing estate he turned into was called Silverwood, and all the streets and avenues were named after places on the Bowland Fells – Tarnbrook Close or Whitendale Avenue; the one he was after was Brim Clough Close on which a certain family resided, namely Dale and Andrea Renshaw, their names being on the voters' register. Anyone under eighteen was not listed, so Henry had no clue if the Renshaws had kids or not.

He didn't know much about Dale, even less about Andrea.

Dale had started to frequent The Tawny Owl in the periods when it was allowed to open during the pandemic. He was mid-forties, Henry guessed, which was a similar age to James Twain, and Henry thought he was a landscape gardener but wasn't certain. He knew nothing at all about Andrea, though he'd seen her with Dale a few times at the pub, and she seemed a bit younger, nice and attractive. As a couple, they came across as morose and unhappy.

'Number eight,' Blackstone said. 'This one.'

He drew in outside a decent but bland detached house, lawned garden, wide driveway, two vehicles on it, one a flat-back SUV with *Renshaw Landscaping* on the side, confirming Henry's vague knowledge of Dale's occupation; the other was a small Renault.

'You want to take the lead on this?' Henry asked.

'Let's keep it fluid.'

'Whatever.' Henry knocked and rang the doorbell, a little fizz of excitement in him as, once more, he would be stepping into another person's world. The joys of policing. Dale Renshaw came to the door in a pair of mud-caked overalls. He looked warily at the pair; he recognized Henry but seeing him out of context made him frown.

'What?' he said abruptly.

'Dale Renshaw?' Blackstone asked. He nodded. She stepped in ahead of Henry, flashed her warrant card and introduced herself.

'OK, but you're the pub landlord, aren't you?' Renshaw asked Henry.

'I am, but I also work as an investigator for Lancashire Constabulary. May we come in for a chat?'

Renshaw sighed. 'I'm assuming this is about James Twain? So just let me get one thing clear: I'm glad the dirty bastard's dead and I only wish I'd had the guts to do it, but I didn't.' Having made his point, he smiled, took a step back and said, 'Come in.' Then called out, 'Andrea, we have visitors.'

'You guessed right, we are investigating James Twain's murder,' Henry said, looking at Renshaw, then at his wife, Andrea, who was sitting meekly on an armchair. Henry and Blackstone were on the settee, Renshaw on the other chair positioned directly opposite Andrea, so she was constantly in his line of sight and seemed to be cowering under his glare.

'And, of course, I'm a suspect,' Renshaw said with contempt.

'With what happened in The Tawny Owl, we'd be remiss not to show you some interest,' Henry said reasonably.

Renshaw nodded.

'So, shall we begin with why what happened in the pub happened?'

Renshaw said to his wife, 'Do you want to tell them or should I?'

She hunched down further and opened her mouth to speak, but Renshaw cut her off with a jerk of his hand and said, 'No, I'll tell 'em because that way it'll be the truth, eh? Fucking bitch!'

Henry could see Renshaw was almost boiling with rage and he cut in, 'We keep this civil, Dale; otherwise, we talk at the cop shop.' Renshaw seemed on the verge of challenging that, but Henry said, 'Yes, we can, in case you were wondering, and yes, we will if we have to.'

That seemed to make him take a breath.

'Right, right,' he said, rocking. 'We came to live here from Manchester – yeah, to get away from all that gang shit our lad was getting into, for a nice, easy, simple fucking life in the country in a new build that has more problems than a fucking maths exam.'

'Language,' Blackstone said.

'Sorry . . . anyway, here we are. I'm a builder, joiner, plasterer and landscape gardener, and I knew I could get work, especially with all these new houses being thrown up, and I ended up contracted to Twain, the cu—' He stopped his profanity mid-C-word. 'Doing all sorts of shit for him – him and his partner have all sorts of stuff going on around the place. Thought I'd hit the jackpot.' Then he glared at Andrea again. 'I was wrong – you hit the jackpot, didn't you, dear? But you got bored first, didn't you? I mentioned this to Twain, who said she could come and do some of his admin.' He paused. 'Which she did . . . only I didn't realize that admin meant blow-jobs and arse-fucking.'

'Dale,' Henry warned him.

'I should've known. Twain had a rep for shagging around – usually clients' wives. Guy had no conscience, just a very big dick. Am I right, love?'

Henry noticed that Andrea's expression had changed from meek and mild to one that mirrored her husband's as a result of the belittling she was enduring.

'Anyway,' Renshaw said, cooling down slightly, 'that's what the thing in Th'Owl was about. He was there, lording it about with his dim missus in tow. I'd just come out for a couple of pints with a few mates after a barney with bitch-face here!' He sneered at Andrea. 'A row during which I told her my suspicions and she cracked instantly, sobbing like the pathetic bitch she is . . .'

'Right,' Blackstone interjected, 'you speak like that again and we're down at the station.'

Renshaw looked at her, sizing her up, then sizing up Henry, and he nodded. 'Anyway, I couldn't resist going for him when he came out of the bogs. Lucky I didn't kill him there and then, actually. It would have saved you the job of finding out who did kill the cunt.'

'I saw you watch him leave later. You were hiding in the shadows,' Henry said.

'I know. I know you saw me, but then I realized he wasn't worth the effort – and you!' He stabbed a finger at Andrea, making her jump. 'You aren't worth it either, are you? So I decided our marriage is over. She can fuck off back to Manchester where she'll be less bored, and she can wallow in shit there because she's getting nothing from me.'

'OK, but what *did* you do after I saw you leave the pub? What were your movements from then up to, say, lunchtime the day after?' Henry asked.

'Came home. Argued. Slept on the settee. Went out to work early next morning – I've got a contract to do some gardens on an estate in Lancaster. I was at work just after six.'

'Witnesses?' Blackstone asked.

'Two workmates. I'll give you their names and phone numbers.'

'OK,' Henry said. 'We still want a statement from you, so come up to The Tawny Owl at, say, two p.m. and we'll take it then. One of the small function rooms is going to be used as a satellite office for the main murder investigation.'

'I'll come.'

'We will want to take your fingerprints and a sample for DNA to eliminate you from the scene of the crime, too . . . just procedure, and I'm sure you'll consent. They'll be destroyed once you've been eliminated from the enquiries,' Blackstone told him.

'No worries.'

Henry glanced out of the front window and spotted Jake Niven doing a slow cruise past in the Land Rover, prompting Henry to change the subject and ask Renshaw some questions about the little gang that seemed to have evolved in the neighbourhood following the influx of new people from other areas.

As he did, he heard a movement upstairs – the shifting of a chair – and then the sound of someone coming down the stairs.

Before he could ask anything, the lounge door opened and a young man stuck his head in.

'Dad? Who's—?' The lad stopped mid-question as Henry turned to look at him. They locked eyes and both froze for an instant in a moment of recognition.

The lad said, 'Shit!' and slammed the door.

Blackstone had also recognized him.

Henry shot to his feet, but Blackstone – younger, quicker – was up a second ahead of him and bounded around the settee and through the door after the lad who had shot out through the front door and was legging it down the avenue.

'What the fuck?' Renshaw said, rising quickly.

'That your lad?' Henry asked, pausing at the door.

Renshaw nodded worriedly. 'Yeah, Callum.'

'Well, he's wanted for several serious offences including assault and burglary and for almost chopping my head off!'

It was obvious that Callum Renshaw knew his way intimately in, around and through the estate as he leapt over garden walls, low hedges and through back gardens in order to escape Blackstone's clutches. As Blackstone ran, she somehow managed to call Jake Niven on her phone as she skidded after the lad.

She was as relentless as Callum was slippery.

Just as she thought she had him in her grasp, he dinked sideways and changed direction, but she was always there or thereabouts, closing in remorselessly like a hunting dog, never giving up, biding her time until her prey was exhausted. And, finally, he ran out of steam when, with Blackstone only feet behind him, he emerged from a back garden to find Jake's Land Rover parked across the bottom of the drive.

He hesitated just long enough for Blackstone to power into the back of him, slam him into the side panel of the vehicle and enjoy wrenching his hands behind his back, telling him he was locked up and putting Jake's handcuffs on him.

From their faces, Henry could tell Dale and Andrea Renshaw knew their son had been up to no good, and although they might not have known the full details of what he was up to, they knew it was serious.

When Jake drew up in front of their house with Callum handcuffed in the back, shouting, cursing and kicking the inside of the cage, Andrea began to weep. Dale had a look of disgust on his face, although Henry wasn't sure who the expression was aimed at.

'How old is he?' Henry asked him.

'Eighteen.'

'In that case, he's an adult and he'll be given his rights when he gets to the station.'

'He's just a baby,' Andrea whined.

Henry went cold and furious. 'Yet old enough to deliberately try to drown an old lady, then attack her in her own home,' he said. His voice quavered.

'Jesus,' Dale Renshaw uttered under his breath.

'I don't believe it,' Andrea said.

Renshaw spun on her. 'That's exactly why we brought him up here, to get him out of the cesspit of Manchester, you stupid woman.'

'What do you mean?' Henry asked.

Renshaw's shoulders slumped, and he shook his head despairingly. 'Among a ton of other shit, he likes hurting old people. You'll find out when you check him out. He's a lost cause.'

Henry pointed at Renshaw. 'Don't forget – two o'clock at Th'Owl, and your son will be at Blackpool police station . . . and if I have my way, he won't be coming home soon.'

Blackstone jumped in with Henry, and Jake set off with Callum in the back of the Land Rover, still kicking and screaming and generally being obnoxious.

'Two birds, sort of,' Blackstone said. 'Result.' She was already interrogating her phone for any mention of Callum Renshaw.

'If he'd come down five minutes later, we'd've walked out of there none the wiser,' Henry admitted. 'Sometimes you just get lucky, but I still think we would've got him sooner rather than later.'

Still concentrating on her phone, Blackstone said, 'What d'you think about Dale Renshaw for James Twain? Suspect or not?'

'He certainly seems like a man capable of hitting someone on the head with a spanner, and I think we need to ask Jake to keep an eye on the domestic situation.'

'Maybe we should have locked him up just to be on the safe side?'

Henry made a 'harumph' noise and said, 'Balancing act. We might yet come back; you never know. Certainly, we need to check with those workmates now before he primes them.'

'I'm on it . . . but I've just accessed Greater Manchester Police's intel system to see if there's any mention of Callum – and there is.' Blackstone read the screen for a few moments and then said bleakly, 'Oh, wow!'

By this time, they had reached the centre of Thornwell village and the burnt-out remnants of The Swan's Neck – just the outer walls with a collapsed roof, the whole sorry mess surrounded by linked industrial but temporary fencing. Henry stopped the car, briefly recalling his time there when he was a real cop investigating the disappearance of a female police officer. That had been a horrific job and the then-landlord, who had run the place down, had been on the periphery of all that. In some ways, Henry was glad The Swan's Neck no longer existed as a pub, and maybe the best result would be to flatten it and turn it into new houses – give it some new life.

Blackstone looked up from her phone, realizing they had stopped. 'What?'

'Why do they want to save this? No one ever went in the place anyway,' Henry murmured.

Blackstone looked at it. 'It'll fall down of its own accord soon.'

'Whatever, it will need demolishing.'

Henry got out of the car and walked nose-up to the fencing. He found a gap between two sections, squeezed through and began to walk around the pub. At the back, there was a large car park, now overgrown. Under some bushes in the hedge, which had previously formed the perimeter of the car park, Henry had found the missing policewoman's cap where it had rolled when she'd been abducted. There was still a gap in the hedge, through which Henry now sidled to find the remnants of a large outdoor eating area where several picnic benches still existed but were clearly rotting away. Beyond that area was a children's playground with a rusting slide and the framework of some swings, but no actual swings.

It all looked very sad.

He made his way back to the car. Blackstone had not moved, but he could see she was speaking on the phone. Henry got in and set off just as she ended the call.

'Renshaw's two workmates confirm his story. He was at work from six that morning, so he's got a good alibi. He was with them until about one p.m.'

Henry thought about it, working through the timeline. 'So Twain was last seen alive, by me, leaving The Tawny Owl at eleven-ish in the company of Celia who was, as far as we know, and according to her, the actual last person to see him alive. She allegedly found his body when she came back from a shopping trip to Lancaster next day and drove to see me immediately in a panic, which, if she is innocent, is just about understandable, but if guilty, was all an act. And I saw her before all that at the war memorial, when she said she hadn't actually seen him that morning but knew he'd got up early and gone into his workshop because she'd heard the sound of the Spitfire engine. She didn't go and see him because she was still angry with him; he had knocked her around after getting back from the pub, hence her bruises. She turns up at Th'Owl smeared in blood consistent with having discovered his body but not with having whacked him with a spanner.'

Blackstone interrupted. 'Is this what's known as stream-of-consciousness thinking or just the incoherent ramblings of an old man on the cusp of losing his mind?' she enquired sweetly.

'It is what it is.' Henry grinned, then checked his watch. 'How do you feel about sorting out Callum Renshaw?'

'I feel good about it.'

'Oh, what did you find out about him?'

'Hmm . . . crikey . . . previous convictions as a juvie for assaulting old ladies . . . released less than two years ago from a young offender institution . . . involved in teen gang activity on Moss Side . . . I'd say he's leader of the pack here, as Jake thought.' Her phone bleeped. 'Ooh, an email from the ballistics people.' She read it to herself. 'Blah, blah, blah . . . well, fancy that!'

'Tell me or your death will be brutal!'

'The bullets found at the scene of James Twain's murder, the ones fired at you . . . which missed . . . match the ones found in Marcus Durham's body and in his pool . . . let that sink in . . . the same gun fired them all, a thirty-eight.'

Henry did let it sink in.

'Which seems to confirm that whoever killed Durham was on track to kill Twain but got there to find the job done, which is very interesting,' Henry said.

'And puts Celia right back in the frame, big style.'

THIRTEEN

Henry drove Blackstone to The Tawny Owl where she got into her car and set off for Blackpool. Meanwhile, Henry made his way to the MIR at Lancaster and spent a couple of hours with a DI discussing tactics. He also checked where everything was up to with searches, house-to-house enquiries and the scientific side of the investigations in the murders of James Twain and Marcus Durham.

There was a lot of stuff coming in, as expected, although there were few eyewitnesses to anything because of the dearth of actual people in the rural locations and the way in which the houses and farms were so spread out; however, looking through the forms, Henry did spot one farm that had been visited by a couple of Support Unit officers that was quite close to the Twain household. The resident there confirmed he'd heard the engine of the Spitfire running that morning and gave approximate times that fitted with Celia's story. The farmer also stated he had seen a motorcyclist haring across his land in the early afternoon, which coincided with the time that Henry had disturbed the shooter in Twain's workshop and then heard a motorbike leaving the scene. Henry immediately deployed the same two Support Unit officers to revisit the farmer and ask if he could point out exactly where the biker had been spotted. If there were any tyre tracks, Henry wanted plaster casts to be taken, which would be a job for a CSI.

When he was more or less happy that things were on track, he called Rik Dean and updated him on the arrest of Callum Renshaw, which was a good one even if it was unconnected with the two murders, and let him know that Dale Renshaw was not a suspect in Henry's estimation, thanks to his alibi.

'And your plans now?' Rik asked. He sounded slightly better.

'Go and see Veronica Gough – we haven't heard from her, and she should have been discharged this afternoon – then on to Blackpool to see how Debs and Jake are going on with Callum. After that, if I've got time, I'll speak to another member of SONAG at random and ask them if they killed James Twain.'

* * *

Veronica was asleep when Henry arrived at the infirmary. Worryingly, he learned from a nurse that she'd had a 'little scare with her heart' earlier but was now once more stabilized. It had put her discharge back a day.

She opened her eyes as he drew a chair up to the bedside.

'I hear you had a bit of a do?' Henry said.

'I'm OK, just a twinge; I'll be out tomorrow.'

'That's good . . . and I have a bit of news for you.'

He told her about Callum Renshaw's arrest, which he put down to good police work rather than a stroke of luck. She seemed impressed but weary and a little distracted.

'What is it?' Henry asked.

Her face twitched with her thoughts. 'I just feel vulnerable and a bit scared, although what you said is good news.'

'You've been through a lot these last few days,' Henry said. 'Only to be expected you're not one hundred per cent.'

'I'm thinking my days of charging around in my wheelchair like Boadicea are over, though.'

'Don't be silly,' Henry began to say, but Veronica raised a weak hand to stop him.

'And my days at that house are numbered, too.'

'What do you mean?'

'Well, I'm all alone there, which I know is obvious, but I've never felt so frightened and incapable of dealing with stuff. I was terrified, Henry, and the worry for me is that if I'd called the police instead of you, I'd still be waiting for them or dead. I mean, the house is all kitted out for me – stairlift, shower and all mod cons for a wheelchair user – but I think the time has come for me to leave, put myself in a care home or sheltered accommodation or something. There's a nice little complex in Caton,' she said, referring to a village near Lancaster. 'I've enough income to move straight away and then sell the house. I'll be OK, money-wise.'

'But you won't be living somewhere you've been all your life. Everything you know is in Kendleton and Thornwell.'

'I know all that, but I'm tired of being alone, almost forcing myself on the community. The place in Caton, I hear, has a good social side and singalongs,' she said, sounding utterly miserable. 'Sadly, I have to wait for someone to die first. Dead man's wheelchair, apparently,' she chuckled mirthlessly.

Henry said nothing. He found the idea sensible, yet bonkers at the same time, and understood both sides of the coin.

'My mum ended up in sheltered accommodation,' he stated.

'You don't sound very enthusiastic.'

'It was OK. Decent flat, decent enough friends, but it wasn't home, though there was enough freedom to suit her, I suppose.'

'But you went visiting her?'

'As often as possible.'

'That's a good thing, then. I haven't got anyone to visit me,' Veronica said, but not in a whiney way. 'I don't mind being alone. Being solitary suits me; it's just when things go wrong.'

'You can install panic buttons.'

'I know, I've done the research . . . not filled with confidence on that one.'

'I get your point.' Henry wanted to say more, wanted to do more, but knew he couldn't get himself embroiled in any responsibility for her because she wasn't his problem.

Yet something gnawing in him told him that she *was* his business, his responsibility, and maybe it was also the village's responsibility to do something for her. Even as he thought this, he wasn't sure how it could work.

'You look puzzled, Henry.'

'Nah, I'm fine.'

'So what's going to happen to this young lad, Callum?'

Glad of the swift change of subject to something on which he was more sure-footed, he said, 'We'll see what he has to say for himself, then hopefully round up some more of his gang, but his offences are so serious that I think we'll keep him in custody and put him before the court. He's got a past history of assaulting older people, so he really needs sorting now before he does something very, very bad.'

'Well, I'm glad you caught him, but I almost feel sorry for him.'

Henry screwed up his nose. 'Don't.'

Callum remained as obnoxious and uncooperative as he had been from the moment of his arrest. Henry guessed he'd brought the gang culture of the big city into a small village and thought he could impose it; the problem was there was nowhere to hide and being a big fish in a small pond, as it were, meant everyone's eyes were on him. Even though Henry conceded it was a stroke of luck finding him, he was sure that the arrest would have come very soon anyway.

Henry arrived at Blackpool nick forty minutes after leaving Veronica and in time to watch the beginning of Blackstone and Jake's interview. The lad said nothing, not even a 'no comment'. He looked hardened to this process and conceded nothing, gave nothing. He'd been allocated a duty solicitor who rolled his eyes throughout the one-sided interview, frustrated by his client's intransigence.

After about half an hour of getting nowhere, the two cops called it quits and ended the interview, returning Callum to his cell and informing the solicitor they would re-contact him when the interview resumed.

Blackstone and Jake wandered back into the CID office where Henry had been watching the audio-visual feed on a computer at one of the desks.

'He's not a helpful young lad,' Blackstone said. Huge understatement. 'What do you think, Henry?'

'Let him fester for a few hours, then let's come back at him, guns blazing, put everything to him, and if he doesn't respond, throw the book at him and chuck him down the hole.'

Jake's sergeant in Lancaster asked if he could be released because there were literally no cops on the streets of the city. Henry reluctantly agreed, deciding he and Blackstone would continue with the interview of Callum. When they got the duty solicitor back, Callum was wheeled into the interview suite, sat down, given a couple of (wasted) minutes with his brief, then Blackstone went in and set up the room.

She started the tape and turned on the video recording system, went through the introductions and cautions again, then paused to look eye to eye with Callum.

'Apologies,' she said, 'there is one more person to join us.'

On cue, the door opened and Henry stepped in. 'So sorry I'm late.'

He sat down next to Blackstone, diagonally opposite the solicitor, but directly opposite Callum, fully aware the lad's eyes were pinned on him, although Henry wasn't looking at him.

Blackstone said, 'For the purposes of the tape, could you please introduce yourself.'

'Yes, yes,' Henry said clearly, still not looking at Callum. 'My name is Henry Christie and I am currently a civilian investigator employed by Lancashire Constabulary. Previously, I was a detective superintendent in the force. I am now retired but continue to investigate serious crimes.'

It was only at that point that Henry slowly raised his eyes and looked directly at Callum, who, wide-eyed, now appeared as if his whole world had crumbled in on itself. Henry gave him a cheeky half-grin.

Callum said, 'I wondered what the fuck you were doing at my house.'

Henry said, 'Coming after you, Callum lad.'

'Do you want to take the lead in this interview?' Blackstone asked Henry.

'Yes, I do, very much, thank you.'

Callum looked at the ceiling and said, 'Shit.'

Henry said, 'I think we've met on a couple of occasions, Callum . . . and now we need you to start telling the truth – OK?'

Callum stared at him, nodded, beaten; Henry cautioned him and asked the first question.

Within half an hour, Callum had admitted everything.

After reviewing the evidence and making a call to the Crown Prosecution Service, they charged Callum with the assault on Veronica by the stream and with burglary with intent to cause grievous bodily harm at her house.

During the interview, Henry had also questioned the lad about the various reports of damage and anti-social behaviour around the villages, including the rotten egg attack on the war memorial, all of which he sullenly admitted. Henry and Blackstone considered charging him with those offences but decided not to because Callum had named the other members of his gang. Henry passed on these names to Jake to arrest at his leisure; the whole lot could be decided on later.

After charge, bail was refused, and Callum was kept in police custody to appear at court in the morning.

Henry left Blackstone to complete the court file, which she was happy to do, not least because she wanted to get to her flat on Preston Docks later and chill at home, alone.

On his way out of the station, Henry passed through the public foyer where he saw Callum's parents sitting in the waiting area, blank-faced. They looked up when they saw him.

Henry went across. 'He's been charged,' he informed them, 'and he's staying in for court tomorrow.'

Dale said nothing, just looked glum and accepting.

But Andrea retorted, 'That's just preposterous. He's done nothing – at least nothing to justify this.'

Henry sat down next to them. 'Let me tell you exactly what he's been up to,' he began, like a storyteller around a campfire.

By the end, they had gone pale and silent.

'He needs help, not a bloody borstal,' Dale said.

Henry didn't bother explaining that borstals no longer existed. Instead, he said, 'Yes, he needs help, but he also needs locking up. He's dangerous, and you probably need to get your heads around that fact. And,' he added, 'he'll need you more than ever, so it's down to you to be there for him, which I agree sounds simple, but it might be complicated for you to achieve.'

'We're not even here for each other,' Andrea moaned. She looked hard at Dale, and he looked down at the floor.

'Up to you,' Henry said. 'I'm not a marriage counsellor, but it seems that while Callum's locked up, you might just have a window of opportunity to . . . I don't know, but you see what I'm getting at?'

'Can we see him?' Andrea asked.

Henry made a call to Blackstone on the mobile, and she spoke to the custody officer.

On his way back north, Henry called a series of people: Rik Dean and Jake Niven to update them; Ginny to say he would be home soon; finally, Veronica, who sounded breathless but pleased by the news that Callum would be unlikely to be out in the near future.

Henry considered going to the infirmary to see her again, but he was getting increasingly weary. Getting there would have meant a journey through the gridlock of Lancaster city centre, which he could do without. He promised to see her the next day.

He was back at The Tawny Owl forty minutes later, planning to do not very much other than bring the murder book up to date, go through the intelligence and information coming in, and help Ginny out, something he knew he'd been a bit lax at over the last few days and felt guilty about. So after freshening up, he put off his murder update part of the evening and wandered back into the pub to find Ginny who, as usual, was busy but easily managing everything. So busy, in fact, she didn't have any time for him other than to give him a peck on the cheek and say, 'Get behind the bar.'

Moments later, he was pulling pints and loving it. He was pleased to see that the amateur murder squad had reconvened and taken over a table in the bar.

Trade tapered off later in the evening, and, with Ginny's permission, Henry sneaked away from the bar and dragged up a chair with the amateur sleuths, who were only too pleased to have him along.

'Solved it yet?' he asked, glancing around the expectant faces and gesturing at the papers strewn around the table.

Dr Lott admitted sadly, 'Regrettably, I think we've gone as far as we can, but it was fun while it lasted. A toast.' The doctor raised what remained of his pint of Guinness and the others also raised their glasses. 'To abject failure.'

They drank, and Henry watched with a smile as he didn't have a glass with which to join them.

'You can only go off the evidence you have,' Henry said.

'Which was very little in this case,' Leonard Barr said. He was the guy who'd once been a saxophonist.

'Why do you think there was a wall of silence?' Henry asked.

None of them had an answer.

'Fear, intimidation?' Henry suggested. 'Usually is.'

'It's possible,' Roger 'The Rabbit' Tyson agreed.

'So, during the course of your enquiries, have you come across anyone who might have held that sort of influence over others?' Henry asked.

'It's hard to say right now, so many years later,' Dave Darbley, the butcher, said.

Henry looked at them all. 'What was the timeline again?' he asked.

They looked a tad confused by that question.

'OK, what was the date of the murder, what time did it happen, what happened before, leading up to it, and what happened after?' Henry clarified the question.

'Oh, I get it,' Leonard said, scrabbling for a bit of paper and finding it. 'The thing is the body wasn't found until the morning of the nineteenth of December, so it looks like it was there all night.'

'Based on what?' Henry asked.

'Based on the fact that the last sighting of him alive was at nine thirty p.m. on the previous evening, the eighteenth, when he left The Swan's Neck to walk home. He never got home, obviously. A search party went out in the morning and found him, dead as a doornail.'

'So, refresh my mind,' Henry said innocently, as if he knew nothing. 'Who was the victim?'

'Lucas Grundy,' they all said in perfect unison.

'And he'd been in The Swan's Neck the night before?'

'Yes.' Again in unison.

'Who with?'

'Eric Grundy,' they said.

'The older brother?'

All nodded together.

'Do we know if anything happened in the pub, a falling out or anything?' Henry asked.

'No reports of anything happening,' Leonard said. 'Two brothers having a drink, one leaves earlier than the other and the next day he's found murdered, two bullets in his brain, which match his own rifle.'

'Did he have his rifle with him in the pub?'

'Would seem so, but these guys were gamekeepers,' Dr Lott said. 'They always had their guns with them, so it wasn't unusual – back then, anyway.'

'Was Eric questioned about the murder?' Henry asked.

'He was . . . but witnesses say he was in the pub for two hours after Lucas left, having a lock-in, and that he set off home by himself,' Tyson interjected helpfully.

'So people witnessed Eric in the pub, which was handy,' Henry thought out loud. 'But they saw nothing later. What time did the pub close?'

'Eleven,' Leonard said. 'But there was that lock-in until midnight.'

'Were witness statements taken from anyone in the pub?' Henry asked.

'Supposedly, but we haven't actually seen them. DS Blackstone said she'd see if she could unearth them.'

They all took another drink in unison.

Henry asked, 'Who here knows Eric Grundy?' He knew the answer. They all did, and all held up their hands. 'Who's known him longest?'

'We all know him, but I'm the one who has probably known him the longest,' Dr Lott said. 'He's one of my patients, has been for probably forty years now.'

'Has he ever revealed anything to you about that fateful night in 1941?' Henry probed.

'No . . . not that I'm allowed to say,' Lott said. 'Patient confidentiality and all that.'

In unison, again, the others uttered derisive snorts. Dr Lott rolled his eyes at them and said, 'But trust me, he hasn't said anything and I haven't ever had occasion to ask him.'

'Has anyone spoken to Eric since you began this . . . this exercise?' Henry asked.

Their eyes all fell and there was a muttered, 'No.'

Leonard admitted, 'This is more a paper exercise than anything. Something to do.'

Like SONAG, Henry thought, but didn't say anything because what they were up to was legitimate and kept their minds occupied. He had no problem with that at all.

'So,' Henry began again, 'two brothers in a pub. One leaves, gets murdered. Witnesses say the older brother stayed in the pub for a couple of hours or so after the first one left,' he recapped. 'But no mention of an argument between them or anyone else in the pub?'

'Nothing,' Roger said.

'So, no falling out?'

'Nope.'

'Eric has to be the main suspect, though,' Henry stated.

'Being a suspect doesn't make you the actual killer,' Leonard said.

'True,' Henry acknowledged. Then, 'Remind me of the date again.'

'Body found on the morning of the nineteenth of December 1941,' Dr Lott said.

'Meaning he was in the pub on the night of the eighteenth of December?' Henry asked.

'Is that significant?' Leonard asked.

'Are you working on a hypothesis?' Roger asked excitedly.

'I'm working on going to bed,' Henry said, then looked round as the pub door opened and Debbie Blackstone trundled in, clad in a dressed-down tracksuit and dragging a small, wheeled suitcase with one hand and a briefcase in the other. She veered towards the sleuths, beaming. Henry couldn't help but grin at her. Her hair was flattened down to her head, not in the usual spikes, and most of her facial jewellery had been removed. Henry had grown to respect her choice of appearance – wild, whacky, 'fuck you' – but seeing her like this made him realize just how attractive she was under the tough veneer. 'I thought you were staying home tonight,' Henry said, 'chilling.'

'I was, but I got bored. I'm showered, clean, got all my damp washing in here' – she lifted the suitcase off the floor – 'which I'll drape over your radiators if that's all right? I've brought my paperwork with me' – she raised the briefcase aloft – 'so if it's OK with you, I'll have a jar and a chinwag with these guys, then "go do" in the guest bedroom?'

'That's great,' Henry said, actually chuffed she'd decided to change her mind. He was more than happy to have her around – someone who had thoroughly enlivened his existence, even though she outraged him mostly.

'And I've got a bit of a pressie for you lot,' she said to the amateur sleuths. She flopped the briefcase on to the table on top of their paperwork and clicked it open to reveal it was crammed with files. She took the top one out, closed the case and put it back on the floor.

Then she dropped the file dramatically on to the table.

'Nipped into HQ, broke into the FMIT archives and extracted this.' She pointed at the thick file. 'To be fair, there's not much in it you guys don't know, but this is the Lucas Grundy murder file as it stands. You're welcome.'

She curtsied as the men drew in admiring breaths and began to applaud her. She held up a hand to stop them just as the barman brought a pint of Stella across to her.

'Put that on my tab,' Dr Lott said.

After all the customers had left, Blackstone and Henry helped Ginny and the staff to clean and tidy up before Blackstone headed for her bedroom and Henry went for one last breath of fresh air on the front terrace.

The village was quiet: no people, no cars. Bliss.

Henry inhaled the clear air but nearly jumped out of his skin when a soft voice said, 'Henry?' and a figure stepped out from the shadows: Maude Crichton, wrapped tightly in a long woollen cardigan, looking frail and upset.

'Maude?' Henry said guardedly.

'Sorry to ambush you,' she said and came up the steps to his level.

'No probs.'

'We need to talk,' she said – that dreaded combination of words that had terrified Henry on so many occasions.

FOURTEEN

'Yes, I'm all right,' Henry said testily in response to Blackstone's query.

'Well, you don't look it and you're certainly not acting it,' she countered just as testily.

It was the morning after, and both were grabbing a quick breakfast in the kitchen of the private accommodation. It was a small, galley-like kitchen, not wide enough for two people to manoeuvre around, and they continually backed into each other, or Blackstone hefted Henry sideways with her hips, as they put the kettle on, dropped bread into the toaster and bent down for the fridge.

Finally, Blackstone raised her hands in submission and said, 'OK, enough is enough. What the hell is eating—?'

She didn't get the chance to finish her remonstration because the living-room door opened and Maude Crichton's face appeared around it, her silver-grey hair tousled and a glimpse of a pale bare shoulder, although it was clear she was wearing some sort of dressing gown and was not completely naked.

'Henry?' Maude called.

'Yeah, yeah,' he said, slithering past an open-mouthed Blackstone, whose expression changed from one of bemused shock to one of complete hilarity.

'I can't find a bath towel, babe,' Maude said.

'Uh, in the cupboard under the washbasin,' Henry directed her.

'Thank you.' She pursed her lips into a kiss, then looked up across Henry's shoulder and gave Blackstone a little wave with her fingers before disappearing.

Henry remained stock-still, facing away from Blackstone, unable to bring himself to look at her.

'Damn!' Blackstone said, unable to contain her mirth. 'I wondered what all that animal-like howling was last night. Now I know, you old dog.'

Henry turned slowly. 'I'm just an old fool, too,' he said.

The toast popped up.

*   *   *

'I can't find a bath towel, babe,' Blackstone mimicked Maude and not for the first time.

'Look, just let it drop, will you,' Henry said through gritted teeth. 'I did it, end of. I've made my bed and I'll lie in it.'

They were sitting in his car, just about to set off, and Blackstone had been remorseless in her ribbing of him.

'I'll back off after a few more digs. I mean, what were you *thinking*?'

Tight-lipped, Henry just shook his head, furious with himself mainly.

'What's going to come of it?' Blackstone demanded. Her tone of voice had moved on from mockery to seriousness. 'I wouldn't mind if you were after her money – at least, that would be a reason.'

'Like I said, let it drop.'

'Fine.'

By this time they were moving. 'Let's just concentrate on work, shall we?' he said as though he had the high moral ground, and as he did, he swerved to a stop alongside the village green, throwing Blackstone forwards against her seat belt.

'Oi, no need to chuck me through the bloody windscreen!'

'I wasn't . . . Hang on . . .' He pulled on the handbrake, left the car ticking over, got out and walked over to the war memorial on the green, pulling out his mobile phone as he got to it.

He was pleased to see there were no more broken eggs on it. He crouched low, read the inscriptions that interested him and took a photograph of them, then all the others, and went back to the car.

Blackstone watched him curiously as he looked closely at the photos he'd taken, zooming in using his finger and thumb, muttering, 'Thought so.'

'What, exactly?'

'Look at this.' He handed her the phone. 'Two people with, shall I say, English names on the memorial – Peter and June Higham – two civilians who died as a result of a "bomb attack" on the seventeenth of December 1941. Then three more with German names on the same date, seventeenth of December 1941.'

'OK, but why is this interesting?'

'Well, my first question is whether these deaths are somehow related through a chain of events. All on the same day in 1941, which I can't get my head around. But I know someone who might be able to tell me what that connection is.'

'Veronica?' Blackstone guessed.

'I was talking to her as I was cleaning up the memorial the other day, and I was about to ask her that very question but got distracted when Celia Twain drove up. I'd forgotten until now.'

'Right.' Blackstone nodded, not getting it. 'What has this got to do with anything?'

'Not sure it has, but you know my mantra, "coincidences is clues"?'

'And the coincidence here is?'

'Well, maybe not an exact coincidence . . . but what was the date of Lucas Grundy's murder?'

Blackstone, put on the spot, hesitated.

'Nineteenth of December, two days later . . . at least, that's when his body was discovered in a ditch, though it's likely he was murdered on the evening of the eighteenth, one day after the two civilians and the three Germans died . . . the circumstances of which I don't know,' Henry said. 'However, is that some coincidence or what? A normally sleepy village in the sticks, where literally nothing ever happens – then wham! Suddenly, we have two victims of a bomb attack – whatever that was – three dead Germans and then a frickin' murder!'

The muscles on Blackstone's face twitched in a way that showed she wasn't convinced. 'Hmm, not the same day, but close to each other, admittedly . . . but I'm afraid I'm going to have to break it to you, Henry – sometimes coincidences are not clues.'

'I beg to differ,' Henry said, taking his phone back. 'Let's go and see Veronica and find out what she can tell us.'

Although still hooked up to a heart monitor, Veronica was sitting up in a chair by the side of the bed looking a little more robust.

They brought her up to date with progress on Callum Renshaw – that he was due in court later that day with an application from the prosecution to have him remanded to secure accommodation, although they expected this to be vigorously challenged by his solicitor. Henry saw Veronica's face react to this, but he assured her that the case for keeping him in custody was very strong, not least because there were others still wanted in connection with the offences. Henry told her that Jake Niven and a team of Support Unit officers were locating these others, and Henry expected them to be in custody by lunchtime. She seemed relieved.

'Now then, Veronica, I want you to fill some gaps for me,' Henry went on.

'I think I've told you everything.'

'I want to talk about something completely different.'

After Henry quickly explained what he wanted to discuss, Veronica, glad of the distraction, said, 'Oh well, let me see. Let me get my brain in order.'

Henry had cadged her a cup of tea from the nurses' station, plus one for himself and Blackstone, saying, 'Sorry, no lemon and ginger tea for you,' as he handed hers over. She gave him an ugly look. He pulled up a chair for himself, and Blackstone perched on the bed, both sipping their hot brews and waiting, breath bated, for story time.

'You've got to remember that I was only nine in 1941, so some things are fuzzy, but a lot is clear and, ironically, becoming clearer as I get older.'

'You often hear that,' Henry said.

'You mean that you can't remember what happened yesterday or why you even went into a room, but details from almost eighty years ago are clear as day?' Veronica said.

'Yep.'

'Right, anyway.' She got herself comfortable. 'I do remember huddling around the wireless with Mum – Dad was away fighting – listening to news of bombing raids being carried out by the Germans in 1941. The Blitz was happening, and mostly they were concentrating on London for obvious reasons, but other places were also targeted by the bombers.'

'Liverpool and Cardiff, for their docks,' Blackstone said. 'They were bombed to shit, if you'll pardon the expression.'

'Coventry,' Henry added, 'for the industry.'

Veronica looked sweetly at Blackstone. 'And on the night of the seventeenth of December 1941, which I remember being a clear, starry night up in the village – an excellent night for a bombing raid, I might add – the Germans came for Liverpool, as you say.'

Blackstone gave Henry a smug 'told you' look.

He rolled his eyes.

Veronica continued, 'I've read about it since, though not recently. A dozen Heinkel bombers came across the North Sea; four swooped on Hull, but the remainder came across the Pennines for Manchester and Liverpool. Quite a big night of destruction – a lot of people dead.'

Henry and Blackstone became a touch more reverential and waited for her to continue.

'However, despite the destruction of the raids, with a lot of bombs dropped on the docks and the Anfield area, the people of Merseyside were ready, and several anti-aircraft guns were used against the bombers with mixed results. Two got hit. One of them plunged into the mouth of the Mersey, killing all the crew; the other one remained in the air but was badly damaged. Amazingly, the young pilot wrestled with the plane, even though one engine was knocked out and there were gaping holes in the fuselage. The plane veered north-easterly, right across central Lancashire, up to the point where the damaged engine caught fire and the pilot began to lose it after his amazing attempts to stay up, and presumably the decision was made to offload the two remaining bombs.'

Veronica paused at this juncture and swallowed some tea.

She blinked. 'And although I've read about it since, I actually watched this plane fly overhead, like watching a ball of fire, a meteorite crossing the sky. I like to think that those last two bombs were not deliberately dropped on Thornwell. I like to think the crew thought they'd reached a point where there were no houses underneath them and no one would be hurt, but they were wrong. One bomb was a direct hit on a house; the other fell harmlessly in a field and exploded. Two people were killed. I saw the explosion from a distance.' She blinked more, remembering. 'It shook the earth, and I felt the blast, which nearly blew me over.'

'What happened to the plane?' Blackstone asked.

'It came down on the moors, on Mallowdale Fell. Its remains are still there.'

'Really?' Henry said, astonished.

'It's just a shell now, mostly looted, but it was never in a location to be recovered, too far away from anywhere.'

'And the crew?' Henry asked.

'The three names you see on the war memorial – the German ones, obviously.'

'And Peter and Elsie Higham? Were they the civilians killed by the bomb?'

Veronica nodded. 'Really nice old couple.'

Henry thought all this through and something that didn't quite fit jumped out at him as he scoured his brain. 'So, three German crew?'

Veronica said, 'Yes.'

Then Henry remembered. He remembered being a lad, one of those nerdy ones who constructed Airfix kits of Second World War planes, then hung them on cotton threads from the ceiling over his bed. At one stage in his childhood, there were enough dangling models overhead to form a mixed squadron of British and German fighters and bombers. This had been a glorious period of his life, and it gave him some knowledge of such machines of war.

'The Heinkel bomber,' he said, thinking back, 'if I remember rightly, had a crew of five – pilot, nose gunner – who doubled as the bombardier and navigator – and, err, a dorsal gunner and a ventral machine gunner . . .'

'Bloody hell, get you!' Blackstone ribbed him, although she was quietly impressed. 'The history man.'

'Signs of a misspent youth,' he said. 'But, yeah, five crew members, I think.'

'It is believed there were five,' Veronica concurred, 'but that two survived the crash on the moors and tried to make their way back across the country, maybe in the hope of somehow returning to the Fatherland. More likely, they perished on the moors on that bitterly cold night – they might also have been injured; even if they were uninjured, it would have been a perilous journey on that terrain. Anyway, their bodies were never recovered, even though the moors were searched. There were and still are plenty of places a body could lie undetected or undiscovered forever or maybe become food for foxes or birds of prey.'

'But the other three were brought down and buried?' Henry asked.

'Yes, in St Andrew's churchyard . . . after the war, their families came to visit the graves occasionally, but the bodies were never returned home.'

'Do we know the names of the missing airmen?' Henry asked Veronica.

She thought a moment. 'You could check with the vicar of St Andrew's. He's keen on military history as well as being the semi-official keeper of village records. If anyone knows the names, he will.' Veronica exhaled, and as the breath left her body, she went pale – recalling and retelling the story had taken it out of her.

'Are you OK, Veronica?' Blackstone asked.

'I'm fine, I'm fine.' She looked at Henry, a bit baffled. 'Why do you want to know all this history stuff anyway?'

He hesitated, and Blackstone stepped in. 'Because he somehow thinks that all those things that happened in December 1941 are linked in some way.'

'And the missing airmen are just another part of the puzzle,' Henry said.

'A puzzle that exists only in his head,' Blackstone finished for him, making Veronica giggle.

'While I realize they were on a bombing mission, it must have been a terrifying journey for them once they got hit,' Henry said, imagining five young men essentially fighting for their lives in a blazing, stricken aircraft. And there was also the possibility that not all of them were alive for that last twenty-odd minute section of the flight. More than one could have been dead even then as a result of the ack-ack fire.

'I don't have a great deal of sympathy,' Blackstone said.

'Me neither as such, but they were just young men on a mission.'

'Which was to bomb the crap out of Liverpool.'

'I get it,' Henry said.

'But yeah, not a happy final few minutes,' Blackstone conceded. 'They certainly didn't break out the champers.'

After bidding goodbye to Veronica, Henry and Blackstone made their way to Blackpool to oversee Callum Renshaw's short courtroom appearance, at the end of which the defence solicitor was told to sit down and shut up by an impatient court clerk, and Callum remained in custody.

Jake Niven and his Support Unit colleagues had managed to arrest a couple of Callum's running mates and were dealing with them, getting quick admissions of guilt, although they pointed their fingers firmly in Callum's direction as leader of the pack and instigator of their crimes.

Happy all this was going well under the watchful eye of a local detective sergeant, Henry and Blackstone headed back to Lancaster and the MIR.

During the course of the journey up the M6, Blackstone found the number of Damian Carter, the vicar of St Andrew's in Kendleton, via the internet, and linked the call to the Bluetooth device in the courtesy car using Henry's phone. Henry knew the vicar was a frequent customer at The Tawny Owl, and after the usual introductions, Henry asked him if he knew the names of the two missing members of the Heinkel aircrew. Carter said he would find them and text Henry the details.

Blackstone disconnected.

Henry caught the look on her face and said, 'What have I done now?'

With a degree of exasperation, she said, 'You do know you're supposed to be investigating two murders that happened two or three days ago, not eight decades ago?'

'I hadn't forgotten.'

'So perhaps we should get back on track; otherwise, Rikky Boy will have your guts, and probably mine, Covid or not.'

'It's just a sidetrack that needed attention,' Henry said defensively. 'We couldn't actually ignore Callum when he came into the lounge,' he continued, trying to justify his deviations. 'And now we're just checking out Eric Grundy as a potential suspect in the murder of James Twain because he's a member of SONAG, and we went on to learn a lot of troubling stuff about him, not least of which is that he is a rapist who has got away with it for almost all his life. Now we know a lot of shit about him that cannot be ignored, we're in a position to go and have a chat with the old man with some pre-knowledge, which is going to be very useful, IMHO.'

'IMHO?'

'In my honest opinion. That's what that means. I think.'

'I know what IMHO means. So are you getting down and groovin' with the kids now?' Blackstone teased him. 'You'll be rapping next.'

'Yo!' Henry said.

Blackstone shook her head in despair and whispered mockingly, 'Watch and learn, my arse.'

They were back at the MIR ten minutes later, where a lot of work was being done in relation to the recent murders by what amounted to a skeleton crew. In pre-Covid days, Henry would have expected to be overrun by detectives and uniforms, but that was now a pipe dream.

There were a few things to catch up on.

In Henry's in-tray in the SIO's office there was a message from the two detectives who had gone to London to interview Sue Daggert, saying that although she had good reason to fall out with Marcus Durham – Durham had gone into drug dealing with the Daggerts but had a bust-up with Sue over a £90,000 payout on a drug purchase – she could have killed him quite happily but didn't because it was known she was under surveillance when the murder happened. She could have planned it and hired a contract killer, but she denied it and there was no evidence of it. The two detectives and the NCA were happy with her story and were sure she wasn't involved in killing Durham. Henry called one of the detectives, thanked them for their efforts and told them to return as soon as possible.

Next, he caught up with the Support Unit search team trying to find the trail of the motorbike that may have been used as a getaway vehicle from the Twain murder scene by the intruder who'd taken potshots at Henry. They had found the probable route used across an adjoining farmer's field and called in a CSI to take casts of the tyre treads in the soil.

Henry contacted the Support Unit sergeant by phone and thanked her for her team's efforts.

The two actual crime scenes were still locked down and being analysed by CSI and forensics, so that side of things was still progressing.

By the time Henry had brought himself up to speed and was as satisfied as he could be, it was almost seven p.m., another day gone and no murderers arrested.

He got up, stretched and went to find Blackstone, who was still working through the files and paperwork seized from Twain's and Durham's offices, to see if there were any leads worth chasing.

When Henry suggested they call it a day, Blackstone scooped everything up, shoved it all into folders and declared herself ready to rock.

'Did you manage to root out any files regarding unsolved rapes and murders from wartime up in the Lancaster area?' Henry asked her. 'If you didn't, that's fine, but if you did, I might just skim through them tonight if I get the chance.'

'You mean if Maude isn't waiting for you, draped across the chaise longue, planning to ravage you again?'

Henry gave her a leery grin and teased back, 'You sound jealous.'

She almost rolled on to the floor in a fit of raucous laughter but managed to keep a grip on the desk. 'Never will I be that desperate,' she said, repulsed by the thought.

'Good, because, as you know, I haven't got a chaise longue. Did you manage to look into the archives or not?'

She gave him one of her piercing looks that, without saying anything, said, *Duh!*

Half an hour later, they were back at The Tawny Owl.

Henry looked at his phone as a text landed. It was from Damian Carter, the vicar of St Andrew's. Good to his word, he'd sent Henry a list of the crew of the Heinkel, and Henry had been right in his boyhood knowledge: there were five of them.

Three were those who had been recovered from the crashed aircraft and whose names were listed on the war memorial on the village green. The names of the other two were the pair who had gone missing and whose fates were unknown and subject to speculation.

The vicar had included in the text a link to a website that was dedicated to locations of military crashed aircraft sites in the UK, and when Henry followed the link, it took him straight to the page about the Heinkel on the moors and showed several photographs of the crash site up on Mallowdale Fell. Some were very grainy pictures taken soon after the crash; others were more recent.

Henry winced as he looked at the images. Although it was clearly a crashed plane, it had disintegrated on impact, and the fact that two people might have survived was a miracle.

Also on the website were black-and-white photographs of the five young men who had crewed the plane – five lads really, posing proudly yet shyly against their plane in their flying suits – grainy photos that seemed especially poignant to Henry; five young guys embroiled in a war and who had never been allowed to grow old. He felt fortunate that his own father had made it home from the war to have a family, a career and a fulfilled, ordinary life. Although he didn't get to a ripe old age, he'd had a good life beyond the army.

Henry looked at the photographs, zooming in on their faces.

From the accompanying caption, he saw the two 'missing' crew members were called Ernst Muller and Wolfgang Achen. He looked closely at them, wondering sadly what had become of them. The other three had been accounted for, their bodies recovered and given decent burials, and at least their families had some sort of closure. His own heart seemed to miss a beat.

'Soft arse,' he chided himself. 'Getting emosh' – as Blackstone might have said – 'over long-dead people.'

But Henry knew what this feeling was about. The same thing that had driven him when he had been a 'real' SIO, the thing within him that wanted to fight for the rights of the dead. The thing that drove him to bring some sort of closure for families and now seemed to extend to two German airmen who had gone missing so many years ago, despite the mission they had been on.

He moved around the photograph of the airmen, trying to focus on details. There seemed to be name tags sewn on to the left side of the chests of the flying suits, although he couldn't be certain. In the end, he sighed with annoyance and gave up, came out of the website and texted a thank you to the vicar who responded with a thumbs-up emoji and asked why he was interested.

Henry said he would come and see him in a couple of days to explain.

Another thumbs-up came.

With a grunt, Henry returned to what he'd been doing before the vicar's text had landed, which was looking through the unsolved files for murders and rapes during and a few years after the war. Henry had taken about half the files, Blackstone the other half.

She was currently in the guest bedroom, and Henry was working at the desk in his lounge.

The number of unsolved rapes terrified him – almost thirty cases over a period of only a few years, although the number of unsolved murders was less of a worry with only two in that period, both of which looked to be standalone, stranger murders.

That left Henry looking at fifteen rapes. For various reasons, such as method, it was easy to discount ten, leaving five to analyse more deeply.

He managed to filter out two more.

Three left.

One in the village of Caton, two in Lancaster city centre, all with similar MOs: lone females targeted on quiet side streets. A male offender, a big guy, who dragged the victims into back yards and raped them and then threatened them with death if they reported the incident, which fortunately they had the courage to ignore, even if the end result from the police was less than satisfactory. The offender wore a rough jacket, maybe tweed, and smelled of what each female described as 'meat', whatever that might have meant.

On each occasion, the man had stolen something of value from the victim, although this nugget did not quite fit with what Veronica had told him about her terrible experience. Had Grundy taken anything from her? Henry did not know.

Henry read the three files again, annoyed at what seemed a pitiful yet half-expected response by the cops back then. He looked at all the similarities and was convinced it was probably the same offender on each occasion, although there was nothing to say any of the crimes had a connection with Eric Grundy.

But it did seem there was a serial rapist at large in the forties, which was probably a phenomenon the police back then would not even have heard of, let alone be equipped to deal with. Henry knew that serial criminals were thought of mostly as a modern phenomenon even though they had always existed.

He read the files again.

The ones he was looking at were definitely connected.

Rubbing his weary eyes, he rose from the desk, took the files across to the sideboard and helped himself to his first JD of the night before crossing the hallway and lightly tapping on Blackstone's door.

He heard a grunt from behind, and a few moments later she opened the door, already in her night things. 'You need to stop coming to my door at strange times.'

Henry ignored the remark and held up the files. 'How are you getting on?'

She held up some files she'd been holding behind her back. 'Swap.'

They did and retreated to their respective rooms.

Ten minutes later, Henry was tapping on her door again.

'What did I tell you about knocking on my door?' she demanded.

He held up the two files she had given him, and she held up the ones she'd taken from him.

Both smiled. A little victory, maybe.

'Thoughts?' Henry asked.

'First one: he's a trophy hunter.'

'Question is, though . . .' Henry began.

Blackstone finished for him: 'Is it Eric Grundy?'

'Only one way to find out,' Henry said.

FIFTEEN

Next morning, before doing anything else, Henry visited the scene of Lucas Grundy's murder in Thornwell with Blackstone.

He parked at the front of the remains of The Swan's Neck and, using a map hand-drawn by one of the detectives (now long gone from this world) who'd originally investigated the murder, he traced the route Lucas Grundy had taken from the pub that night back in 1941. As well as the map, which he had taken from the file that Blackstone had snaffled, Henry also had copies of the murder scene photographs. They were not the originals but photocopies, and the images in them were blurred, even though it was apparent what was in the photos. Henry assumed the originals would be impossible to track down.

Blackstone trailed him, regaling him with the timeline.

'So, about nine thirty on that December night, Lucas Grundy left the pub where he'd been with his brother, Eric. That is the extent of the eyewitness evidence, which comprises a statement from Eric and one from the pub landlord. The two brothers had been drinking. According to the landlord, they had no disagreement and were laughing and joking. This was the day after the bombs had hit the village and the bomber itself crash-landed up there somewhere.' Blackstone gestured towards the rising moors. 'We don't know if the bodies of the aircrew had been recovered at that point, but it's an assumption we might make. So . . . the Grundys lived on a small-holding – still do – two miles from the pub. Lucas sets off in complete darkness, no streetlights in those days, especially in wartime, but it's probably a journey he'd done numerous times: up the main road for half a mile, then left into Partington Lane and another mile and a half, on a rough track in those days, to the house.'

With the map and the photographs held in front of him, Henry began to retrace that final, fatal walk.

The pair reached Partington Lane, which was now a tarmacked single-track road with passing places, yet still with drainage channels either side to catch water coming off the fields. They turned and walked up.

'Hard to say how much this has changed,' Henry said. 'Road surface, yes; otherwise, not that much. What do you say, Debs?'

She shrugged and almost collided with him as he stopped suddenly in front of her.

'According to the police report, Lucas's body was discovered one hundred yards up the lane in the drainage channel on the right and his rifle, a twenty-two, was found with him, so round about here. Looks like he'd been disarmed, shot in the back of the head somehow. Strange,' Henry mused, trying to imagine how this might have happened. He peered at the photocopied pictures of Lucas, face down in the drain with his rifle thrown diagonally across his back; there were other ones taken from different angles and more of the body once it had been recovered from the drain and laid out on the track. Even though the images were not clear, the wounds to the back of his head were very visible.

'Learned anything?' Blackstone asked.

'That we need to track down the original photos,' he muttered, then shrugged. 'Ambushed walking home from the pub, but I can't quite work out how he was disarmed, then shot in the back of his head . . . unless he handed over his weapon willingly . . .'

'To someone he knew?'

'Yep.'

'Eric, maybe?'

'One hundred per cent. Even though his story is that he walked home drunk from the pub later in complete darkness, did not see Lucas's body – which I admit is possible – fell asleep in his bedroom, found him next day after a search and called the police.'

'And I say again, Eric, maybe?'

'One hundred per cent,' Henry also said again.

When they arrived back at his car, a Support Unit personnel carrier was waiting with half a dozen constables and their sergeant, all kitted out in dark-blue overalls and boots, eager to assist in any way.

Henry briefed them quickly before he and Blackstone got into his car and drove up Partington Lane to Eric Grundy's home, a smallholding called Under t'Meadow. It was also now a cattery, a kennels and a dog-sitting business, with a number of outbuildings housing these activities surrounding the main house, which was a large, double-fronted bungalow with an extension at the back.

'Busy shop,' Blackstone noted as they got out of the car and heard a cacophony of dog howls and cat shrieks. A broad man with a hefty chin, dressed in a thick check shirt, jeans and wellingtons, and with an ancient-looking golden retriever hobbling behind him, strode over. Henry could see the family resemblance and guessed this could well be one of Eric Grundy's grandsons.

Blackstone did the introductions, then handed over to Henry, who'd decided that the best way in was via the thin end of a wedge: polite, then less so.

'I'm in charge of the investigation into the murder of James Twain,' he began.

'Oh, that twat,' was the man's initial dull response, but which pleased Henry because there was nothing better than strong, negative feelings towards the victim; such emotions often provided a portal into the mindset of a possible murderer.

'Why do you say that?' he asked sweetly.

''Cos he tried to get us to sell up and we told him where to stick it. He wanted to demolish this place and rebuild it as part of a housing estate. Nasty git. Glad he's dead.'

'Really?'

'And as far as his plans for The Swan's Neck, he was just out to screw all the locals and make a ton of dosh for himself.'

'Any idea who burned the place down, just out of interest?'

'Probably him . . . a good arson job usually speeds things up, doesn't it?' The man grinned, and Henry could see he had a distinctive underbite to his jaw. 'Anyway, I'm Tom Grundy . . . what d'you want?'

'We'd like to have a chat with Eric Grundy.'

'My grandad? Why would that be?'

'We're speaking to all the members of the Save Our Necks Action Group,' Blackstone said.

'About Twain's murder?' Tom asked, highly amused.

'What's so funny?' Blackstone asked, deadpan.

'Well, if you think any of them could have done it, you're pissing in the wind.'

'Meaning?' Henry asked.

'They talk. They blow hot air. They plan, but they do sod all; none of 'em's capable. They're all well-old gits . . . only one could have, I suppose – that one who used to be a scenes of crime cop or summat, but even he's a wimp.'

'Maybe one of them contracted someone to commit the crime

for them,' Blackstone suggested, eyeing Tom up and down, weighing him up as a potential hitman.

'What are you suggesting?' Tom squirmed uncomfortably.

Blackstone gave him a pointed look, and Henry said, 'Whatever, we'd still like to chat to Eric about it.'

'You do know he's a hundred years old, don't you? He's had a message from the queen.'

The queen's message was mounted in a picture frame and displayed proudly on the mantelpiece over a wood-burning fire.

'Do you mind if I have a look?' Henry asked politely.

'Help yourself,' the old man said. This was Eric Grundy's seventy-five-year-old son, Benjamin, who had replaced Tom once Henry and Blackstone had been shown into the bungalow. Eric was apparently in the extension, a small, self-contained apartment with all mod cons and where the old man lived. He had been told there was someone to see him and said he'd be through shortly.

Henry crossed the room, which was very dated and depressing, with old furniture and fittings, the walls brown, smoke-stained and covered in woodchip wallpaper. As he read the royal message, he wondered if he would ever be the recipient of such a thing.

Obviously, getting to a hundred was the first hurdle.

Next was if the royal family still existed by then. Henry thought they were hanging by a thread as it was.

'You say you're speaking to all SONAG members about Twain's murder?' Benjamin asked.

'We are. Routine,' Blackstone answered. She was sitting on a big, wide, old leather armchair, so soft it seemed to envelop her within its cushions, like a Venus flytrap. She felt like a character from Alice in Wonderland.

Henry's eyes took in every trinket on the mantelpiece, all sorts of everything on the wide surface, from porcelain figurines to an old clock, to brass models of war planes, one at each end, a Spitfire and a Heinkel, two deadly enemies facing each other. He then looked slowly around the room. The walls were full of paintings of all sizes, 3D display frames with medals in them, photographs in frames, plus a selection of animal heads on shield-shaped mounts, including a huge stag, a couple of foxes and a badger. None of them looked particularly new or well-maintained; nor did the two rifles mounted on the wall on a gun rack.

He turned to Benjamin, who seemed to be doing well for his age: fit-looking and alert – probably had to be to keep pushing his wheelchair-bound father around all the time.

Henry gestured around the room. 'Do all these belong to your dad?'

Benjamin nodded. 'Pretty much.'

'Bit of a collector, then?' Blackstone commented, catching Henry's eye as both detectives thought the same thing: *trophies*.

'A hoarder, by the looks,' Henry said.

'You collect lots of things by the time you're a hundred,' Benjamin said. 'Too bloody much if you ask me, but it keeps him happy, gives him pleasure.' He eyed the two interlopers. 'I know this is routine, but you're not going to put him under any pressure, are you? His hearing isn't great and he's not always with it.'

'Just a few questions. We're obviously aware of his age, so we'll tread carefully,' Henry assured him, just as a double door slid open automatically, specially made to allow Eric Grundy to come and go into the main house from the extension in his wheelchair.

Henry had seen and spoken to him before when he had turned up at The Tawny Owl for the SONAG meetings, pushed by Benjamin. Until the recent delvings into the man's past, Henry had pretty much taken him at face value. Ageing but still quick-witted, pleasant, like-able to a degree, but obviously determined to stop an unpopular development at an age when most people would not, or could not, be bothered. And Henry didn't think the claims that SONAG members were just a bunch of old-fogey shouters were true. He thought they could have been a real handful if they'd got really motivated.

Eric pushed himself through the doors into the living room and gave the visitors a dirty look. He was wearing grimy-looking clothes and pants with a stained crotch. He also stunk of body odour.

In a gravelly voice, he said to Henry, 'I thought you were a landlord, not a cop.'

'I was a cop, then a landlord. Now I'm a bit of both.'

'Investigating a murder? What's all that about?'

'Two murders actually, one of which is James Twain's.'

'If you think I did it, you must be deluded.'

'We just want to ask you some questions, that's all. Just routine.' Henry shrugged. 'Only because you're a member of SONAG.' Even as he spoke and looked at this man, Henry felt his dislike growing because of what he knew he'd done in the past.

Grundy snorted a laugh. 'Right, but don't expect me to remember everything.'

'Your brain seems pretty sharp to me.'

'Up to a point, then not so much. I am a hundred, you know?'

'And with a message from the queen to prove it,' Blackstone quipped.

She got a scowl from Grundy, who said, 'Who are you?'

'DS Blackstone and I'm a full-time cop.'

Grundy adjusted his thick-lensed glasses, which were smeared with fingerprints, and said, 'You look more like a Liquorice Allsort.'

'Dad!' Benjamin piped up. To Blackstone, he said, 'Sorry, love. Old man, old-fashioned, thinks he can say anything he likes and get away with it.'

Blackstone nodded, but her face had the look of a thunderstorm coming.

However, the old man, in spite of his son's remonstration, said to her, 'You look stupid and unprofessional in those ridiculous clothes and with that hairstyle, pink and spiked. No standards! What's the world coming to?'

'That is definitely enough, Mr Grundy,' Henry said, stepping in, although he knew full well that Blackstone didn't need him to stand up for her. It was the other way round if anything, as he'd discovered over the last months.

'Henry!' she snapped. Then she stood up and spoke to Grundy. 'I didn't come here to be insulted or to insult you, Mr Grundy. I know you're an old guy and probably have very traditional views about what people should look like in various professions, but what they look like doesn't mean they can't do a job, does it?'

He looked at her, a smile playing on his lips, clearly pleased by his button-pushing.

'I mean,' Blackstone went on, 'for example . . . what do you think of women in general . . . just wondering?'

'Why ask that?' He slavered down his chin.

'I'll lay odds you think they're second-class citizens.'

'Debs,' Henry interrupted, 'let's stop this.'

She shook her head angrily, much to Grundy's enjoyment.

Henry looked at him and said, 'Let me ask you my questions, eh?'

'If you must.' He was still scowling at Blackstone, who had turned away and walked across to the back wall to look at the many photographs displayed, as well as some small stuffed animals and birds in display cases.

'Why are you so interested in stopping the proposed development of The Swan's Neck?' Henry asked him.

Eric tore his eyes away from Blackstone and looked at Henry. 'Bad for the community. More traffic. More fucking kids. More shit all around. Not going to happen now, though, is it?'

'Because of James Twain's death?'

'Couldn't have happened to a nicer cunt.'

'Dad! For Christ's sake,' Benjamin pleaded.

Grundy made a flicking gesture with his right hand, dismissing his son's words, and then he looked at Henry and said, 'And no, I didn't kill him.'

Henry nodded thoughtfully. 'But you're very glad the development is less likely to happen now?'

'Result, isn't it? OK, have we finished now? I'm tired of all this and anything more will just be harassment of an old man.'

'Nah, not by a long shot,' Henry said.

'What's that supposed to mean?'

Henry took a breath, but Blackstone filled the void for him. 'You won't be aware yet, but Lancashire Constabulary has reopened the investigation into your brother Lucas's murder in 1941, which I'm sure you'll be pleased to hear. We're like a dog with a rat.'

'Well, best o' luck with that,' Grundy said, unfazed. 'I take it you think I did it?'

'Did you?' she asked.

'Fuck y'on about? No, some bastard shot him in the head on his way home while I were in the pub, boozing.'

'The Swan's Neck? You seem to have a very long-standing affinity with that place,' Henry said.

'It were my local, so obviously!'

'Who do you think killed Lucas?' Henry asked.

Grundy shrugged. 'Don't know or I'd have said eighty years ago, wouldn't I?'

'No ideas at all?'

'He was an unpopular guy, but nobody saw owt, and if they did, they didn't say owt. Most of them are dead anyway, so trust me, you're on a pointless task wi' this one. It's been reopened more times than a prossie drops her knickers in the rush hour,' he snorted, 'and the rozzers have asked me more times than I care to mention if I killed Lucas. Answer – no, I didn't.'

Henry glanced at Blackstone who was watching the old man as he spoke, but then she returned to her perusal of the things on the wall.

'But your mind is still clear about the events of that night?' Henry asked.

'Clear as day. My memory hasn't faded yet and, you know, it was a pretty big event, your brother being murdered, so it kind of sticks with you. My mind's OK; it's my flesh and blood that's on the way out. And my hearing. And my prostate.' He screwed up his nose.

Behind him, Henry heard Blackstone gasp.

'You OK?' he asked her.

'Yep – just stubbed my toe.'

'OK.' He refocused on Grundy. 'Lucas's murder took place a day or so after that German bomber crashed on the moors after dropping its last bombs on Thornwell, didn't it? Two civilians killed . . .'

'By murdering Nazi bastards.' Grundy swore.

'Well, at least the crew died, didn't they?'

'And good riddance. They got their just deserts.'

Behind him at the wall, Henry heard a scraping noise where Blackstone was standing.

'Oi! What the fuck are you doing, Bertie Bassett?' Grundy demanded of Blackstone.

Henry twisted and saw she was carefully lifting a small glass-fronted display case from the wall. It had two items in it which he couldn't quite make out from where he was sitting. However, he kept his focus on Grundy, wondering where best to take this after Blackstone's whopper of a lie about the reopening of the murder case; he felt a responsibility to keep the dialogue going as he guessed Blackstone had taken that tack because the old man had severely pissed her off by insulting her, and she now wanted to rattle his cage. Henry got the feeling, though, that Grundy was well versed in fending off questions – and allegations – about Lucas's death. Over the course of many years, he'd been spoken to by detectives and journalists and was in his comfort zone.

He'd kept his story simple: he was in the pub when Lucas was shot, and eighty years down the line no one was going to prove anything different.

What he'd never been questioned about was rape, and the old man would be unprepared for that.

Henry wasn't under any illusions that he and Blackstone would suddenly crack the murder case after all these years, but he knew they had a bloody good chance of cracking the rape cases, and if they could find one or more of the 'trophies' that had been taken from the victims in Grundy's possession, that would be awesome.

Yet, strangely, Henry wasn't completely sure how to broach this. Maybe he was out of practice.

The Support Unit team were ready and waiting to be called in, and Henry thought that maybe he should just let that happen and see how it panned out. He was mentally skimming through his options when the whole thing was completely skewed by Blackstone.

Henry sensed her standing behind him, just to one side.

He also sensed she had something in her hands.

The expression on Grundy's face had changed, too: from cocksureness to apprehension.

Blackstone said, 'You're a real collector, aren't you?'

'Is that a crime?'

'I mean, like dead stuff, yeah?' She stepped forward so she was level with Henry's shoulder and wafted a hand around the room, indicating the stuff on the mantelpiece and the walls. Then she pointed directly at a mounted fox's head and a stag's head. 'Did you shoot those poor creatures and kill them?'

He leaned forward in his wheelchair, squinting at her. 'It's called culling. I was a gamekeeper. That's part of what we did – cull things that were a nuisance – and yes, sometimes I kept the trophies.'

Henry glanced quizzically at Blackstone as she breathed the word, 'Trophies.' Then she went on, changing tack, 'That crew of the German bomber? The bodies of the three dead ones were recovered from the plane, weren't they?'

'Yes. Me and Lucas helped bring the bodies back. Gave 'em a proper burial at St Andrew's, though I don't know why. Murderers!' he almost spat.

'But two of the crew were never found, were they?'

'They were the lucky ones, survived somehow, escaped. I only hope they died up on the moors somewhere because that was one cold night.'

'So you never came across them?' Blackstone asked.

'Uh, no . . . Look, what is this?' he demanded, his eyes flickering to what Blackstone had in her hand.

'Yeah!' his son interjected. 'Where is all this going? What are

you both playing at? My father's an old man; he doesn't need you
playing games with his head, getting him all confused.'

'Shut up and fuck off, Ben,' was how Grundy senior responded
to his son's attempt to protect him. Grundy tapped his own head.
'I'm compos mentis; I know what's going on.'

'I know you are, Dad,' Benjamin said painfully.

'Well, shut it, then.'

Blackstone waited patiently for this exchange to peter out, then
said to Henry, 'Can you recall the names of those missing crew
members?'

Henry still wasn't quite getting it, but he was more than happy
to trust her and go along with whatever it was she was doing. 'I
do,' he said. 'Ernst Muller and Wolfgang Achen.' The names the
vicar had found for him, now etched into his mind.

Blackstone was still clutching the 3D box frame of the type used
to display military or sporting medals.

She had the glass side of it pulled to her chest and she tilted it
slightly to look at what was mounted within the frame.

Henry watched her carefully, instinctively knowing this was a
huge moment.

He was shocked to see she was actually shaking, and he knew
that despite all he had been through with her over the last few
months – uncovering a huge paedophile sex conspiracy going back
thirty years, during which he had discovered much about her, what
made her tick, what had affected and changed her into the person
she now was – he had never seen her like this.

'What is it, Debs?'

She looked at Grundy, who squirmed under her gaze. A century
of living, something that should be celebrated – oh, the fucking
irony of that, Blackstone thought, now despising him with every
fibre of her soul.

Was there a flicker of terror in his eyes? She hoped so.

Was this a time he had known would come? She hoped so.

Again, Henry asked softly but firmly, 'What is it, Debs?'

Blackstone turned the frame around so Henry could see what
was displayed properly for the first time. Initially, he wasn't sure
what he was looking at, but then he knew.

Two items were in the frame, one above the other.

Henry's mind flipped back to the grainy black-and-white photograph of the five members of the Heinkel aircrew lounging about

by their plane. And how he had tried to look at the sewn-on name badges on the chests of their flying suits but could not quite bring the focus up to read them.

Henry knew what he was looking at in the display case.

Two ragged name badges which had been cut from the khaki-coloured flying suits.

Bloodstained.

The actual names embossed in the material in silk thread.

Top name: Ernst Muller.

Bottom name: Wolfgang Achen.

Almost unable to breathe, Henry gasped to Blackstone, 'Get that search team in here now.'

He reached into his jacket and pulled out a folded piece of printed paper: a search warrant issued by a magistrate that morning.

They commandeered the evidence storeroom off the MIR, so everything was kept under the strict supervision of the exhibits officer, who was selected by Blackstone.

It was eight p.m. by the time Henry and Blackstone stood at the table in that room – under the watchful eye of the chosen DC – and began to really analyse what had been seized from Grundy's home.

Everything was about to be bagged up and sealed, but before that happened, Henry wanted a good look at what they'd got. Both wore disposable gloves.

They were silent. Not because of what they were actually looking at, because everything was pretty innocuous in its own right, but because of the sickening implications of each item.

In an old shoebox: a high-heeled shoe, circa 1946. Blackstone pointed to it and said, 'As described by the woman who was raped in Lancaster city centre, one of her shoes stolen by the attacker.'

Henry nodded and picked up the scrap of paper underneath the shoe, now yellowing with age, but on it the words *She was excellent – screamed*, and dated 1946.

He replaced the shoe and paper carefully, then pointed to another item on the tabletop, a mock-pearl necklace of a style dating to the late forties. There was a note, again on yellowing paper, torn from a pad, attached to the necklace with an old-style safety pin.

Blackstone consulted her notes and said, 'Caton Road, again as described by the victim.'

The note pinned to it said, *Another screamer, had to gag her.* This was dated 10 January 1949.

Henry swallowed, not liking this process at all, but realizing its importance. He exchanged a glance with Blackstone. Her face was tight. She pointed to the next item, a powder puff . . . and it went on until they reached the sixth item. This was a folded letter with a few lines of text written on it in pencil, in its own envelope, now in a clear plastic evidence bag. Henry shuffled this out on to the table and picked it up carefully with a pair of tweezers and gently pulled out the letter inside, which he flattened just as gently.

There was a name and address on the front of the envelope, but on the back were scribbled the words *First one, always the best.* It was dated simply *VE Day.*

Blackstone said, 'Don't you love it when criminals can't resist detailing their own crimes? Makes it so much easier for us dim cops that crims are usually dimmer than us. Like mafia dons getting an accountant to keep financial records . . . you must have had a lot of that in your time as a super cop?'

'Not as often as you would imagine,' Henry said, looking at the contents of the letter, the paper now so delicate that mishandling it would have caused it to crumble to nothingness. It was only a short letter, hardly anything, but to its owner it had meant everything, and the man who had raped the owner of the letter must have known that when he cruelly took it from her as a souvenir. With his phone, Henry took a photograph of it. Then he carefully put the letter back in the envelope, took a photo of the address side, but not what was on the back, and slid the whole thing back into the evidence bag.

He then pointed to the name and address on the envelope and shared another look with Blackstone and saw her swallow back her emotions.

'She didn't mention this,' Henry said.

'Perhaps it was one step too far?'

'I need to give her a ring about this,' Henry said and held Blackstone's gaze as something jarred his memory. 'Shit!' he said. He looked at his phone, tapped the gallery icon to take him to the photographs stored on the phone and opened one of the latest ones he'd taken. To Blackstone, he said, 'Remember me taking that photo of the war memorial yesterday?'

She nodded.

'This rang a bell, but I've only just realized why.' He expanded the photograph, handed it to Blackstone and said, 'Look at the name of that soldier.'

She did and emitted an emotional sigh and said, 'Bugger!'

There were more similar items seized matching the descriptions of items stolen during rapes in the late forties to early fifties, plus others that needed further investigation into other unsolved rapes or indecent assaults in that period.

And when the police had done that, Henry had already decided that the timescale would continually be extended forwards five years at a time because he was convinced that Eric Grundy would turn out to be one of the most prolific sex offenders ever.

The Support Unit search of Grundy's house, which had been meticulous, had also discovered, hidden in a box in the cellar, the remains of the two flying suits, which had ragged holes where the name patches of the airmen had been cut and torn away. Both suits were covered in blood, the staining now black with time, with bullet holes in the chests, four in each.

The two suits had been carefully transferred into modern-day suit-protector bags with transparent windows and were now hanging side by side on hooks on the wall of the evidence room.

Henry looked at them side by side, as the two men might have been on the day they died. Brothers in arms and all that crap, he thought.

He looked at Blackstone again. She said, 'I want him to stay alive long enough to answer all this in a court of law.' She made a sweeping, all-encompassing gesture. 'I want each and every one of his victims – even the German airmen – to be heard, to get their day in court.'

'Let's make that happen,' Henry said.

Henry held his mobile phone as far away from his ear as possible because a newly invigorated Rik Dean, his Covid symptoms waning by the hour, was shouting so loudly down it that there was every chance of a burst eardrum.

'A what?' the detective superintendent screamed. 'A hundred-year-old suspect? An eighty-year-old murder? German bloody warplanes. Unsolved rapes from the forties and fifties. Jesus H., Henry. You were – are – supposed to be investigating two murders that happened less than a week ago, dammit!'

'I got sidetracked and I've already been castigated for it,' Henry said along his extended arm. 'Anyway, we haven't arrested him yet, but arranged for him to attend Blackpool nick tomorrow morning – then be arrested.'

'You don't have permission to get sidetracked, though I might castrate you.'

'Well, it's happened – and just think of the kudos.' Henry tried to woo him.

'The kudos? Investigating crimes hardly anyone can remember?'

Henry muted his phone so he could hear Rik, but Rik could not hear him. He looked at Blackstone and said, 'This isn't going well.'

'I told you he'd want your guts, though I never thought he'd want your balls.' She laughed.

They were back in the SIO's office off the MIR, and Henry was attempting to update Rik with progress so far, but the boss wasn't impressed by the unexpected turn of the investigation.

Henry thumbed off the mute button as Rik was saying, 'And how the hell are you going to manage it? You haven't got time to go around interviewing a hundred-year-old bloke who's probably got dementia and a hearing aid, and even if he hasn't, he probably can't remember sod all . . . and where's the kudos in that for us – cops harass frail old man? I can see those headlines now.'

'Well, there is something else,' Henry said.

'Such as?'

'His computer was on and we got a peek,' Henry said. 'And we found literally thousands of child pornographic images on it, videos and stills. He might be a hundred but that doesn't stop him being a pervert.'

Henry grimaced as he recalled the moment when the search of Grundy's house moved into the old guy's bedroom in the extension and the laptop on the bedside cabinet. The moment when Henry went innocuously to the device, and Grundy burst in behind him, rammed Henry's legs with the footrest of the wheelchair and used the footplate to launch himself off the chair towards the computer in order to close it down before any cops could see what was on the screen.

Henry moved slightly quicker, having almost forty years on the guy.

He snatched up the computer, and the old man's hands simply grasped thin air and he crashed on to his big, unmade, very stained bed, groaning with the effort. Meanwhile, Henry, balancing the laptop on the palm of his left hand like a waiter negotiating tables, opened the screen fully and tapped a key to reveal the sordid images Grundy had been perusing in the minutes before Henry and Blackstone arrived at his home. Henry tapped the return key and another, equally horrific image came up.

'I think we'll be having this,' he told Grundy.

'You can't, it's not mentioned in the search warrant,' Grundy bleated.

'That's the beauty of a search warrant issued in England and Wales,' Henry explained coldly. 'It allows us to seize anything else we may find that we suspect is evidence of a crime, not just what is specified in the warrant. A lovely catch-all, really.'

Henry knew it was an important moment, not least because it gave him a stranglehold over crimes being committed in the here and now, not just those from the dim, distant past, which could be easier for Grundy to wriggle free from.

'He's a paedophile, and I'm sure that when we start digging, we'll find he's been committing offences of a sexual nature all his life, perhaps aided and abetted by his kith and kin, who are probably bricking themselves as we speak.'

'Right, that's all well and good, but what about the two recent murders?' Rik demanded.

'I have an action plan I'd like to run past you on that,' Henry announced, thinking on his feet. 'If you OK it, I'll be able to concentrate on those two murders, which I feel we are very close to solving . . .' To Blackstone, he mouthed, *We are, aren't we?*

She mouthed back, *No*, and shook her head.

'All right, what is this action plan of yours?' Rik asked cagily. 'Some form of BS designed to make me think you are actually doing something constructive?'

'No, no . . . it's a good one, but I do need your clout.'

'My clout? You and I both know the clout of a detective super is highly overrated.'

'I'll run it past you anyway.'

Rik paused. Henry could imagine his pained face. 'Go on, then.'

'Do the names Eddows and Cattle mean anything to you?'

Admittedly, they were not names to conjure with. Not like Batman and Robin or Starsky and Hutch. Eddows and Cattle, not names that tripped off the tongue, were two detective constables based in

Preston CID, whom Henry had encountered when he had just started as a civilian investigator and he'd had to hand over the reins of an enquiry to them.

Henry knew there were many DCs just like these two scattered throughout Lancashire Constabulary's CID offices who, day in, day out, unflashily, professionally, investigated crimes and were experts at interviewing suspects and witnesses and searching for the truth.

To Henry, they were superheroes who operated mostly under the radar, solving crimes using acquired skills and knowledge and persistence and good humour; superheroes dressed in Marks & Spencer suits.

Henry loved detectives like them. They were the backbone of many investigations. Detectives who could be briefed, then unleashed, and be guaranteed to come back with a bone.

Because, as Henry knew, interviewing was a dark art of sorts.

Most cops were proficient at it at best, and that was fine. Their skills were adequate and, more often than not, certainly when dealing with low-level crime, used successfully.

Yet there were those detectives who had something special.

That way of applying a metaphorical crowbar and gently prising open a box of secrets until the suspect was enveloped first without knowing it and then, when they realized they were in boiling water, just giving up everything.

Henry believed he had once been a skilled practitioner of that dark art. He knew he had been good, maybe one of the best, but the thing with such a skill was that it needed constantly honing like a samurai sword and perfecting by daily use. He would now happily concede he was rusty, and therefore it made common sense to hand over the case to officers in the thick of it daily, who would also relish the job.

Hence Eddows and Cattle.

Needless to say, they were busy men, dealing with their own cases in Preston. Fortunately, Henry's request came at an opportune moment when they had a slight lull in proceedings, having just charged two very nasty men with aggravated burglary. They were finishing the court file when Henry phoned. Their desks faced each other, so they were able to listen to Henry on speakerphone as he pitched the job to them.

Without hesitation, they agreed. An hour later, Henry and Blackstone dashed down and met them at Preston nick to tell them a story about a hundred-year-old man suspected of committing terrible historical offences, possibly including murder.

The two detectives were fascinated, relishing the unusual challenge, and Henry knew he could not have left Eric Grundy in safer hands.

SIXTEEN

enry had planned on making a detour to visit Veronica on the way home – he knew she was still in hospital – but by the time he and Blackstone were on the M6 northbound, it was getting late and he decided to shelve the idea until the next day.

Instead, he went straight back to The Tawny Owl and updated the murder books in relation to Twain and Durham with everything that had happened so far, which, he hoped, would enable him to refocus his mind so he could concentrate solely on those cases.

Blackstone sat beside him quietly, in a different world. Before he could ask what was eating her – though he could hazard a guess – his phone rang. She answered it.

'Civilian Investigator Henry Christie's phone,' she answered primly.

'Jake Niven . . . hi, Debs . . . I'm assuming you're on the move?'

'Correct.'

'Can Henry hear?'

Blackstone said he could.

Henry called, 'Hey, Jake, how's it going?'

'Good. One more lad in custody, charged for court, some of the other kids released but under investigation . . . Village gangland has crumbled, hopefully,' he chuckled.

'That's great.'

'But that's not what I phoned to tell you.'

'Go on.'

'I've been looking through the CCTV footage from Mrs Gough's cameras around her house and' – he paused for dramatic effect – 'I think I've solved James Twain's murder for you.'

'This is one of the key moments,' Jake said.

He, Henry and Blackstone had met up in the MIR at Lancaster

where Jake had connected a laptop to an interactive whiteboard at the front of the room so the image on the laptop was transmitted to and appeared on the board.

It was divided into quarters, all images taken from the security cameras fitted around Veronica's house. Three were from cameras screwed under the eaves of the house, angled down and covering the gardens, and the fourth was fitted to a high gate pillar at the bottom of her drive.

'I'd been skimming through to see if there was anything useful in terms of getting one of Callum Renshaw and his gang invading her property, but there was nothing of much use,' Jake explained. 'On the night they broke in, they had their hoods pulled down over their heads and faces, tightened with drawstrings . . . Anyway, as I said, key moment.'

Jake pressed play.

The pictures showed daytime images from around the house. 'I went back a few days earlier just to see if there was any footage of the gang casing the joint, but there was nothing . . . However . . .'

Henry saw the time stamp was eight forty-two a.m., the date one week ago.

'What am I looking for, Jake?' he asked.

'Top right . . . just about now.'

This was the view from the camera on the gatepost, looking back towards Veronica's house.

Not much happened for a few seconds until a delivery van from a well-known supermarket appeared in shot and reversed into the drive. The van went all the way back to the house, and Henry saw Veronica come to the door as the van driver opened the back of the van and hauled her delivery of groceries into the house for her. They had a chat, then the van driver climbed back into the cab and Veronica closed her front door.

The camera caught the van driver cheekily lighting up a cigarette before setting off slowly down the drive, but as he turned out of the gate into the road, he caught the CCTV camera with the top edge of the van, dragging it around on its fitting. He drove away, probably not knowing what he'd done. Then, instead of pointing at the house, the camera was pointing outwards at a strange angle, across the road towards the drive of the house opposite.

Blackstone said, 'Veronica mentioned this happening.'

'Yeah, I recall.' Henry nodded. 'How relevant is this, Jake?'

'Keep watching,' he said mysteriously. He tapped the keys of the laptop, making the images blur and jump until he finally said, 'Watch this.'

The four frames came to a halt. Three showed the views from underneath the house eaves, whereas the fourth was still recording the view across the road as it had still not been repositioned.

Henry looked at the time and date stamp. The morning of the day of James Twain's murder.

The time was nine forty-seven a.m.

Nothing happened. Until a car came into view and turned on to the driveway of the house opposite Veronica's.

The displaced camera was in such a wonky position that the whole of the car could not be seen, just the bottom half of it, but when it stopped on the driveway of the house, the rear registration plate could be seen and read; the driver's door opened and someone got out; legs appeared, then the door closed and the legs disappeared as the person walked towards the front of that house.

Henry and Blackstone looked at each other and, unknown to Blackstone, Henry's arse twitched repeatedly. Henry looked at Jake who arched his eyebrows a couple of times. 'The car stays there until five past eleven,' Jake said. 'I'll fast-forward to this time.'

He did until he released the button and returned to real time. A few moments passed and they watched the same pair of legs appear and get into the car, which then reversed out into the road and set off towards Kendleton, but the picture only showed the bottom quarter of what was an unmistakable vehicle. A sporty Mercedes.

'That's it, basically,' Jake said. 'Case solved.'

'Well, well, well,' Henry said, scratching his scalp. 'What a bang-up job,' he complimented Jake. 'Nice one.'

Despite this new development, they did exactly as Henry suggested earlier: chill, hit the sack, awake refreshed, power on, solve two murders.

The last item on the agenda was perhaps the most difficult to achieve, but all the preceding ones were easily done, so after spending time with Jake, Henry and Blackstone made their way back to Kendleton for food and drink, then sleep, with an early morning rendezvous in the living room for coffee and toast, and a quick chat through their plans for the day.

Throughout the discussion, Henry picked up strange vibes from

Blackstone, who seemed not totally engaged with the chat but had
a smug look on her face, a half-grin that began to irritate Henry.

He challenged her. 'What's going on?'

'What do you mean?' she asked innocently.

'I mean – hah! You know exactly what I mean.' He gestured at her
face. 'That look. That expression. Like the cat that's licking the cream.'

'OK, I'll come clean.' She wiped the butter from her lips. 'You
know how you said we'll go and solve two murders today?'

'A laudable but probably not achievable ambition.'

'All I can say is this, Henry Christie . . . you never know your
luck – but for the time being, let's just concentrate on James Twain.'

Henry surveyed her as though she was bonkers and said, 'Whatev.'

Blackstone drove the courtesy car with Henry in the passenger seat.
He had to make a few phone calls and wanted to be able to concentrate on them and not be distracted by driving, even though the first
journey of the day was a relatively short one. Less than five minutes
later, Blackstone drew up on the road at the bottom of the driveway
opposite Veronica Gough's house.

Henry looked at the security camera on Veronica's gatepost and
saw it was still skewed towards this driveway and would now be
recording the bottom edge of his car. He grinned and said thanks
to that careless delivery driver.

'Gut instinct?' Henry asked her.

'As we did yesterday – play it like we know nothing, see how it
pans out, then screw him down.'

'Agreed – just another routine visit and see if any rats run out
of the aqueduct.'

'Eh?'

'One of those "before your time" references,' Henry said. 'Monty
Python?' She shook her head. '*Life of Brian*?' She shook her head.
'Forget it.'

Henry knocked on the front door at exactly nine a.m. Blackstone
hovered behind him. The door opened after a short delay, and Tom
Derrick stood there in his dressing gown and slippers.

'Henry!'

'Morning, Tom.'

The retired CSI narrowed his eyes as he looked at Henry and
Blackstone. 'What can I do for you?'

'Mind if we step in, Tom? You know DS Blackstone, don't you? I know it's Sunday and all that, but needs must.'

'Yeah, yeah, course. Come in.' He stood aside and waved them through with a sweeping gesture. 'Left into the living room . . . and forgive the mess.'

Henry turned, followed by Blackstone, followed by Derrick.

'Sit, sit,' he bade them.

They did so while he remained on his feet. 'What's this about? You look and sound so serious,' he tittered nervously.

'Murder is a serious business,' Henry said, stone-faced. 'You're aware that I've been asked by Lancashire Constabulary to investigate James Twain's murder?'

'Yeah, of course . . . the great detective steps back into the fold and all that,' Derrick quipped.

'Something like that,' Henry said humourlessly.

'Exactly like that,' Blackstone said ominously.

'So . . .?' Derrick asked. 'What has this to do with me?'

'The thing is, Tom, so far suspects are not exactly flinging themselves at us,' Blackstone said. 'I can call you Tom, can't I?' she asked and Derrick nodded. 'So it's down to us to do some old-fashioned detective work, old-fashioned "going round, talking to folk, seeing what we can uncover" kind of detective work.'

'And you may be aware that one of our lines of enquiry is to speak to every member of the Save Our Neck Action Group – SONAG – because of the friction and bad feeling caused between the group and Mr Twain,' Henry explained.

'Oh, yeah, course,' Derrick said and seemed to relax a touch as though he was suddenly on firmer ground. 'Hey! What about a brew while we chat?'

'No,' Henry said, pausing before he added, 'thank you. We're fine. How about you take a seat, Tom?'

'Ooh, OK. Back to serious,' he said. He perched on the edge of an armchair. 'Serious, serious.'

'It's routine, Tom,' Blackstone said, 'but still serious, yes.'

'I get it. I was in the game once . . . well, sort of. SOCO, you know? Call it CSI now. But I prefer SOCO. CSI is very Americanized.'

'So you'll have a good idea of how things operate?' Blackstone said.

'I'd say so,' he confirmed.

'So,' Henry began, 'how come you're a member of SONAG and what is, or was, your relationship with James Twain?'

'Wow! Straight in, Henry – BOOM!'

'No point in beating around the bush.' Henry smiled thinly. 'Time is money and all that.'

'True, true.' Derrick nodded sagely. 'Well, the SONAG thing – that development is just down the road from here and it's going to cause real problems for us locals who've been here for a while and recall when the place was peaceful. I heard about the group, decided to join forces and add my voice. Nothing sinister.'

'And your relationship with James Twain?' Blackstone kept probing.

'Non-existent, really.'

'But you did know him?' she persisted, not knowing if he did or didn't.

'Well, yeah. I met him a few times in passing, but that's all.' Derrick fidgeted as the two detectives looked him over with continuing serious expressions.

'Where and when did you first meet him?' Blackstone asked.

'Err . . . he was a member of Yealand Golf Club.'

'As you are?'

'Yes, um, I think I once had a four-ball with him . . . can't remember my partner . . . ages ago. He played with his poor wife, Celia, as I recall.'

'So your relationship was slightly more than non-existent?' Henry said.

'Hey! Look, what is this?' Derrick demanded. He shot up on to his slippered feet.

'It's just a few questions, Tom. Like DS Blackstone said, routine,' Henry assured him. 'Just because I know you and what you used to be in the police doesn't mean you'll have it easier than anyone else. You know that.'

Derrick exhaled. 'No, no, course not.'

'We're just very thorough,' Blackstone added. 'It is a murder, after all.'

'Fair enough.' He sat back down but remained uncomfortable.

'So, what did you think of him?' Henry asked.

Derrick shrugged. 'In what way?'

'In any way.'

'Bit brash,' Derrick said after a moment's thought. 'Full of himself. Ladies' man.'

'Do you have evidence of that ladies' man thing?'

'Just rumours, tittle-tattle around the villages.'

'Saying what?' Blackstone wanted to know.

'Er, look, I don't want to speak ill of the dead, but, frankly, he was supposed to be a bit of a shagger, if you'll pardon the expression, DS Blackstone. Cheated on his wife.'

'Is that why you called her "his poor wife"?' Henry cut in.

'Yeah, I guess so.'

'And you know her well?' Blackstone asked with a rising inflection in her voice.

'No, not at all really,' he said unconvincingly.

'What does "really" mean, Tom?' Blackstone asked.

'It means I don't know her,' he replied coldly.

There followed a brief but intense 'stare-out' between him and Blackstone, from which he withdrew quickly and averted his gaze. His face seemed to have acquired a number of tics: his left eye, his mouth and his chin all started doing a coordinated dance.

After a short silence, Henry said, 'Tom, what were you doing on the morning of James Twain's murder? That would be last Monday.'

'You know what I was doing,' he said, affronted. 'I attended SONAG at The Tawny Owl. You saw me, Henry; we talked. I even kept an eye on Mrs Twain with Ginny when you went to the murder scene.'

'OK, Tom, let me be more specific. I saw you come to the meeting with the other members just before eleven thirty. What were you doing before that, say between six a.m. and eleven a.m.?'

'I was here, at home.'

'Doing what?'

'What I always do – *this*, pretty much,' he said, opening his arms wide and indicating his attire. 'Mooching around in my night things, having breakfast, listening to Radio Four, doing a bit of surfing – stuff a guy my age does.'

'Were you alone? Can anyone verify this?' Blackstone asked.

'Yes, I was alone. I'm a widower, and no, it can't be verified . . . So, are we done?' Derrick asked frostily, beginning to get agitated, which greatly pleased the two detectives who liked it when people they interviewed got ants in their pants.

Henry and Blackstone looked at each other, then looked back at Tom Derrick and said, 'No,' in unison.

'Why the fuck not?' he responded furiously.

Panic was beginning to set in – something else the detectives liked.

'Don't start swearing, Tom,' Henry warned him. 'That'll only get our backs up.'

'OK, OK,' he said, trying to calm himself down, but his eyes flicked from Henry to Blackstone and gave the game away: he now realized this was more than just a routine visit on a murder enquiry and his life was about to implode.

Henry observed the sweat roll out of Derrick's hairline and down his forehead, making his skin glisten as all his pores opened. 'I'll ask that question again and I want you to think really carefully before answering, Tom. It's important. Were you alone that morning?'

Now Henry watched as Derrick's jawline tensed, relaxed and tensed again. And again. And the tics continued to jive. Henry almost expected hives to start popping up, too.

'Sometime today would be good,' Blackstone said, urging him.

'Yes, I was alone,' he said testily. 'And now I am asking you to leave. This feels like a fucking interrogation by the bloody Gestapo, and no, I won't watch my language, girlie,' he sneered at Blackstone.

Probably not the right thing to say.

'So let me get this right – you don't "really" know Celia Twain?' Henry said quietly, persistently.

'As I clearly said, no,' Derrick said with fast-rising exasperation.

'And you were alone here on the morning of James Twain's death? Here? Mooching?'

'*Yes*, as I said!'

Wickedly, Blackstone, who had now reached the end of her tether, especially after the 'girlie' putdown, said to Henry, 'Can I ask him?'

'Ask me what?' Derrick demanded.

The two detectives pretended to ignore him and continued to look at each other.

Then, after a period of consideration, which to Derrick must have seemed like an aeon, Henry said, 'OK.'

Blackstone cleared her throat, turned to Derrick and said, 'Are you having an affair with Celia Twain?' She smiled innocently.

'Wha—? No, I'm not,' he blustered. 'Why? What makes you think that?' His voice now had a tremor of uncertainty in it.

'OK, prior to Celia turning up at The Tawny Owl with a spanner in her hand and covered in blood, had you been in any sort of contact with her that morning, Tom?' she asked next.

'No.'

'Would you like to reconsider that answer for just one teeny-weeny second more?' Blackstone offered, holding her thumb and forefinger up with the most minute of gaps between them.

Derrick did just that. His mind whirred and clicked, churning the past ten minutes over very quickly and realizing something very important: they definitely had something on him. He said, 'What have you got?'

'The first thing is this,' Blackstone said, winging it slightly and adding a bit of literary licence to what they did know. 'We suspect that you are involved in the murder of James Twain. To what extent, we are not sure yet, but we know that so far all you've done is tell us lies, which does not bode well for you.'

'Preposterous! I've told you the absolute truth.'

Henry shook his head sadly. 'Tom, you haven't. One last time – one opportunity to tell us the truth is now open for you, but that opportunity is ending in about ten seconds.'

'I've told you . . .'

'All right, all right, stop the clock,' Henry said, now suddenly wanting to yank his collar and have a more formal chat with this man, who was incrementally driving him up the wall. You could only go so far with conversations like this, Henry knew. He nodded at Blackstone, who took up the running.

'We know for a fact that Celia came to this house on the morning of her husband's murder.'

'No, she didn't. I swear on my dead wife's grave.'

'In which case, I feel you're shitting on that poor woman's memory,' Blackstone said, 'because Celia was here and we need to know why, Mr Derrick.'

'And I'm telling you,' he began, not about to concede anything.

But before he could finish, Blackstone said, 'We've got her on CCTV, Tom.' She spoke blandly, hiding her feeling of triumph.

'Impossible.'

'Well, let me, a girlie, tell you something, Tom, something you'll be well aware of: in the event of a murder, these days the police automatically comb routes for CCTV cameras that might be useful in terms of victims' or suspects' movements or vehicle movements which might be related to the offence. I imagine you've seized a few in your time.'

'I have.' His face drained of all colour.

'We were lucky in that the footage from a camera just sort of dropped into our laps without us even trying,' Blackstone told him.

'And, Mr Derrick, I now believe this discussion needs to continue at a police station, under caution and under arrest . . . What do you say?'

'Whatever,' he said glumly.

Blackstone told him he was under arrest on suspicion of murder and cautioned him. He did not respond, although his face showed how stunned he was.

Henry stayed with him while he changed out of his dressing gown into proper clothing and reminded him on several occasions to say nothing. He failed to add there was a little scenario awaiting him when they arrived at Blackpool police station.

When they were ready to travel, Blackstone cuffed him and led him out to where, as prearranged, Jake Niven was waiting with the Land Rover, which Derrick instantly railed against.

'I'm not going in that shit-heap.'

Blackstone opened the back door, unlocked the inner cage and gestured for him to climb in or be chucked in.

With a look of resignation, assisted by Henry, he began to clamber up the step, and as he did, he glanced across the road and spotted the misaligned CCTV camera on Veronica Gough's gatepost. Henry noticed that he'd seen it, and the two of them looked at each other.

'That one,' Derrick said.

Henry smiled sadly at him and helped him into the back of the vehicle. Jake slammed the cage shut and locked the back door.

'Blackpool nick, rear yard,' Blackstone said to Jake.

The journey began with Henry and Blackstone following Jake. This time, Henry drove and Blackstone made the calls to coordinate the timing, and to try to get a search team together to hit Derrick's house when the authorization came through.

Finally, as they reached the point where the M6 joined the M55, Blackstone sighed. She glanced at Henry, giving him a wink, and said, 'Girlie, my arse.'

Blackstone opened the rear door of the Land Rover and then pretended to have a problem unlocking the inner cage door.

They had reached the yard at the back of the new police station, and Jake had pulled in so there was a view from the back of the vehicle across to the entrance to the custody office, where a police van had pulled up a minute before them and two detectives and a couple of uniformed constables were overseeing the arrival of another prisoner.

The rear door of this van was open, and one of the detectives was helping the handcuffed prisoner out.

Henry, seeing this, rushed up to Blackstone at the back of the Land Rover and said hurriedly, 'Shit, close the door,' and gestured across at the other van.

Blackstone said, 'What? Why?' and looked over towards the prisoner who was stepping out of the van.

'Bugger!' She slammed the Land Rover door shut and moved to stand in front of the rear window in order to obstruct Derrick's view.

It was too late. With his face pressed up to the cage door, Derrick had already spotted the prisoner in the other van who was now entering the custody office.

It was Celia Twain, who, looking over her shoulder, had also fleetingly glimpsed Derrick in the back of the Land Rover.

Blackstone gave Henry a secret grin. Timing was everything.

Ten minutes later, having got the all-clear from the detectives who had arrested Celia – now sitting in a female cell, having been quickly booked into the custody system – Blackstone unlocked the rear door of the Land Rover, and the still-cuffed Tom Derrick stepped out, shooting her a snarling, contemptuous look that told her and Henry all they needed to know: the charade was over and the pressure was now fully on because Tom Derrick and Celia Twain would be played off against each other until the real truth came out.

'Bastards,' Derrick hissed as Blackstone steered him towards the custody office door.

In the end, the truth came out quickly and no play-offs were necessary as each prisoner tried to get their story in first.

Their affair: James's treatment of her, plus his affairs, had driven her into widower Tom Derrick's arms and then into love. No accounting for taste, Henry had thought, but he kept that to himself.

The murder: what had been a passing remark – 'We should kill him' – grew into a plot. They knew there would be many suspects because James was so disliked in and around Kendleton and Thornwell for his affairs and his unpopular building projects.

The plan: if only they could come up with something that would fool the cops.

The expertise: Tom Derrick's career as a SOCO was crucial and would come in handy.

*   *   *

After the interviews, Henry, Blackstone and the two detectives who had arrested Celia listened through the tapes again, watched the video recordings and pieced together what had happened leading up to and including the day of James's murder.

'I said to her, the best thing would be a double bluff,' Tom Derrick said as he began to open up with some pride about his idea to kill James. 'Best thing is to be covered in blood, I told Celia, so it looks like you found the body and the murder weapon.' He took a sip of water from a plastic cup. 'See, I know about blood splatter and patterns and all that because I've been to so many murder scenes in my time – probably more than you, Henry – and I knew just how to do this . . . See, thing was, Celia really wanted to do it, to kill him, to have that pleasure, and I couldn't for the life of me deny her that, could I?'

Henry and Blackstone, the interviewers, waited.

'So it was a given. She had to do it but in such a way, obviously, that you lot could never prove it.'

'And how did you achieve that?' Blackstone asked.

'Preparation, planning, all that sort of thing. My experience. Her desire. And the right moment. That was crucial, and it seemed just right after the argument in Th'Owl.'

'With the steak knife?' Henry asked.

'The very one. After the tussle with Renshaw and when they got home that night, the fact that James assaulted her.'

'That was the straw that broke the camel's back, knocking me around like that. It just seemed it had to be done. James had to be killed and I had to do it. Even so, I wanted to get away with it, which is where Tom came in. He knew how it might be done.'

'So what happened?' Henry asked Derrick.

'Celia phoned me in the early hours from burner phones we had ready, saying that if it could be done in the morning, we should do it. Thing is, everything was ready. I was ready, we were ready – all it needed was for things to fall into place. Tell you what,' he chuckled, 'I didn't sleep that night.'

'I knew James had gone out to mess with his plane,' Celia said. 'And I knew Tom was ready, parked down the road. I knew it was going to happen, that I would kill James that morning . . . I even knew which spanner I was going to use because I'd hidden it ready in one of the offices. A heavy one, but I knew I could handle it because I'd practised a few times hitting sacks of potatoes. I got really good, and I knew I could bash his head in with it. I was looking forward to it.'

'He'd gone into his workshop, y'know, where that plane of his was – which me and Celia had planned to sell, incidentally, worth millions – and because he'd switched the engine on, it was impossible to hear anything else, so if he was looking in the right direction, sneaking up on him was easy.'

'Tom drove up and stopped outside the workshop, then we got ready.'

Henry said to Derrick, 'How did you get ready?'
'I'm still in demand for my SOCO knowledge and still run courses for police forces, so I have all my gear in the back of my hatchback. Have knowledge, will travel . . . So we pulled on forensic suits with elasticated boots, nitrile gloves and hoods fastened tight. We gave each other a hug . . . I mean, even then it could have gone pear-shaped. If James had come out and found us, that would have taken some explaining.' Derrick chortled at the thought. 'But the gods were with us, and he didn't, so we went and peeked into the workshop. Celia had the spanner ready and then the right moment came.'

'Tom held the door open for me. I ducked in under his arm and quickly walked over to James.' She blinked at the memory and smiled. 'Then I just beat him to death, and once I'd started, I couldn't stop. Felt so good, so right, pounding the back of his head with the spanner, blood spraying everywhere, all over me . . . warm and lovely, in my face . . . until finally I stopped for breath. I was absolutely covered in blood, and he was dead as fuck, and I just looked to the door at Tom and waited where I was, didn't move, like he said I should.'

Tom Derrick shook his head in sheer admiration.
'She was beyond terrific. Maybe a little OTT. She could have stopped after the sixth blow, but she needed the release until it was all out of her system . . . actually, she was magnificent. Killer Queen, I call her now.

'Anyhow, once she'd finished, I told her to stay put, don't panic, wait for me to get to you . . . I came into the workshop and spread out a sheet of polythene then laid out a change of clothing and all the time, I'm like, "Stay there, let's do this right."

'Then, when the sheet was laid out, I laid a row of stepping plates from there to the crime scene, told her to drop the spanner, then I led her carefully back along the plates to the sheet where she stripped off, cleaned her face with a kitchen towel, then put her forensic suit into a bag and then put on the change of clothing. I did the same, too, then collected the stepping plates, rolled up the polythene and Bob's your uncle!'

Blackstone said, 'Then what?'

'Well, the adrenaline was flowing, tensions were high, but I said we needed to chill. Obviously, we wanted to fuck like rabbits, but that was a DNA no-no. That, I told her, would have to wait. Best thing, I told her, was for me to go home and for her to chill, then do the' – here Derrick used the ubiquitous air quotes – '"shopping thing", making sure she called on you, Henry, on her way to Lancaster while I sorted out disposing of the forensic suits and cleaning the stepping plates. Then, when she'd done that, she'd come home with some sandwiches for James and "find"' – more air quotes – 'the body and react in the way a loving wife would. The blood covering her clothing would be consistent with finding the body of a loved one . . . you know?

'Obviously the problem was she called round to my house. I'd told her not to, but she needed reassurance. If she hadn't come round, it would have worked – you'd be none the wiser, and we'd have ridden out the investigation. Plus,' Derrick said excitedly, 'when you went to the scene, Henry, and found some other bugger there, that was just another useful distraction . . . whoever the hell that was.'

Derrick paused wistfully at that point. 'If only she hadn't called to see me.'

'If only,' Blackstone said with no sympathy. 'You might have got away with murder . . . but you didn't.'

'There's a search team on its way to your house, Tom,' Henry said. 'Do you want to save us some trouble? I assume the stepping plates haven't been destroyed yet?'

Derrick looked glum. 'Still in the back of my car, which is parked around the back.'

'And the plastic sheet and forensic suits?'

'Fuck . . . there, too. I never got round to destroying them as I should've.'

'Because you never expected to get caught,' Blackstone said.

He nodded.

'What was the idea of trashing the offices?' Henry asked. 'To put us further off the scent?'

'We didn't do that.'

'Which seems to indicate that the other intruder did,' Blackstone said in relation to the trashing of the offices.

They had finished their review of the interviews and were now in the CID office hypothesizing about Marcus Durham's murder, the links between the two dead men and the significance of the extra intruder at the Twain murder scene.

The prisoners, Celia Twain and Tom Derrick, were stewing in their cells, while charges were being prepared after liaising with the CPS. Other enquiries were still ongoing, but the search of Derrick's house had found the incriminating, bloodstained evidence in the back of his car.

'So it would seem,' Henry agreed. He narrowed his eyes, remembering that Blackstone had said something tantalizing about solving two murders over breakfast that morning, but so far she had not expanded on that.

He was about to ask when he was distracted by the arrival of DCs Eddows and Cattle into the office, fresh from interviewing Eric Grundy. They came in, loosening their ties, looking weary, but brightened up when they spotted Henry and Blackstone.

They sat down opposite and Eddows said, 'Wow, guys.'

'If you ever feel like dropping any other stuff our way in the future, can I just say one thing? Do it!' Cattle told them.

'This is absolutely incredible,' Eddows said, shaking his head.

'What a nasty piece of work this old guy is,' Cattle added.

'We're listening,' Henry said.

To begin, Eddows placed a folder on the desk and extracted a photograph of the display frame containing the name tags of the two German airmen from the Heinkel. He pushed the photo across to Henry and Blackstone and said, 'These two young men were executed like dogs.'

SEVENTEEN

'I'm beat,' Henry confessed.

Blackstone regarded him for a few moments, weighing up whether or not to respond with an age-related jibe, but thought better of it, not least because the day had also sapped her energy, drained her of emotions she never dreamed she had – with the exception of rage, which she knew she possessed aplenty. Instead, she went up on her tiptoes and kissed him affectionately on the cheek. She said, 'Moi, aussi – but you won't hold it against me if I grab a pint and a chaser, will you?'

Henry shook his head.

'Tempt you to a snifter?'

'No, but cheers . . . ha! You youngsters! Go and enjoy yourselves.'

'I beg your pardon. Have you seen the age demographic out there?'

'You be careful. They may be past it, but they could still have thoughts.'

She gave him a lewd wink and spun away, and he watched her walk down the corridor and out into the bar of The Tawny Owl. He turned into his living room, poured a shot of JD, necked it in one, wiped his mouth with the back of his hand and said, 'You bastard, Eric Grundy.'

He poured another very generous measure, and this time took it into his bedroom, placed the glass on a chest of drawers and went for a long, hot shower.

Then, in his shorts and dressing gown, he inserted the DVD that Cattle and Eddows had given to him into the player attached to the TV on the wall opposite the bed and settled back to watch the edited contents of the interviews with Eric Grundy.

Henry could not have asked anything more of Eddows and Cattle. He'd given them their brief and let them loose. They knew what to do.

The DVD he was now watching was taken from the interview-room cameras recording the detectives interviewing Grundy. They were the edited highlights, which was OK, though Henry would have liked to see every minute. That would come, so he contented himself with what he had.

The detectives had risen splendidly to the challenge.

Prior to the interview commencing, they had hung the two flight suits, still in their clear plastic suit hangers, on the wall of the room.

Henry looked at the set-up while the room was empty of any of the participants. The screen was divided into two halves, one camera focusing directly on the space where Grundy would be positioned and the second a more general, all-encompassing view, which included the wall on which the suits were hanging, with ragged rectangular holes where their name tags had been removed. Henry gave a sudden involuntary whimper when he realized the name tags would have been sewn on to their flying suits over their hearts. It was as if they'd had their hearts cut out, too.

He took a sip of the JD and watched the highlights unfold.

The interview-room door opened. DC Eddows led the way in, followed by a duty solicitor, then Eric Grundy pushed in his wheelchair by his grandson, Tom; DC Cattle came in last.

Grundy had been seen by a police doctor and declared physically and mentally fit to be detained, and his grandson had been given special dispensation to be in the interview on the understanding he did not interrupt proceedings: if he did, he would be ejected.

The two detectives sat side by side on one side of the interview table, Grundy and his solicitor on the other, with the grandson on a chair behind.

Henry looked closely at Grundy. The old man's expression was impassive, bland and also cocksure, as if he was untouchable, yet Henry saw his eyes flicker occasionally to the flying suits hanging there.

The two detectives began with the usual pre-interview formalities, the introductions, the cautions, after which the solicitor leaned forward and asked of the flying suits, 'What is the significance of those?'

'It's something we'll come to later,' Eddows said calmly.

'This already feels like intimidation of sorts – psychological games,' the solicitor whined. Henry smiled to himself: it was exactly that.

Henry knew the two detectives would be pleased that the presence of the suits was already unsettling Grundy and his brief.

'It's what we call evidence, and we will come to those exhibits in due course,' Cattle said, and Henry grinned again: no self-respecting detective was ever intimidated by a duty solicitor. Often, under much pressure, cops had to be steadfast and hold their ground, and these two were not for budging.

The solicitor sat back with a lemon-sucking face.

'Now then, Mr Grundy,' Eddows began. 'You have been arrested for being in possession of indecent, pornographic images and videos of children, which were found on your computer and also in several photographic albums in your bedroom. Do you wish to say anything about that?'

'No comment,' he grunted.

To the solicitor, Eddows said, 'Is that your advice to your client. A "no comment" interview?'

'It is.'

Eddows nodded. 'So be it.'

The interview began. Eddows pulled on a pair of nitrile gloves, reached underneath the table and lifted a large, padded envelope, which he opened. It contained the aforementioned laptop, which the DC extracted and placed on the table.

'This laptop computer,' Eddows said, 'was seized from your bedroom. Is this your computer?'

Grundy didn't even look at it. 'No comment.'

'I need to tell you that a fingerprint expert has dusted the lid and screen of this computer; just so you know, she tells me there is only one set of prints on it. Although we have yet to take your finger-prints, Mr Grundy, I'm willing to bet that when we do, those prints will match yours.'

'No comment.'

'We've also had the contents very quickly checked by our specialist department dealing with online abuse, and they say there are thousands of vile images stored on this computer. They also say that there are at least a dozen email addresses, all of which relate to you, Mr Grundy. So, did you download and view these images?'

Grundy swallowed. Henry saw his chin wobble.

He glanced sideways at the flying suits, then back at the detect-ives and then at his solicitor and over his shoulder at his grandson, who averted his eyes and would not look at his grandad directly.

Henry wondered if Grundy felt as if this was one of those moments in a torture chamber where the walls started to come in and crush you to death. He hoped so.

Grundy whispered the name of his grandson weakly.

Behind him, Tom said, 'I can't help you.' His voice was tinged with disgust, his facial expression filled with cold horror. He said to his grandfather, 'Just tell them everything.'

Henry knew this was the first, early, crucial breakthrough.

'For the moment, we are going to leave the issue of the abusive photographs because we would like to discuss something else with you, Mr Grundy,' Eddows announced at the start of one of the interview sessions. They were five hours into the process, which had been spread out over the day. Although Grundy was a monster, he was old and frail and had to be looked after. The interview sessions were not long and drawn-out, and he was given plenty of rest, refreshment and toilet breaks – but those walls kept inexorably moving in.

'My client is a very old man,' the solicitor cut in, as he had done many times, 'and I think we've had enough for today, don't you?'

'We understand that,' Cattle said sympathetically, 'and if you have any complaints about the way in which your client has been treated, then please make your representations to the custody officer.' He didn't add, *Otherwise, shut it*, but those unsaid words hung there.

Grundy scowled at the detectives. He'd been unpleasant, obtuse and nasty, but he had finally admitted the computer was his and he'd downloaded the images and videos. 'What the fuck are you going to do about it?' he demanded. 'I'm a fucking hundred years old. I've got a letter from the queen. There is nothing you can do to me!'

He was certain his age was his protection.

Eddows' response to that had been, 'Don't be too sure.'

Henry sat up at this point as, on screen, Eddows picked up a plastic bag from down by his feet, opened it and took out the 3D picture frame seized from the wall of Grundy's living room which displayed the two nametags from the flying suits.

Eddows stood the frame up on the interview table, angled so Grundy and his solicitor could see it. The old man seemed to shrink into himself.

Eddows said, 'I'd like you to explain this to me, please. This frame, in which two blood-soaked name tags are displayed, was on your wall.' He described it for the benefit of the audiotape that was running alongside the video. 'There is a metal plate underneath the tags with the date etched on it, that date being the seventeenth of December 1941.'

'No comment.'

Eddows pointed across at the two flying suits. 'Those name tags were cut from those two flying suits which belonged to two members of the German aircrew of a Heinkel bomber that crashed on the moors above Kendleton on that date. Three crew members died in the crash; two other members were unaccounted for.'

'They were called Ernst Muller and Wolfgang Achen,' DC Cattle added.

'Look, what is this?' the solicitor demanded.

One look from Eddows silenced him.

'The suits, as you can see, Mr Grundy, have bullet holes in them,' Cattle said.

'No comment.'

The two detectives waited.

Then Cattle said, 'I know from a conversation you had with the two detectives who arrested you that you have a very deep hatred for Germans.'

'Nazi bastards,' Grundy said quietly.

Cattle had touched a button. 'Excuse me?' the detective asked.

'I said Nazi bastards. They' – he jabbed an arthritic finger towards the flying suits – 'got what they deserved . . . They were lined up and executed by me and Lucas . . .'

Watching the screen, Henry tensed up and said, 'Caution him, arrest him.'

As if Eddows had heard him, he said, 'I must remind you that you are under caution, Mr Grundy, and I am arresting you on suspicion of murdering these two airmen, Ernst Muller and Wolfgang Achen. Did you and your brother murder these two men?'

'Yes, but only after they'd bombed our cities and dropped two bombs on Thornwell . . . We were on the moors hunting when the plane came down. Three were dead, two alive and we frogmarched them back to Thornwell, lined 'em up behind The Swan's Neck and shot the bastards. And you know what?' Grundy leaned forward, his face gurning. 'I'd do it again.'

Henry's blood bubbled.

Cattle said, 'I must remind you that you are under caution and you are now under arrest for their murder.'

Grundy made a dismissive 'Phh' noise. 'I'm a hundred, you can't do a damned thing to me, so you might as well arrest me for murdering my pathetic, simpering brother Lucas as well, because guess what? I did that, too.'

EIGHTEEN

'Henry, you're like a cat on a hot tin roof,' Blackstone said irritably. 'Just chill, will you?'

'Not sure I can.'

'Just let those two guys do their jobs; when they have something for us, they'll let us know. In the meantime . . .' She allowed her words to drift into nothingness. 'There is nothing else we can do. As regards Celia Twain and Tom Derrick, their court files are done, CPS have been briefed, and they're not due to be put before the magistrates until four this afternoon.'

'I'm on pins, end of story,' Henry said as though he hadn't heard her.

'I fucking know you are.'

It was the morning after, and they were back in the MIR. Henry knew what was going to happen that day. He'd spoken to Eddows and Cattle who'd run their interview strategy past him for the next round with Eric Grundy.

Because of his age, the old man had been allowed to go home for the night rather than be locked in a cell, released on bail on condition he returned to Blackpool police station at ten a.m., brief in tow, for more fun and games.

Henry now knew that over the course of the day Grundy would be interviewed about the rapes, including that of Veronica Gough, although she would not be the first one they would talk about. And the prospect was filling Henry with dread, feeling he should be the one in control of it, be the one doing the interview, but also that it was only right that two experienced detectives of the calibre of Cattle and Eddows should be trusted with it.

They'd promised to keep him abreast of all developments, but not to expect any update for a few hours.

At nine fifty-five a.m., Eddows texted Henry to say Grundy had arrived at the station and was being booked back into the custody system.

'Let them do it,' Blackstone cooed. 'Let them get on with it.'

'I know, I know.'

'And in any case, I want to show you something that might just keep you occupied for an hour or two. It might be nothing of value, but see what you think.'

'Is this what you were being all mysterious about?'

'Yep. Follow me.'

They were in the SIO's office, and she led him out into the MIR to the back of that room to two tables she had shoved together to form one big one. On one corner of the table was a small stack of files containing the documents seized from Twain's and Durham's offices, which Blackstone had been studying for the last few days when she got the chance.

She picked up one of the folders and began to lay out the papers from inside it along the length and breadth of the two tables.

'Chronological order,' she mumbled as she placed the last sheet out. 'Bear with me,' she said as she scanned them all again to make sure they were correct. Satisfied, she said, 'Right, pin your ears back, matey.'

Henry stood behind her, watching as patiently as he could.

'First thing,' she said, pointing to the sheet of paper in the top left corner. 'Almost ten years ago, you arrested Marcus Durham for a botched, amateurish kidnap job, yeah? This is a copy of the original crime report.'

Henry nodded.

'That whole shebang,' she continued, 'related to an argument that Durham had with a guy called Josh Price over the purchase of a house at auction, which Price bought against Durham's wishes.' She looked at Henry. 'You remember that, don't you?'

'I do. I led the job, but it was quickly over, and when Durham was locked up, I had to delegate it to a local DS. I was running a murder at the time.'

'Phew. Right, now, the property in question was called Nine Elms,' she said – and Henry's eyes narrowed because the name meant something to him, but he wasn't sure why. It was on the edge of his memory and it was annoying him. Blackstone looked at him, also with her eyes narrowed, and asked, 'Does that ring a bell at all?'

'Sorry, being dim here,' he admitted.

'OK, no worries. We'll come back to that. So, Marcus gets locked up and goes to prison for eight years and he's out after four – fuck the system and all that – but he's ankle-tagged for another two years . . . However, in that period he and James Twain meet and become on-off business partners, doing a few renovations together in and around Clitheroe and the Ribble Valley: farmhouses, normal houses, shops, all sorts of things.

'Durham's tag comes off and then here' – she pointed to the next sheet of paper – 'we have a missing-from-home report of a certain Josh Price who disappears into the ether from his home in Clitheroe. Despite lots of media, social media and the usual bog-standard police enquiries, he was never seen again, and the assumption is/ was, because he was in financial difficulties, he took his own life. Body never found, which is unusual but not unknown. However, my question here is: was Durham involved in that? Did he snatch, kill and dispose of Josh Price? Maybe, maybe not, but knowing what we do about Durham, he was definitely capable of killing, certainly, and bearing a grudge, definitely.

'Now' – she picked up the next sheet along – 'it gets interesting. This' – she waggled the paper – 'is the name of a company set up by James Twain. It's called Vale Holdings and did not do very much business at all, other than buy a property in a private sale and sell it on to another company called' – here Blackstone picked up another piece of paper – 'Supermarine Holdings, which in turn sells the property on to another company called CTJT Holdings. With me so far?' she paused to ask. 'Buy – sell – buy – sell, yeah?'

'So far, so good.'

'It's pretty basic stuff, really. I mean, we're not talking about multinational companies or anything like that, but what we are talking about are shell companies all set up by Twain, and they existed for one purpose, which, I believe, was to cover something up – that's often what shell companies are for.'

'The "something" being the purchase of a property?' Henry guessed.

Blackstone nodded. 'I've had our financial people have a quick look at this too and they've found' – she held up the next sheet of paper – 'a list of payments, first for the property and then payments made from each of these shell companies to the other, all via bank accounts owned by James Twain, one of which is offshore in Jersey.

'Anyway, the point is that, finally, another company set up by Twain then sells the property once more to another company called Poolside Holdings, which lists its one and only director as . . . go on, guess.'

'Marcus Durham,' Henry said as the pieces fell into place for him.

'Poolside then sells the property – which, incidentally, has been sold each time for the exact same amount that Vale Holdings first bought it for – to the private individual who is none other than Marcus Durham. Each of these shell companies is then dissolved but Companies House and various other websites on the internet still have details of them, so they're not that well-hidden for someone who's a bit dogged and determined' – Blackstone let her tongue loll out and she gave a few dog-like pants – 'like me, but off-putting enough for most people.'

'So the property first bought by Vale Holdings was Nine Elms?' Henry said, beginning to get excited.

'Correct, and in one of the later transactions – the sale between Supermarine Holdings and CTJT Holdings – the property is referred to as "the property formerly known as Nine Elms, now known as Chipping View".'

'Got it,' Henry said, better late than never. 'Nine Elms was the house that Josh Price outbid Durham for at auction, which is now called Chipping View. I remember looking at the gatepost when I went up to the scene of Durham's murder the other day and seeing that the original name had been filled in and replaced by Chipping View, but I'll hold my hand up: I knew it meant something, but it didn't click then.'

'Correctamundo!' Blackstone said. 'So Durham eventually gets the property he wanted but hid the trail of how he bought it, for whatever reason. And he got it cheap, too.'

'How cheap?'

'Well, Josh Price paid a hundred and seventy-five thousand at auction when he outbid Marcus – bearing in mind the place was a total wreck then, but with potential – and James Twain, via Valley Holdings, managed to purchase it for just under ninety grand, which is a stupid knock-down price.'

'Who was the seller at the start of this chain?'

'Margaret Price, Josh Price's wife, or maybe widow – dunno.'

'Wow,' Henry said.

'There is something else of interest,' Blackstone said. She picked up another sheet of paper which had a news item copied on it from the *Clitheroe Advertiser*. She handed it to Henry.

'Not good.'

It was the report of the suicide of a teenage girl called Hannah Price who had hanged herself in some woods on the outskirts of Clitheroe.

'Another common denominator in this series of business set-ups, purchases and dissolutions is a solicitor in Clitheroe called Donald Warhurst who specializes in businesses and commercial property conveyancing. He did some work for James Twain and Marcus Durham for some of their renovation projects. I've checked him out, and, by all accounts, he's a shit-bag. There are some customer reviews on a solicitor review site, warning folk not to get involved with him. These reviews are tempered by some very glowing ones, though, which I would say are false and have probably been posted by Warhurst himself.'

'So what are you saying about all this?' Henry asked her.

'Maybe nothing.' Blackstone shrugged. 'I'm not saying any laws have been broken, but we're investigating a murder, trying to find a motive, and it would be remiss of us not to go and have a chat with Warhurst and maybe see Josh Price's wife, Margaret, at the same time. I've got her address. To me, it seems like a lot of work has gone into this from Durham's point of view, kind of covering his tracks. Could it be something that got him murdered? If nothing else, it'll give you something to do rather than skulking round here like a caged lion.'

The drive took just short of an hour, taking the picturesque route from Lancaster across the Trough of Bowland and dropping down into Dunsop Bridge before skirting into Clitheroe and looping round into the one-way system up the hill and into the town centre, passing the 1,200-year-old castle as they bore right into Castle Street, which was the main thoroughfare running through the lovely town, a place Henry knew well. He'd ventured there many times as a teenage lad with his friends, mainly to drink and carouse.

Warhurst's Solicitors was on a road called Wellgate, which was on the right as they came back down the hill. Henry had driven and Blackstone had made a phone call on the journey to try to secure an appointment at short notice with Mr Warhurst, but had been told by his secretary he was busy all day, including going out to visit a client, and that he would not have time to see them – even when Blackstone told the woman who they were, though not what they wanted to see him for.

'We'll wait, then,' she'd informed the woman curtly and hung up on her.

She sat back then to enjoy the ride in Henry's courtesy car through some of the most glorious, unspoilt countryside in England.

'Have you heard about your real car yet?' she asked him.

'Hoping to hear today,' Henry told her. 'Not sure they quite know what to do, but I guess they'll have to write it off, which means a new car. Yay!' he finished without enthusiasm. 'Got a bit of "can't be arsed" syndrome about that, as fun as it might sound. I'd just got used to that one.'

'You could buy my Mini,' she suggested.

'As if.'

By the time they'd reached Clitheroe, Blackstone still hadn't convinced him that buying her car would be a good move for someone at his time of life, plus she'd made him tune the car radio into some strange (to him) music channel playing stuff he thought had no melody. It turned out to be Radio 1.

Henry managed to find a space a couple of hundred metres away from Warhurst's office but as he was about to get out, his phone rang: his insurers with an update. He gestured to Blackstone that he needed to take the call, and she gestured back she would go and see Warhurst and sauntered away without him.

Henry sat back and prepared to do battle.

A couple of minutes later, he spotted Blackstone strolling back just as he came to the end of his little bit of to-ing and fro-ing with Scott, the same insurance guy he'd given an earbashing to a few days earlier; it seemed that Scott was more than just a call taker.

Blackstone flopped into the car.

'He's out visiting a client,' she informed Henry. 'Should have been back an hour ago, and the lady behind the desk is getting a bit frazzled because she can't contact him and there are three clients waiting for him, all getting a bit nowty. I said we'd pop back if we got the chance.'

'No worries.'

'Shall we go and see Mrs Price?' Henry said.

Blackstone said they should and read the address from a piece of paper.

Ten minutes later, with the help of the satnav on her phone, they found the house in the Low Moor area, not far from where Edisford Bridge crossed the River Ribble. It was the middle in a row of terraced houses on an old, cobbled street that, Henry vaguely seemed to remember from a bit of local knowledge, were built to house workers in a nearby mill, long demolished.

He drew in behind a very nice-looking Maserati sports car that looked completely incongruous in this location.

Blackstone peered at the numbers on the doors. 'It's that one, just further along,' she said and began to get out just as Henry's phone rang once again.

It was Rik Dean calling.

'Rikky Boy. I'd better take it,' Henry said to Blackstone and thumbed the answer icon.

She shrugged, got out and walked down to the address.

Rik, now almost fully recovered from his Covid symptoms, wanted a detailed update on progress, and Henry settled in for a long chat. He didn't mind much because, so far, it was all pretty good news, even adding – in order to gild the lily somewhat and keep Rik off his back – that he and Blackstone were out and about following a good lead in the Marcus Durham investigation. As he spoke, he could see Blackstone beyond the Maserati at the door of Mrs Price's house. He saw her push it open and slowly step inside.

Henry began filling Rik in with all the details he was demanding. Apparently, the chief constable was on Rik's back, and the crime commissioner was on the chief's back, a situation Henry remembered well from his days on the force. Everybody was on everyone else's back, and Henry guessed that in the current climate, when the cops were under so much scrutiny, it was even worse than ever.

As he brought Rik up to date – getting some nice, appreciative noises from him – his phone beeped to indicate someone else was calling, and when he glanced at the screen, he saw a message to say Blackstone was on the line.

'Rik, hang fire just one sec, will you?'

Henry thumbed the icon and said, 'Yep?'

'Mr Christie, it's DS Blackstone here . . . you, er, might want to come in here, please . . . there's a bit of a situation . . .' The line went dead, and Henry looked quizzically at his phone, wondering what the hell Blackstone was on about, calling him Mr Christie and herself DS Blackstone. A bit formal.

A lot wrong.

He flipped the phone call back to Rik Dean and said, 'Got to go, mate . . . I think something's up here. Call you back.'

He ended the call without further explanation, got out of the car and walked quickly to the house, passing the Maserati. Because of the position he'd pulled in behind the Maserati, he hadn't seen that parked beyond the sports car by the kerb was a very knackered-looking, muddy trials motorbike, which at that moment did not make him do a double take, but perhaps should have done.

The front curtains were fully drawn at the ground-floor front window, and Henry could not see inside.

Henry tapped on the door, which was traditional-looking with a fanlight design and a lever-type handle. He waited a moment, got no reply and knocked a little harder, noticing then that the door was actually open a fraction of an inch. He pushed it with his knuckles. It swung open with a creak into the narrow hallway of the two-up, two-down house, and although the hallway was probably less than a yard wide, it was plenty wide enough for the bulky corpse that lay there, face down on the linoleum floor, with a gaping wound in the back of the head and a large pool of deep red blood underneath it.

First thing – it wasn't Blackstone.

It was a heavy-looking man dressed in a suit, and Henry had seen enough gunshot wounds to know he'd been shot in the back of his head and that the bullet had entered the cranium at such an angle it had skewered up through the occipital bone and exited through the parietal bone, making a terrible mess.

'Debs,' Henry called worriedly, '*Debs.*'

'Henry . . . in here, front room . . . you'll have to step over the body, I'm afraid.'

'Debs, you OK?' he called, remaining at the front door.

'Yes, yes, but you need to come in, Henry, please . . . erm, or I'll get shot, I think,' she replied. 'And, uh, don't do anything silly like calling for back-up, eh?'

'Fuck,' Henry said quietly, then raised his voice. 'OK, will do.'

There wasn't much room to manoeuvre, but he managed to edge carefully around the dead man and take a few more steps to the living-room door, which was open. Inside, he could see Blackstone on a tired-looking armchair. She was sitting upright, rigid, and her fingers gripped the ends of the armrests, knuckles white with tension, nails digging into the fabric.

Henry stood at the threshold and whispered, 'Debs?'

Blackstone's head turned very slowly towards him, and he saw abject fear in her expression as she tilted her head to indicate for Henry to enter, which he did, slowly, and saw a pale-faced woman sitting on a dining chair directly opposite Blackstone, pointing a gun at her, then at Henry as he came into view. Behind her was the front window with the closed curtains.

'Sit on the chair arm,' the woman ordered him with a grating, unemotional voice, 'next to your colleague.'

Henry moved across the room. Blackstone tucked her arm in, and Henry perched on the edge of the chair arm as instructed. Although he kept his eyes firmly on the woman and the gun, he did manage one quick scan of the room and saw a discarded forensic suit, white colour, on the two-seater settee, plus a hockey goal-keeper's mask and a motorbike helmet.

The gun followed him, unwavering, and stayed on him as he settled down.

'Good,' the woman said.

'Henry, this is Mrs Price . . . Josh Price's wife,' Blackstone said nervously. 'Margaret, this is Henry Christie, my boss.'

She nodded. 'We've met.'

Realizing she meant at James Twain's workshop, Henry said, 'Yes, we have, haven't we? I obviously don't know what's going on here, but if you could put the gun down, might we talk?' He made pacifying gestures with his hands, open palms.

Margaret Price sneered and shook her head. 'I have no talk left in me,' she said simply, and a tear rolled out of her eye. 'I have nothing left.'

Henry looked at her. Her face was thin and drawn, and seemed to have a yellowish tinge to it, and he could tell she was a long way down a road that might not have any turning circles unless he could get through to her.

'I'm sure we can talk, Margaret. We can always talk,' he said gently.

Again, she shook her head and closed her eyes despairingly for a moment, but not long enough for Henry to even consider hurling himself across the room in an effort to disarm her. He was too old for that kind of shit anyway.

'Who's that in the hall?' he asked, knowing it was probably not the best opener in the world, but that it was imperative to start a dialogue here, especially as he was trudging in dark treacle for the moment.

Margaret gave a snort and a sneer. 'The glue,' she said. 'The glue that made it all possible. The facilitator.'

'Donald Warhurst?'

Margaret nodded.

'Tell me,' Henry encouraged her.

'I've no energy. I've got nothing,' she said, then looked squarely at Henry. 'Know why?'

'Not until you tell me, Margaret.'

'Marcus Durham took everything from me. Everything – and now, on top of that, God – I suppose – has put the boot in. So I just wanted to make the last effort to put some things right, including luring that bastard to my house and killing him. He tried to run but not fast enough.'

The gun was still pointing at Henry and Blackstone.

'And that's a joke, too. *My house?* Not my house. My rented house that the social pay the rent for.'

'Tell us about Marcus Durham,' Blackstone said.

'What can I say? He kidnapped Josh to teach him a lesson. I mean, Josh was no angel; he was a rogue, but underneath he was a good guy – he was, honestly.'

'We believe you,' Henry assured her.

'Anyway, he was no tough guy either. He'd walk away from physical trouble, wouldn't mix it, didn't like it . . . and thing was, y'know? We had our hearts set on that house. It was going to be our forever home, the one we'd never leave. We'd have tons of kids and dogs, and even though we couldn't really afford it, Josh went for it and stupidly outbid Durham, who'd supposedly told everyone it was his for the taking. But we wanted it. It was ours if we paid for it, so we arranged a crippling loan and it was ours. Until Marcus came along and kicked down our door at the house we were in back then and dragged Josh out and beat him up bad, threatened to kill him. And you know what? Soft Josh never got over it. Never. He lived in fear every day after, and all Durham got was eight years, out in four. And Josh wasn't the same man, not the man I married.'

She rested the gun on her lap but kept it pointed towards the detectives.

'I'm not saying he wasn't a drinker or a gambler or made some rash business decisions, but they got worse until our financial predicament was horrific . . . and then one day, he disappeared and his – our – debt was ten times worse than I thought . . .'

In the hallway, Warhurst's mobile phone began to ring. In life, the ringtone would have been amusing to him and his golf club mates. In death, it was tragic – 'Money, Money, Money' by ABBA. It stopped after a few seconds.

'And the house – the one we believed was going to be our forever home, the one Josh financed with that loan, and we'd never even started to renovate – was just a dead weight now, and I had to get rid of it. That man out there convinced me that it wasn't worth anything, so I sold it to him and used the money to pay off some of the debt.'

'That's so sad,' Blackstone said.

'In the meantime, our daughter, Hannah, was off the rails, couldn't accept that her dad would go missing, and it screwed her up more each day . . . and then, the final nail in the coffin – my coffin – was my diagnosis.' Margaret's eyes dropped tiredly. 'Pancreatic cancer.'

'Jesus,' Blackstone said.

'I'm so sorry,' Henry said.

'Hannah couldn't take any more of it. Six months ago she went into the woods and hanged herself, and after that, even though my own mind was screwed, I began to think more and more about Marcus Durham and what he'd done to us, and one day I went to look at Nine Elms and saw it was now called Chipping View, and it was renovated and looked like our dream – until I saw Durham arrive one day with a woman on his arm, and I realized that he killed Josh, he killed Hannah and now he's killed me.

'Didn't take much to uncover that chain of purchases by non-existent companies for him to hide behind, and I decided to kill him, kill the other guy who was part of it—'

'James Twain?' Henry asked.

She nodded. 'And that solicitor in the hallway who put it all together, which he admitted to me before he ran and I put two bullets in his brain. Didn't get to shoot Twain, the guy with the Spitfire, because he was already dead when I got there, and when you arrived and surprised me, I panicked and took a few potshots at you and legged it.'

'On the motorbike?' Henry asked.

She nodded. 'But I did get to shoot Marcus Durham, and I will never regret that because he killed my family. And now . . . I'm done.'

Margaret raised the gun, and Henry knew she had said everything she was going to say. She pointed it at him. He winced and braced himself as her finger curled on the trigger, but then she angled it away from him, turned it to herself and jammed the muzzle up into the soft skin below her jawline.

*   *   *

Henry leaned against the car, making a call to Rik Dean as he watched the activity outside the house, a busy mix of police cars, uniformed personnel, crime scene van, an ambulance, crime scene and cordon tape.

The front door was open and crime scene investigators were in the early stages of erecting a forensic tent to cover the front of the house.

Two forensic-suited bods came out of the door, followed by Blackstone, her arm around the blanketed shoulders of a very poorly looking Margaret Price, who could hardly stand. Blackstone took her across the pavement and helped her into the back of the ambulance, and a paramedic took over and closed the doors.

Blackstone watched as the ambulance drew away from the kerb, followed by a section patrol car, then she walked towards Henry, dragging her feet and not looking him in the eye. He moved out of her way as she opened the passenger door and dropped exhaustedly into the seat.

Henry finished his call, walked around the car and got into the driver's seat, then leaned back and exhaled and looked at his partner. 'You did brilliantly there, Debbie, talking her down from that,' he told her, bursting with admiration.

She didn't react, but then said, 'It's all about people taking things from other people, isn't it, Henry?'

'Yes, yes, it is,' he replied.

NINETEEN

It was a long time since Henry Christie had been into a church. Mostly he'd been to places of worship to investigate the theft of lead from the roof or gold crosses from the altar. He was not a religious man and, in spite of the many bad things he'd witnessed and dealt with, had no intention of becoming one.

It was eight p.m., and four days later when he walked up to St Andrew's Church in Kendleton alongside the vicar, Damian Carter, who had been so helpful in naming the aircrew of the German bomber that had crashed on the moors, Henry was now, in confidence, explaining why he'd needed the information.

Damian listened to the terrible story in silence, then, as they reached the church, he opened the inset door and allowed Henry to step in ahead.

'She's there,' the vicar said, pointing down the aisle to the front of the church, where the single figure sat alone in a wheelchair.

'Thanks,' Henry said, shaking the vicar's hand. 'We'll talk some more over a pint soon.'

The vicar nodded and stepped back out of the door. Henry walked down the aisle, glancing up and around at the old church, impressed as ever by the architecture and stained-glass windows of such places, until he came alongside Veronica Gough, who was sitting there in quiet contemplation.

Over the last few feet, Henry had coughed gently so she knew he was there and would not startle her. The last thing he wanted was to give her another heart attack.

'Hello, Henry.'

'Hi, Veronica.' He sat down at the end of the pew next to her wheelchair. 'How are you feeling?'

'Not bad, actually. Fighting fit, I think.'

'I'm sorry we couldn't get to the infirmary when you were discharged; we both got very much tied up with things.'

'Not a problem. Damian came for me. He's been lovely, but I imagine part of that could be because of my generous donations every Sunday.'

They smiled at each other.

'I believe things have moved on,' she said.

'You could say that.'

'So, how is my friend, Eric Grundy?' she asked ironically.

'Hmm, where do I begin?' Henry pondered. 'First of all, it seems he had a vested interest in seeing the development at The Swan's Neck crushed because he and his brother buried the two German airmen they executed in what is currently the kids' play area at the back, which has never been dug up in eighty years.'

'Oh my!'

'His worry was that one of the bodies would have bullets in it from his rifle, which he still owns, and that the other body had bullets in it from his brother's rifle, which he also still owns. To be honest, it probably wouldn't have taken any self-respecting detective two minutes to unravel that particular tale, which would then have moved on to Lucas's murder because it's all interlinked.'

'Which you did.'

'Me and Debbie, yeah. Tomorrow a forensic team will be moving in to dig up that area,' Henry told her. 'Anyway, turns out that Lucas got the jitters after they'd killed the airmen and wanted to go to the authorities to confess the deed, but Eric didn't want that, so he followed him home from the pub. Partway up Partington Lane, he ambushed him, shot him in the head with Lucas's own rifle, then went back to the pub for more drinks. The publican, who's been dead for years, backed up his story, and it could never be proved that Eric killed Lucas unless he confessed, which he now has done.'

There was a lull in the conversation.

'And you have more to tell me?' Veronica asked.

Henry nodded. 'It turns out Eric was a serial rapist' – Veronica gasped in shock – 'and that you were his first victim.'

'Oh my God.' Veronica looked quickly at Jesus on the cross, crossed herself and said, 'Sorry.'

'It's all ongoing with his solicitor and the police and the Crown Prosecution Service, and we haven't yet decided what to do, but I'm pushing to get him in front of a Crown Court and let a judge make the decisions for us . . . but I'm just a voice in the wind,' he admitted. 'Only right that a murderer and rapist should stand trial, even if they're very old.'

'I agree.'

Henry took out his phone. 'Now then, Veronica,' he began gently, 'me being a bit dim, it only recently dawned on me that one of the names of the soldiers on the war memorial was Rupert Arkholme and that Arkholme was your maiden name. Was Rupert your father?' Henry had only clocked this after he'd stopped to take a photograph of the names on the memorial when he was with Blackstone. He'd taken the photo for another reason but had noticed the name Arkholme and only then remembered that Veronica had mentioned it was her maiden name when she was telling him about the rape on VE Day.

'Yes, he was. He was killed in Belgium in 1945. His unit was ambushed by a German patrol. It was a terrible blow for me and my mother because we were expecting him to come home, but, of course, lots of fighting still went on, even after VE Day.'

'I'm sorry,' Henry said. 'That's terrible.' He sighed and wondered how best to do this, looked at the old lady and saw tears rolling down her cheeks at her memories. 'Eric Grundy,' he began, 'took things from the girls he assaulted – trophies, we call them. He took a necklace from one girl, a ring from another, things that meant something to the victim. It was all about power with him and his very twisted personality. If you remember, I phoned you and asked if he'd taken something from you?'

She nodded. 'He did, something I cried over all my life, the last thing I ever had from my dad. I'm not sure why I didn't tell you about it to start with.'

'That's OK . . . but the thing is, people like Grundy, who think they've got away with these offences, like to keep these "trophies" to drool over, I guess, and he did, and we found a lot literally under his bed.'

She looked at Henry. 'What does that mean to me?'

'What sort of phone have you got?'

Puzzled, she said, 'A smartphone, obviously. I may be ancient but I'm tech-savvy, as they say.' She rooted the phone out of her handbag and waggled it at Henry.

'Let me send you this photo. The thing is I can't give you the real thing back yet because it's evidence, but I promise that once we've finished with it, I will return it to you. In the meantime, I took this photo of it.'

Henry fiddled with his phone, and a moment later Veronica's phone pinged as a message landed.

Henry watched as she tapped on the screen and opened the photograph Henry had taken of the letter he and Blackstone had found in Eric Grundy's possession.

She began to read it.

Henry sat back on the pew and also read it on his phone: the letter found by him and Blackstone in an envelope on the back of which had been scribbled, *First one, always the best*, and dated *VE Day*. Henry had not sent these images to Veronica, just the contents of the letter. When he came to return it to her, he would somehow have those words obliterated because he never wanted her to see them.

It was a letter from a soldier, a father, fighting a war in another country, to a young daughter at home who was waiting desperately to see him again.

It was only short, hardly anything really. But to its owner it meant everything, and the man who committed the rape on the owner knew that when he cruelly took it as a souvenir.

It read:

Dearest Ron.

Not long now. Missing you so much.

Quite a long journey, but I'll be home soon.

Then I will twirl you around and dance with you, which I know you love.

Can't wait. Love you so much.

Dad xxx

Henry closed his eyes momentarily, then looked at Veronica.

'He used to call me Ron,' she said. Then, simply, 'Thank you, Henry.' She paused, then asked, 'Will he ever have to know he made me pregnant?'

'Not if you don't wish it,' Henry assured her.

He said goodbye and left her sitting at the front of the church, just one last look over his shoulder to see her shoulders shuddering as she cried, then he stepped out into the darkening night, taking a deep breath on the porch, trying to work out how he was feeling. Numb, mostly.

He was then aware of a shape, a shadow, a movement behind him, coming at him quickly from the recess, and before he could respond, he felt three very hard punches to the right side of his back. He twisted, trying to grab whoever it was – a dark figure in a hoodie – but they stepped away from his fingers and fled through the tombstones, and Henry went after whoever it was.

Except he didn't.

His legs did not respond as a huge, all-encompassing pain seared up through his back into his chest cavity. He reached around instinctively, bending his right arm around to where there was a thick, pulsing wetness on his back. His hand came away and he looked at it, covered in blood.

He groaned, sank to his knees, knowing that what he'd thought were three punches were in fact three stab wounds through his ribcage, and although he tried to fight it, everything went from him, all strength, all reason, and he slumped forward, trying to hold himself up on all fours, but his arms had no strength, his elbows would not lock, and he slithered forwards and then rolled slowly on to his back, looking upwards at the stars beginning to twinkle in the night sky, his eyes blinking as he tried to focus and not drift into blackness.

$29.99 –